$\mathcal{Y}$ou're  a

$\mathcal{P}$rivileged

$\mathcal{W}$oman.

INTRODUCING
PAGES & PRIVILEGES™.

It's our way of thanking you for buying
our books at your favorite retail store.

— $\mathcal{G}$ET ALL THIS $\mathcal{F}$REE —
WITH JUST ONE PROOF OF PURCHASE:

◆ **Hotel Discounts** up
to 60% at home and
abroad ◆ **Travel Service**
- Guaranteed lowest
published airfares
plus 5% cash back
on tickets ◆ **$25 Travel Voucher**

$50 VALUE

◆ **Sensuous Petite Parfumerie** collection

◆ **Insider Tips Letter**
with sneak previews
of upcoming books

$\mathcal{Y}$ou'll get a FREE personal card, too.
*It's your passport to all these benefits– and to
even more great gifts & benefits to come!*

There's no club to join. No purchase commitment. No obligation.

Enrollment Form

☐ *Yes!* I WANT TO BE A *PRIVILEGED WOMAN*.

Enclosed is one *PAGES & PRIVILEGES*™ Proof of Purchase from any Harlequin or Silhouette book currently for sale in stores (Proofs of Purchase are found on the back pages of books) and the store cash register receipt. Please enroll me in *PAGES & PRIVILEGES*™. Send my Welcome Kit and FREE Gifts -- and activate my FREE benefits -- immediately.

More great gifts and benefits to come like these luxurious Truly Lace and L'Effleur gift baskets.

▼ DETACH HERE AND MAIL TODAY! ▼

NAME (please print)

ADDRESS   APT. NO

CITY   STATE   ZIP/POSTAL CODE

PROOF OF PURCHASE

SAMPLE ONLY

Please allow 6-8 weeks for delivery. Quantities are limited. We reserve the right to substitute items. Enroll before October 31, 1995 and receive one full year of benefits.

**NO CLUB!
NO COMMITMENT!**
Just one purchase brings you great Free Gifts and Benefits!
(More details in back of this book.)

Name of store where this book was purchased_____

Date of purchase_____

Type of store:

☐ Bookstore   ☐ Supermarket   ☐ Drugstore

☐ Dept. or discount store (e.g. K-Mart or Walmart)

☐ Other (specify)_____

Pages & Privileges™

Which Harlequin or Silhouette series do you usually read?

Complete and mail with one Proof of Purchase and store receipt to:

U.S.: *PAGES & PRIVILEGES*™, P.O. Box 1960, Danbury, CT 06813-1960

Canada: *PAGES & PRIVILEGES*™, 49-6A The Donway West, P.O. 813, North York, ON M3C 2E8   **PRINTED IN U.S.A**

One of them was a murderer

One of them, a person in this room, had held a gun and fired point-blank into the dead man's chest. Trina glanced at the figurines in her hand—a wedding cake groom and a tiny shattered bride. Would she be next?

Trina leaned against the wall, closed her eyes and listened to the bickering wedding guests. She'd come to Alaska seeking a new life, filled with love. Instead, she'd found murder.

A callused hand slipped into her own and she heard David St. John whisper, "This will all be over soon."

When she opened her eyes, his dark gaze embraced her with a warmth that should have been reassuring. But Trina had to wonder if David was the murderer....

Dear Reader,

One of the greatest rewards of writing for Harlequin Intrigue is the chance to travel in your mind to places you would never dream of going. Like Alaska. Since I live a quiet life in Denver, where we usually get plenty of snow, a trip to glacier land wasn't my number-one priority. However, after working on *The Suspect Groom*, a MAIL ORDER BRIDE book, my priorities have changed. I envy the two main characters in this story, Trina Martin and David St. John.

The country near Juneau is remarkable and beautiful, a wonderland filled with incredible wildlife. Just think of being caught in a blizzard with a gorgeous, rugged male, like David St. John. Think of snuggling in front of the fire with nothing to do but share bodily warmth. Of course, Trina Martin has to worry about solving a couple of murders and surviving when the killer comes after her. But David and Alaska make her struggle worth it.

I wouldn't mind being Trina. I'm tempted to respond to one of those ads for MAIL ORDER BRIDES!

Sincerely,

Cassie Miles

The Suspect Groom

Cassie Miles

Harlequin Books

TORONTO • NEW YORK • LONDON
AMSTERDAM • PARIS • SYDNEY • HAMBURG
STOCKHOLM • ATHENS • TOKYO • MILAN
MADRID • WARSAW • BUDAPEST • AUCKLAND

If you purchased this book without a cover you should be aware that this book is stolen property. It was reported as "unsold and destroyed" to the publisher, and neither the author nor the publisher has received any payment for this "stripped book."

ISBN 0-373-22332-3

THE SUSPECT GROOM

Copyright © 1995 by Kay Bergstrom

All rights reserved. Except for use in any review, the reproduction or utilization of this work in whole or in part in any form by any electronic, mechanical or other means, now known or hereafter invented, including xerography, photocopying and recording, or in any information storage or retrieval system, is forbidden without the written permission of the publisher, Harlequin Enterprises Limited, 225 Duncan Mill Road, Don Mills, Ontario, Canada M3B 3K9.

All characters in this book have no existence outside the imagination of the author and have no relation whatsoever to anyone bearing the same name or names. They are not even distantly inspired by any individual known or unknown to the author, and all incidents are pure invention.

This edition published by arrangement with Harlequin Enterprises B.V.

® and TM are trademarks of the publisher. Trademarks indicated with ® are registered in the United States Patent and Trademark Office, the Canadian Trade Marks Office and in other countries.

Printed in U.S.A.

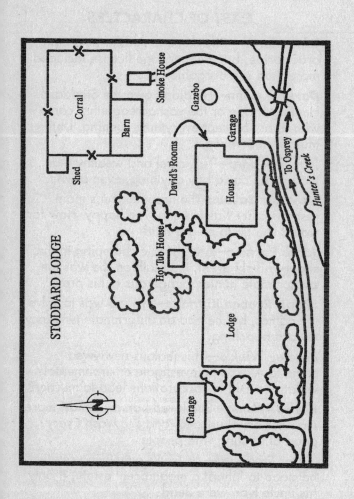

CAST OF CHARACTERS

Trina Martin—She came to Alaska as a mail-order bride, but the marriage license included more than she bargained for.

David St. John—He didn't own the Stoddard Hunting Lodge or the vast acreage that came with it, but he kept everything running. Until murder intervened.

Ivan Stoddard—This cruel and wealthy man thought he could buy anything, even a wife.

Maybelle Ballou—The housekeeper's main responsibility was to keep Ivan happy. How far would she go to please him?

Jacob Poynter—An Olympic champion in the shoot-and-ski event, the biathlon, he was the consummate hunter, dangerous to his prey.

Sheriff Reuben Kittridge—His job was to solve the crimes, but he had an unfortunate tendency toward poaching.

Bradley Winkle—This jealous newlywed came to Alaska to investigate environmental violations. Did his accusations lead to murder?

Phyllis Winkle—She loved horses, almost more than her new husband, and she wasn't very good at dealing with people.

Victor Stoddard—As Ivan's only living relative, he stood to inherit a magnificent estate, if only his uncle Ivan were dead.

Prologue

A bitter wind from the Alaskan coast mountains tore through the night. Black velvet skies, studded with crystal stars, loomed over the stark snow-covered horizon, but Darien Greenlee saw only the glare of headlights in his rearview mirror. Like the glowing eyes of a predatory beast, the lights had tailed him for the past eight miles on this desolate road that led to Ivan Stoddard's hunting lodge.

From a distance, Darien heard a timber wolf howl at the waning February moon, and he shivered. His grip tightened on the steering wheel of his rental car. This idiot behind him was following too closely, tailgating as if they were in a traffic jam instead of being the only two vehicles for miles and miles. Darien hadn't seen another car since he passed through the main street of Osprey and circled the edge of Crowberry Lake. What was wrong with this guy?

Darien lessened his speed by five miles per hour, so that the other car could pass him. But the driver stayed tight on his tail. Swinging wide on a curve that was rimmed by ice-covered berry thickets, Darien slowed even more. The vehicle behind him did the same. They were creeping along the dark road. *Was the driver Ivan himself? Was this his idea of a joke?*

Suddenly, without warning, the headlights behind Darien came close. The other car nudged his bumper, and the studded snow tires of Darien's rental car skidded on the icy road.

"Hey!" The exclamation burst through his lips. What was going on? This wasn't funny! Darien stomped hard on the accelerator and shot forward. He'd driven this route often enough to be familiar with the twists and turns in the narrow road that led through an old-growth spruce and hemlock forest. Beyond the trees, a two-lane road shot straight as a harpoon. The lodge was only a few miles farther away.

With satisfaction, Darien saw the headlights fall behind.

He chuckled. *Try to keep up with me. Just try it.*

His rental car burst past the trees. Far away, Darien saw the glow of lights from the lodge. Up close, too close, there was an obstacle in the road. A log. A fallen tree. He pumped frantically on the brakes and came to a stop only inches from the jagged pine boughs.

The car behind him halted.

Outraged, Darien flung open his car door. He charged toward the other vehicle, a Jeep, ready to confront the person who was stepping out. "What the hell were you doing? I could have been killed. I have a good mind to—"

His words stopped when he saw the shimmer of starlight on the gunmetal gray barrel of a Winchester rifle. The raw wind, the Taku wind from the mountains, sliced through his parka and chilled his heart.

The driver of the other car raised the night sight and aimed at Darien's chest. The voice was a whisper. "Seems that you've fallen into a trap."

Though the shape was well-padded in winter gear, Darien recognized the person. "You!"

"I'll give you a sporting chance, my friend. I'll count to one hundred before I come after you."

"Don't be absurd. I won't play games with you. It's freezing out here."

"Twenty-eight below zero."

"Come on, now. Enough is enough." Darien fought the terror that rose in his chest. "Let's get this road cleared," he continued reasonably. "We can use the winch on your Jeep."

"I'll make it even easier for you. I won't use the rifle with the night sight." The rifle disappeared into the Jeep. "I'm only armed with this handgun. A Colt .45. That's fair."

"You're insane!"

"One. Two." The whisper was firm. The cadence of the count was steady. "Three. Four."

"You'll never get away with this." Searching for a way out, Darien stared at his rental car, neatly hemmed in by the log and the Jeep. There was no way he could escape, but his own rifle and hunting gear were in the trunk.

"Don't even think it" came the low whisper. "Touch your car and the game's over. You die right now." The count resumed. "Five. Six."

"It would be more fair if I was armed." Darien tried another tactic. "You said you wanted to be sporting, didn't you?"

"Seven. Eight. You're talking yourself to death, my friend. Nine. Ten."

Darien started running. He had two choices—into the trees or toward the lodge. The trees would provide shelter and make him a more difficult target, but he couldn't hide there long. It was too cold. Still running, he zipped his Gore-Tex parka and pulled up the hood. There were bears in the forest. And wolves. Night hunters.

Still, he chose that direction.

The lodge was nearly two miles away, and the landscape was flat white with nowhere to hide.

He heard the echo of the first shot ring out. The stillness of the Alaskan night shattered like glass.

Chapter One

He was exactly the way she'd imagined. Trina Martin peered through the window of the single-engine Cessna at the tall, long-legged man in a shearling coat who stood beside the Osprey airstrip. Behind him, the glacial landscape of Alaska, north of Juneau, glistened in the midday sunlight. The sparkle of crusted snow matched the two-carat diamond in the ring she wore on her fourth finger, left hand.

Trina couldn't believe she was actually here, couldn't believe that she was finally going to meet him. Though the brim of his black Stetson obscured his features, she had the impression of a strong jawline. What would he look like? Was his hair blond or brown or red? Was it streaked with silver? She knew he was in his mid-forties. She knew he was healthy and fit. But, in all their correspondence, she hadn't seen a photograph, hadn't been brave enough to ask. Was he handsome?

The plane taxied forward and she could no longer see him. She leaned back in her seat, trying to catch her breath and to calm the tremulous quiver of anticipation in her stomach. Finally, she thought. Finally, she would be face-to-face with her future husband, Ivan Stoddard.

"We're here," the pilot announced from the cockpit.

Trina was the only passenger in the small plane, and she was struck with a sudden reluctance to disembark. What if Ivan didn't like her? What if he thought she was plain or clumsy or boring? Worst of all, she thought, he might take one look at her and discover the lie she'd perpetrated since the very beginning of their correspondence.

"I got to tell you," the bush pilot said as the plane slowly glided to a stop. "I've transported a lot of weird stuff to people out here. A pair of matched apricot poodles. A frozen cheesecake from New York City. And the skull of a prehistoric man to some archeologist. But this is the first time my cargo has been a mail-order bride."

"I'm nowhere near as interesting as those other things."

"Beg to differ, ma'am. You're plenty more exciting than a poodle or a prehistoric head."

"Thanks, I think."

"Oh, that was a compliment, ma'am. You mind if I ask you one thing?"

"Go ahead."

"Why? Why would a pretty woman like yourself agree to come up here and marry a man she's never even met?"

The answer wasn't easy. When Trina first replied to the advertisement for a mail-order bride, she might have been undergoing the first prickles of an uncomfortable mid-life crisis. She was thirty-five, unmarried and stuck in a dead-end job. Taking off for Alaska appealed to her, and she'd started a correspondence with Ivan Stoddard.

Over the course of a month, he wrote to her almost daily, and she fell in love with his letters. Maybe not *in love,* she thought now, but deeply *in like.* He was witty, honest and sensitive. His occasional attempts at poetry, though perhaps not brilliant, were charmingly sincere. Most of all, his letters showed that he loved his life-style, without reservation and fear. Trina wanted to share that excitement. She was tired of petty whining and complaining. She longed to embrace her future, and Ivan seemed to be the man who could show her how to live. When she received the engagement ring by special courier, she slipped it on her finger, quit her job and made her travel arrangements.

"Well?" the pilot prodded.

"Adventure," she said.

"You're surely going to have that wish come true. If there's one thing we've got more of than snow in Alaska, it's adventure."

While he jostled the switches and shut down the engines of the Cessna, Trina lifted her large canvas purse onto her lap. Digging through her makeup, she found a small compact and checked her appearance. Her cheeks were flushed, which deepened the blue color of her eyes. Her minimal makeup was okay, but her long brown hair, pulled back in a single braid, was something of a mess. She tried to tidy the straggles that had come unfastened, then gave up, pulled out the rubber band at the end of the braid and shook her head. The untamed thickness cascaded halfway down her back. Her long hair was her best feature, but right now it seemed too wild. Should have had a trim, she thought. Should have had a hairdresser add russet highlights to the dull brown color. It was too late now, and Trina didn't expect to find stylists in attendance at the secluded game preserve where they were headed.

She took off her gold-framed glasses and stashed them in their case. Perhaps her vision of Ivan would be an unfocused blur, but she didn't want his first impression of her to be of a bespectacled former secretary. Besides, she needed to look younger, and the glasses added years.

The pilot flipped down the exit hatch. "Here you go, ma'am. Best of luck to you. Many happy returns."

Too excited to speak, she nodded her thanks and stepped from the Cessna. The ridged rubber sole of her boot crunched on the hard-packed snow beside the tarmac runway. An icy wind coiled around her and nipped the tip of her nose. She shivered. This would be her home now. Alaska.

The man who stood waiting held his hat in his gloved hands. His eyes were a deep, moody brown. Sunlight sparked golden reflections in his dark blond hair.

She tried not to stare, not to squint myopically to bring his features into clear focus. Truly, she didn't need to look too hard to see that he was wonderfully masculine, as strong and rugged as the land he called his domain. It was nearly impossible to believe that this virile man had written the twenty-eight thoughtful letters she'd received.

"Afternoon, ma'am. I'm David St. John."

"You're not Ivan?"

"He sends his regrets. There was a crisis this afternoon, and he couldn't get away." David stuck out his hand. "I'm the foreman at the hunting preserve."

Her red mitten disappeared into his thick leather glove, and she gave a firm handshake, suppressing her disappointment. Throughout this long journey, she'd been anxious to see Ivan, to finally meet him. It didn't seem like she could hold off for one more minute. But there was no choice. "I guess an occasional crisis can't be avoided."

"Afraid not."

She forced the smile onto her face. Trina needed to be strong, to be prepared for anything. In his letters, Ivan had explained, several times, that life in Alaska didn't follow the predictable rules of politeness.

"I'm sorry," David said, and she detected a note of sympathy in his voice. "I'm sure if Ivan was here, he'd tell you that you were some sight when you were coming off that plane. You looked like Alice, taking her first gander at Wonderland."

"That's how I feel. This land is so beautiful. Last night, when my plane landed in Juneau, it was too dark to really see anything. But this morning we flew over the Mendenhall Glacier. It's so amazing and it looks blue. There's so much water, too! And the Cathedral Peaks. And the forests. I can't wait to see the green fjords in the springtime. I've read all the books on Alaska that I could get my hands on, but this is... well, it *is* like Wonderland."

"And Ivan would probably tell you..." He cleared his throat. "If you don't mind me saying it, Trina, you're prettier than your photograph."

Her eyebrows arched in disbelief. The picture she'd sent was from ten years ago when she was twenty-five, and that little white lie had prevailed throughout her correspondence with Ivan. In his advertisement for a mail-order bride, he'd said he wanted a young, healthy, strong woman to be his wife. Trina fulfilled the requirements, except for the youthful part. "That was a posed photo," she said, hoping that explanation would cover the ten extra years. "With makeup and special lighting."

"I like you better this way. You look real."

With the pilot's help, he loaded her two suitcases and steamer trunk into the back of a four-wheel-drive Jeep Cherokee. Then he turned to her. "Is this all of it?"

"Yes." Those few cases held all her earthly belongings. Trina had been ruthless in discarding everything that wasn't absolutely essential. She'd sold all her furniture, had given away her trinkets and mementos.

In Alaska, she wanted a completely fresh start. A brand-new life, full of promise and adventure. And maybe she'd even find love.

David held open the door on the passenger side. "Let's roll."

She fastened her seat belt and settled back for the ride, noticing that he peeled off his heavy leather gloves and wore only a light thermal pair for the drive. "How far are we from the lodge?"

"Not far."

"In terms of miles?"

"Time and distance don't mean much out here. In a blizzard, it can take an hour to go a mile. In clear weather, like today, we'll be at the lodge before your eyes get accustomed to the glare off the snow. Have you got sunglasses?"

"Yes." Prescription sunglasses! These would be the perfect thing to wear. Not only would she be able to see clearly, but the dark lenses would disguise the faint traces of laugh lines around her eyes. She fished them out of her canvas bag and put them on.

The snowy panorama, though muted by the sunglasses, was spectacular. She scanned in all directions, absorbing the view, then turned her gaze to the man who was driving. She'd been right about the strong jawline. His profile appeared to have been chiseled from granite. He was remarkably good-looking. "Have you lived up here long, David?"

"I was born near Skagway at the foot of the Yukon Trail. I left for a while, but I came back home. It's funny how that happens, how the place where you have roots calls you back. No matter how far you roam, there's one place on earth where you really belong." He smiled. "What about you, Trina? I know you're from Colorado, but is that where you were born?"

"I was born in Los Angeles, but I don't consider that home." Her father had been in the military, and they had lived in dozens of places. She wasn't fond of her personal history and preferred not to remember her family's unsettled life-style, ruled by a dictatorial father. She changed the subject. "So, David, what does a foreman on a game preserve do?"

"It depends. Mostly I take care of the livestock."

"The moose and the bear?"

He laughed. "They take care of themselves. We have domestic animals. Horses, a couple of beef cattle. We tried sheep and chickens, but the wolves found them too appealing."

"Appealing?"

"Succulent," he said.

Aware that she was in a different land with different rules, Trina swallowed the automatic exclamation of disgust that rose in her throat. Succulent? Yuck! Though she knew the food chain was a part of nature, she'd never been a farm girl, and she hated to acknowledge the natural fact that meat came from a living creature. Rather, she liked to believe that it grew on trees in prepackaged cartons, which were then available in the butcher's section of her local supermarket.

"Also," David said, "I maintain the property. Do some carpentry, some building, some repairs. Mostly, at this time of year, I run the snowplow. And I handle the hiring and firing when we need help. During slow times, I do a lot of the paperwork for Ivan, setting the appointments for the hunters who stay at the lodge."

"The hunters." There was another source of possible conflict. Trina had tried not to dwell on that part of her future husband's business. His land wasn't a pristine game preserve where the Alaskan version of Bambi and Thumper scampered free. The lodge was a hunting operation.

She had reread the letter several times wherein Ivan told how he had stalked and killed a bull elk. Though he described the skinning and processing of the venison in detail, she had sensed an obvious admiration for the magnificent animal that provided its meat. He'd mentioned another hunter who'd accompanied him on that expedition—David St. John. Though Ivan didn't say much about him, it made Trina feel more familiar with the foreman. "Ivan mentioned you," she said. "In his letters."

"Did he?" David pointed to a fence post. "That's the beginning of Stoddard land."

She peered along the fenceline that stretched farther than the eye could see. "All this?"

"It's a big place. Over two thousand acres."

"Why is it fenced?"

"Mostly to keep the poachers out."

"Well, of course." She tried to make sense of this vast, bizarre land. "I don't suppose a scrawny little bit of barbed wire would hold something as big as a moose."

"You'd be surprised. There are two things you need to remember about moose, Trina. They're a whole lot more dangerous than Bullwinkle. However, they are just exactly as dumb as they look."

He turned and they drove through a gateway that stood open. "Not much farther," David said. "The lodge is over this ridge, just through the forest and straight on from there."

They entered a corridor between tall spruce trees, so thick that the forest blocked the sunlight. The branches started high on the trees, and the dark trunks seemed to surround David and Trina in an ominous, impenetrable fortress. Amid the trees, there was silence and so much less snow that patches of the narrow road's surface were visible. "Taming this land is quite an accomplishment," she said.

"Alaska is never tame. At best, we puny humans have momentary control. But the environment is king. The Haida Indians understood that. They always made peace with the local spirits of trees and wind and water. But nobody ever really expects to conquer the land. No more than they can change the weather."

"If it was that bad, no one would live here."

"There are rewards. The sight of the first snow. Ever held a snowflake on your glove and watched it melt?"

She shook her head. "Never have."

He continued, "There's a special smell in a winter camp fire. No sparkle of a diamond mined in Africa is as beautiful as sunlight on a waterfall or the northern lights. And the springtime? It's heaven. You can taste spring in the air. In the melting snows, the fjords are lush and inviting. You want to run across the remaining ice floes and roll around in the green. But then, crack! The ce breaks. And you're stranded. Trapped."

He glanced over at the woman who sat so primly beside him. Her full lips were slightly parted. Her head was cocked slightly to one side, like a curious fawn. "Stop me, Trina. I'm beginning to sound like a damn poet."

"Like Ivan," she said.

"Oh, yeah." David couldn't keep the sarcasm from his voice. "Ivan's real poetic. A regular bard."

"In his letters, he is."

He didn't want to argue with her. It wasn't right for him to be thinking about her at all. She was Ivan's woman. Not his. "Just remember, Trina. Southeastern Alaska can be very beautiful, but it's dangerous, too."

When they came out of the trees, their way was blocked by several four-wheel-drive vehicles and pickup trucks. David pulled to the side of the road and parked. "Let's check it out. This must be the big crisis."

"Is that a police car?" She gestured toward a beat-up truck with police lights on top and a sheriff's star painted on the side.

"Belongs to the sheriff from Osprey."

"Fascinating," she said. Though he started around the Jeep to open the door for her, Trina opened her own door. She needed to assert her independence.

David escorted her toward a burly man with a dark walrus mustache. He was huge, as tall as David and half again as wide. Was everybody extralarge up here? Or was it just the padding of parkas and snow gear? Though she was above average height at five feet, eight inches, she felt positively petite as David introduced her to Reuben Kittridge. "Reuben's the sheriff."

The big man shook her hand. Beneath eyebrows that were nearly as bushy as his mustache, he studied her with penetrating eyes. "You're the mail-order bride," he said, "and I'll be doggoned if you aren't a pretty little thing."

"And you're a pretty big thing."

"You're right about that." He glanced at David. "She's a beauty. Ain't Ivan got all the luck?"

"Just so. What's the problem here, Reuben?"

"Early this morning, at first light, a couple of kids came through here. Cross-country skiing, they said, but I expect they had their rifles with them. No way to prove it, though. So, you tell Ivan not to press charges for poaching. They were good boys to come forward even though they might get in trouble."

"I hope nothing happened to them," David said.

"They found a body. A man's body. Or what was left of it . . . after the wolves."

"Anybody we know?"

"I don't think so. If he was carrying a wallet, it's gone now. His face and hands are pretty well torn up."

Trina shuddered. The cold wind swept around her, but the icy feeling came from deep within her heart. What a horrible way to die! Being eaten by wolves. The trembling froze her blood, and she folded her arms across her waist, holding tight to keep the bones from rattling against each other. She tried to be braver. This was beautiful Alaska!

And yet, she was frightened. This sort of thing never happened in urban Denver where she'd worked as a secretary. Her voice squeaked like a rusty hinge on a door that she was trying with all her might to keep closed. "Wolves, you say?"

Reuben nodded. "It was wolves, all right."

She felt David's presence nearby. Though he didn't touch her, he was close, shielding her from the fearful chill.

The sheriff continued. "He had some high-class snow gear. His parka was shredded, but it was one of those fine Gore-Tex things. Good boots. Thermal everything. Not that all the padding in the world could save him from hungry wolves."

"He was careless," David said. "Really, Trina, this sort of thing doesn't happen every day."

"Every other day?" she said, trying to be rough and ready despite the tremor in her voice.

"Seldom," David said. "Most people know better than to go wandering off at night and get themselves lost. That must have been what happened. Right, Sheriff?"

"Don't know. My guess is that he died at least a couple of days ago. Maybe even a week. Hard to say. We've had some light snowfalls at night."

They stood and watched. About two hundred yards from the road, Trina saw a group of men trudging through ankle-deep snow. Two of them glided a litter across the rolling field. Though the body on the coffin-size sled was completely covered, she too easily imagined the dead man.

Her stomach lurched. Trina closed her eyes rather than turning away. She didn't want to betray any weakness. This was her new home. If she wanted to stake her claim, she needed to be strong.

"But it wasn't just the wolves that got him," Reuben said. "Nope, this good old boy was dead before he hit the ground. Three bullet holes right in the back."

DAVID HAD BEEN looking forward to meeting Trina and showing her the wonders of Alaska, a little piece of heaven. Instead, he had introduced her to a hellish murder.

Though she had exclaimed enthusiastically when they first beheld the buildings of the Stoddard Lodge and Hunting Preserve, her voice held a high note, a tremble like the sound of a startled thrush. She'd been tense, stiff. When he'd showed her the bedroom in the big house beside the lodge, the bedroom that was to be her own, she asked for a moment alone.

David left her, went downstairs and through the front room to the study. He rapped on the door. "Ivan!"

"What the hell is it?"

Pushing open the door, David entered. "I've got her."

"Her?"

"Trina Martin. The woman you're going to marry."

"Oh. Her." Ivan peered through hooded eyelids that always reminded David of a hawk or a falcon. A predator. That was Ivan. Though he could be vicious and demanding, he never apologized for his attitude. And David respected that. Ivan was what he was—no worse and no better. "What's she look like, David?"

"If you cared, you could have come to the airfield."

"I was busy. I had a crisis to attend."

David glanced around the quiet office. The fax machine was still. The copier, untouched. The screen of the computer, equipped with up-to-date software, stood dark and blank. On the desk top in front of Ivan, a game of solitaire was spread but unfinished. "Light seven to dark eight," David said. "I can see how busy you are."

Ivan moved the cards and flipped through the deck again. There were no more moves.

"Looks like you've lost," David said.

"By now, you know me better than that." Ivan manipulated the layout of the solitaire game and won by cheating. "There. That's better."

"By the way," David said, "about the crisis ... Reuben says the dead man isn't easily recognizable and has no identification."

"So they don't know who it was."

"Not a clue. And he was shot."

"Murdered?" There was a singular lack of surprise in Ivan's question. He scooped up his deck of cards. "When?"

"They can't tell. Reuben said they'd probably go all the way to Juneau for forensics."

"A forensics team? My, my, a real homicide. That must be a big deal for Sheriff Reuben Kittridge."

David settled himself into the chair opposite the desk. Over the past five years, he'd sat here so often that the leather was worn to the shape of his rump. The distance was exactly right for David to stretch out his long legs and prop his boot heels on the edge of the desk. Usually, he was content, even pleased, by Ivan's lack of attention to business because it left more for David to work on. But this was different. Trina was different. David couldn't allow Ivan to run roughshod over her life.

"Reuben probably thinks he can give me a hard time about this," Ivan said. A slow, evil smile curled his lips. "I'll look forward to his feeble attempts."

"This is murder, Ivan. Take it seriously."

"One more dead trespasser. Who cares?" He looked up. "Tell me about the girl."

"She's okay."

"Only okay? I wanted somebody who'd make the rest of you backwoods yahoos sit up and notice. Is she going to do that?"

David cleared his throat, paused. He wanted to say that Trina was more than a trophy. One look had told him that. She was warm and bright with an inner beauty that outshone her lovely exterior. But David couldn't admit his feelings. Ivan would laugh and tell him to forget it. He'd marry Trina just to spite David.

Damn it, there wasn't time to come up with the right words to express the effect Trina had had on him. And that was a great irony in Alaska where—during the dark cold winter—time stretched into a slow infinity. Since Trina arrived, every moment seemed to speed as quickly as sand in an hourglass. Every moment was sparkling.

"So where's my bride?"

"Upstairs in her room, making herself pretty," David said.

"For me." Ivan grinned. "I'm going to like having some sweet young thing fluttering round, catering to my every whim. I don't know why I didn't do this years ago."

David's jaw tightened. Ivan didn't deserve a woman who was as sweet and sensitive as Trina. He wouldn't appreciate her. He'd ordered up a bride with the casual disregard he might use in placing a catalog order. As long as she was approximately the right size and shape, he didn't care about what was inside. If it weren't for those letters, those damn letters...

Trina stepped lightly into the room. She'd changed from her travel clothes into a long, purple and white sweater and matching purple leggings. She wore a large silver locket at her throat. On her feet were beige suede boots that were very stylish, but unsuitable for going out in the snow. Her long mane of brown hair rippled past her shoulders, and her eyes danced with the same happy excitement David had seen when she left the airplane.

David rose to his feet and so did Ivan.

She moved toward them with a fetching shyness, so eager to please, and David hoped with all his heart that Ivan would be gentle with her.

"Trina Martin," he said. "At last we meet."

"At last."

He took her hand, raised it to his lips and lightly kissed her fingertips. "What did you think of your bedroom, Trina?"

"It's very...pink," she said.

"Women like pink."

"Well, yes. And I don't mean to criticize. But I'm not a Barbie doll."

"It's Maybelle's fault. She's the housekeeper, and she ordered the bedspreads and curtains. Made David work overtime putting up that rosebud wallpaper."

"The housekeeper?" Trina brightened. "This place comes with a housekeeper?"

"Maybelle Ballou," he said. "But she's leaving at the end of the month. Going south." He regarded Trina with that hooded stare. "That won't happen with you."

"Why wouldn't it?" she asked.

"You'll be my wife. You can't just up and quit because the winter's too cold. Or you're lonely." He sneered. "A wife needs a home, and that's what I'm giving you. A home and a lodge and a barn and several outbuildings. Not to mention the two thousand acres of land. That's a pretty damn good bargain, Trina."

"Yes, I suppose it is." But she wasn't sure if she believed that she'd just made the deal of the century. Ivan Stoddard wasn't at all what she had expected. Though he was an attractive man, tall and lean, with sharp features, there was a harsh, intimidating light that emanated from his dark eyes. His short-cropped hair was iron gray. He was most definitely older than his letters suggested. Though Trina had subtracted ten years from her own résumé, she suspected Ivan was closer to sixty-five than forty-five.

"How many employees do you have?" she asked.

"Up to twelve when the lodge is full. Which isn't often. In the wintertime, it's usually just me and David and the housekeeper. When Maybelle leaves, that would be David, me and you."

"Me? Then, am I expected to act as housekeeper?"

"Well, you wouldn't want some other woman messing with your house."

"I didn't sign on to be an employee, Ivan. There's more to being a wife than—"

"Sure, sure," he interrupted as he returned to the chair behind his desk. He stared at her. "Turn around, Trina."

"What?"

"I want to inspect you. I'm making an investment here."

"To inspect me?" She felt her cheeks grow red with embarrassment and anger. This man was nothing like his letters. Ivan was crass and rude and...

"You heard me, honey. Turn around."

Finally David spoke, "Come on, Ivan. Knock it off."

"I have the right."

"Well, why don't you ask her to open her mouth so you can check out her teeth like a horse you might buy." David stepped up beside her and squeezed her shoulders protectively. "He's joking."

"I'm not," Ivan said. "Little Trina here claims to be twenty-five, but she looks a damn sight older."

She cringed inside. Her lie! She'd already been caught in her lie!

"Does it matter?" David asked.

"Hell, yes. I want my wife to give me some legal heirs. Sons, of course."

"I see," Trina snapped. "And do we drown the daughters?"

"What?" A perplexed frown crossed Ivan's face, then he said, "Don't take me wrong, Trina. I've got nothing against women. I like women. Living up here, I've learned that a strong woman can do almost anything a man can do. But I'd prefer little boys. I'm an older man. I'd like a kid to play with, and I don't much care for dollies and dress up."

"Talk about your mixed messages," she said under her breath. In one quick statement, Ivan had credited women and discredited them at the same time.

The telephone on Ivan's desk rang and he snatched it up. As soon as he recognized the caller, his voice softened like butter in the sun. "And I'm real pleased to hear from you, too. You hold on for just a second, okay?"

He turned his gaze on Trina. His gaze scoped from the top of her head to the tips of her toes. "I guess you'll do just fine. I'll see you tomorrow at the wedding."

"But—"

"That's all, Trina." Ivan nodded to David. "Get her some dinner and put her to bed."

A dozen protests sputtered behind her lips, but she was too confused to speak, and David was turning her gently toward the door. She gazed up at him and saw a wellspring of sensitivity in his dark eyes. If only he had been the man she'd come to marry, everything would be wonderful. She could have forgotten the dead man in the field, could have been truly happy.

Had she expected too much? She touched the silver locket at her throat. Inside, folded tight, was a scrap of paper from one of his letters. One word was written upon it—love.

When she reached the door, Ivan called out. "Hey! Your backside looks just fine to me."

What had she gotten herself into?

Chapter Two

Trina marched along beside David, not speaking. She kept her chin high. Her encounter with Ivan reminded her, more than anything, of those years in her childhood when her military father barked out orders and it was her job to obey without question. During that time, she'd learned self-control. Trina knew, from experience, that she could grit her teeth and stand anything—*anything!*—for a brief period of time. But this was marriage, and marriage should be for a *long* time. A lifetime.

David directed her through the entry and down a hallway. They passed an arch that led to the kitchen where they could hear the housekeeper, Maybelle, at work. From there, David took Trina down a few steps to another, narrower corridor.

She tripped on another small stair, recovered her poise and said, "This floor plan doesn't make sense. Up a half flight, down a hall, up another. It's like a house put together with children's building blocks."

"Makes sense when you consider the weather," he said. "In the summer, it's possible to build and add on. So the houses up here tend to expand in spurts. This addition was my special project three years ago."

He opened a door to a spacious room, paneled entirely in faintly redolent cedar. The most striking features were a large moss rock fireplace and wide windows that showed a view of the barn. David opened a door on the right side of the fireplace. "In here is my office. The other closed door leads to my bedroom."

She watched him warily as he added another log to the blaze in the fireplace. "Why did you bring me here, David?"

"I thought you might need a friend. I know you're disappointed. Your first meeting with Ivan didn't go exactly as you wanted."

An understatement if she'd ever heard one. "It could have gone worse. I mean, he didn't bite the head off a live chicken or anything."

"I might have a solution."

"Murder Ivan?" she suggested.

"The thought has crossed my mind—a number of times. But I don't think we need to try anything so drastic."

"Okay, David, what do you think I should do?"

She glanced at him. Even though she couldn't see him clearly without her glasses, he appeared to be uncomfortable, and he spoke with hesitation,. "Sometimes, Trina, things aren't as they seem."

She nodded. *What was he trying to tell her?*

"Sometimes, a person can make an honest mistake. It occurs to me that things might not work out with you and Ivan. Now, if that happens to be the case—"

"I don't want to think about that." She perched on the wide stone ledge beside the fireplace and sighed. "It's true that Ivan isn't all that I had hoped for, but I really haven't given him much of a chance. I felt much the same way about him after our brief phone conversations, but then I'd read his letters again. I know the man has a kind, gentle heart.''

Maybe Ivan just needed a good woman to bring his shining qualities to the forefront. Maybe he just had a gruff exterior. Or maybe she was kidding herself and Ivan was an irreparable jerk. If he really intended to marry her tomorrow, she didn't have much time to figure out which was which.

''He seems to be a generous man,'' Trina finally ventured.

''When it suits him.''

''I mean, you heard all the things he offered me. The house. The lodge. The land.'' She lifted her hand, turned it toward the fire. ''Look at this ring, this diamond. It had to be expensive.'' But the ring felt heavy on her finger. And the diamond glittered with a cold, harsh light.

''Ivan's a wealthy man,'' David conceded. ''I don't know his liquid value, but his assets make him a millionaire. He made his money in oil thirty years ago. He's owned this lodge and all the acreage for twenty years. He's rich, all right.''

Comforting, she thought, but money didn't really matter. Character was more important in a husband than wealth. She stuck to her initial, hopeful assessment. ''He's generous.''

''And rich. I guess that's enough to make you go ahead with the wedding.''

''What are you suggesting? That I'd marry a man because of his assets?''

''I've been told that it's just as easy to fall in love with a rich man as a poor one.''

''It doesn't matter to me.''

''Right. Sure.'' He sounded disbelieving. ''If not money, what do you want?''

"A home."

"You had a home. In Denver."

"A place to live isn't a home. In any case, it's not there anymore. I quit my job, gave up my apartment and sold my car."

"Why?"

"Because . . ." Her voice trailed off. She couldn't tell David that she'd been foolish enough to fall in love with a man based on a stack of letters, but that was the truth. With his written words, Ivan had captured her heart.

"Is it because you knew you'd be coming into money?"

"Why do you keep harping on that?"

"I'm looking at the facts, Trina. You're a mail-order bride. Why? Money. Why else would you come here and offer yourself to a man you'd never met?"

How dare he insinuate that she could be bought! She bounded to her feet and strode toward the door.

"Trina, wait!"

"I won't sit here and be insulted. Not by you."

"But by him? By Ivan?" David caught up with her at the door. "You heard what he wants from you. A live-in housekeeper who will bear his sons."

"Leave me alone, David."

He grasped her arm and she pivoted quickly. In reflex, her hand rose to slap his face. He caught her wrist, stopping the blow before it landed.

When she looked into his blazing eyes, sparks ignited between them. She staggered backward a step, shocked by the unwarranted passion she felt. What was going on in her head? She was furious with David, so mad she'd almost slapped him. And yet, she wanted nothing more than to fling herself into his arms, to taste his lips, to feel his strong, lean body against hers.

This couldn't be! Though David was undeniably handsome, she couldn't succumb to this terrible, inappropriate attraction. This was the eve of her wedding day. She shouldn't even be looking at another man.

"I'll be in my room, David. I don't want dinner. I'm not hungry."

She wrenched away from his grasp and fled through the mazes of stairs and corridors to find her ridiculous second-floor room that was all flounces, fluff and pink, pink, pink.

She'd never been so confused. Pacing back and forth on creaking floorboards, she felt trapped by her irrational emotions. She fought to calm the thumping of her heart against her rib cage when she thought of…David. Not Ivan, but David St. John. From the moment she'd seen him through the window of the Cessna, he'd been everything she wanted in a man. But it wasn't right! She needed to ground herself, to make sense of this.

She grasped the silver locket, unfastened the catch and opened it. Carefully, she unfolded the tiny piece of paper. When Ivan had been writing to her, the body of his letters was typed on a computer, but the signature was written. At first, he'd signed his letters with "sincerely," then he progressed to "cordially." On the letter he wrote on Valentine's Day, he signed with the single word she treasured in her locket. "Love, Ivan."

No matter how horrible he'd seemed when they met, he had written to her of love.

Trina dug through her suitcase until she found his letters. She threw herself across the pink satin bedspread and read the promise he'd written on Valentine's Day. "The nights in Alaska are the worst. Long, cold and dark. I lie in my solitary bed, wishing for the warmth of someone beside me. Wishing for you. Wishing I could touch your long, silken hair. Wishing I could hear your gentle heart, beating in rhythm with mine. If you marry me, Trina, I vow that your nights will never be lonely...."

In other letters, he had talked about seeing the reflection of a waterfall in her eyes, sitting together on the porch, holding hands and watching the migration of Canadian geese. He wanted to show her the snow foxes and river otters at play. But she couldn't reconcile his prose with the man who had callously asked her to turn around for inspection.

And what about the phone call he'd received before he dismissed her? His sweetened voice and furtive manner made her think that the caller was a woman. Was he in love with someone else? Was he planning his own special bachelor party in the arms of another woman?

Exhaustion descended upon her like a heavy cloud. Trina kicked off her boots and crept under the covers, sleeping fitfully throughout the night.

The next morning, the skies were still blue, but the snow clouds were rising. Gazing from her window, she marveled at this magnificent land and wished she could be happy. Today, after all, might be her wedding day. But her emotions crashed around her. Her wedding day? "What have I done?"

Her father would have told her to buck up and get on with it, and—for once—Trina figured that was good advice. She needed to meet with Ivan, to assess his attitude and make her decision.

But first, she needed to dress. She stripped, grabbed her terry cloth bathrobe and headed across the wide landing toward the bathroom. She knocked on the door and waited for a response. When none came, she twisted the knob.

A man stood just inside. It was almost as if he were waiting for her.

"Oh, I'm so sorry." Trina stepped back, averting her gaze from his bared chest. All he wore was a robe.

"You must be the blushing bride," he said.

"Blushing is correct." With one hand, she shielded her eyes. With the other, she clutched her bathroom supplies and tried to hold her robe closed. "I didn't know I was barging in on you."

"I don't mind. After all, you're practically family. I'm Victor Stoddard, Ivan's nephew from Juneau."

She hadn't even thought of Ivan's family arriving for the wedding. To call it off would be dreadfully embarrassing.

"Aren't you going to shake my hand, Trina?"

"Of course, I don't mean to be rude." If he wasn't embarrassed, why should she be? She stuck out her hand and looked directly into his eyes. The family resemblance was unattractive on Victor. Where Ivan's sharp features gave definition to his face, Victor's were exaggerated. His cheekbones jutted outward, creating sunken cheeks. His nose was too large and pointed for his weak chin. She shook his hand quickly. "Pleased to meet you, Victor. I'm Trina Martin."

"Soon to be Trina Martin Stoddard. My Auntie Trina."

His weak grasp clung to her. His skin was still damp and clammy from the shower. She suppressed a sense of revulsion. "Are there other family members here?"

"There are no other family members. Both of my parents and my brother were killed in a small plane crash. About two years ago."

"I'm sorry."

"That makes me Ivan's only living relative." He made no move to allow her into the bathroom. "Except for you, of course."

"If you'll excuse me, I'll go back to my room and wait until you're finished in the bathroom. Again, I'm sorry."

"I'm finished." When he stepped into the hall and brushed past her, he came a little too close for comfort. Trina dodged around him and slipped into the bathroom. She didn't breathe comfortably until she'd locked the door.

Victor Stoddard was a strange and unpleasant man, but he was the least of her problems. Trina pushed him from her mind and concentrated on showering, washing and blow-drying her hair. Though she had already decided to wear her hair down for the wedding—if there was a wedding—she quickly wove a single braid down her back. This morning, she needed to get outside, to breathe the fresh air while she made her decision. If only she could spend some time with Ivan....

Trina dressed quickly and hurried downstairs to the kitchen where she met the housekeeper, Maybelle Ballou. She was a buxom, boisterous woman who immediately plied Trina with fresh-baked, chocolate chip muffins and coffee.

"You don't look twenty-five," Maybelle announced.

"I've had a rough life," Trina countered.

"That's a good thing, honey, because it's about to get rougher. Alaska is no place for wimps." Maybelle's full mouth rolled down in a frown. "I hate to leave. Feels like I'm chickening out. But my kids are grown and gone and I want to spend some time seeing the rest of the world."

"How many children do you have?"

"Six," she said proudly. "And three different husbands. That's another thing I'll miss about Alaska. There aren't many women up here, so even an old biddy like myself has her pick."

Trina smiled into her coffee.

"Brace yourself, sweetie. Even when you're married, they come sniffing around like tomcats." She picked up a muffin and munched absently while she talked. "Now, let me tell you about the plans for today. The weather says we're going to have a big storm, but we ought to be okay until late afternoon. Your guests are going to start arriving at about noontime."

"Guests?"

"People from the town."

"Juneau?"

"Lordy, no. Juneau's nearly a hundred miles away. These are people from Osprey, which is only about twenty miles from here." She winked. "It's going to be fun. We'll have a regular potlatch."

"A what?"

"Potlatch. That's what the Haida and Tlingit call it when everybody gets together to celebrate. In the old days, a good potlatch would go on for days, but I expect this is going to be a short party with the weather turning grim."

"This seems like a lot of work for you," Trina said. Perhaps futile work if she called off the wedding. "Can I help?"

"Certainly not. It's your job today to be pretty and sweet."

There was no point in arguing with Maybelle. This was a formidable woman who charged straight ahead, come hell or high water, like those rough-and-ready gold rush women from Alaskan legends. She was the type of woman who would thrive in Alaska. But what about Trina? Though she didn't consider herself to be wimpish in the least, she wasn't exactly rugged. Was she too citified to live in the backwoods? She'd definitely been frightened when she'd heard there'd been a murder. Ivan's crude behavior affronted her. "I hope I'll fit in."

"Don't worry, honey. You'll do just fine." Maybelle clapped her on the shoulder with bearlike strength. "Okay, so we got a crew from town coming and the people who are staying at the lodge. Only three of them. There's that cute young couple, the Winkles. And Jacob Poynter."

Maybelle dropped a pause. It was as if Trina should be impressed by Jacob Poynter, but she didn't recognize the name.

"Jake Poynter," Maybelle repeated. "He won a bronze medal in the Winter Olympics about ten years ago."

"What event?"

"Biathlon. That's the one where they cross-country ski and then shoot. Jake is quite the celebrity. And a great buddy of Ivan's." Her lips pursed. "That Ivan! Sometimes he annoys the heck out of me. He hasn't even told me if he's going to have a ceremony or what kind of ceremony. But if there's a need for a best man, you can bet your bottom dollar that Jake's got the job."

"That's reassuring."

"And if you're needing a matron of honor," Maybelle said, "I'm free."

"Thanks." In spite of all her doubts, Trina brightened. She might actually be married today. There might be a ceremony where she would be the bride instead of the bridesmaid. "I have a dress," she said. "Do you think I should wear it?"

"You betcha! A woman only gets married once for the first time." Maybelle polished off her muffin. "This is your first time, isn't it?"

"Yes."

"Smart girl! First time I got hitched, I was only eighteen. And I'll tell you this, I never was a little slip of a girl, but I wasn't big enough to carry all that responsibility. No, ma'am. Now the second one, well, he was my true love. Every woman should be married to a true love. At least once in her life. And he was mine...."

Maybelle's words rolled on as she continued with her kitchen chores, and Trina allowed the woman's voice to lull her into a sense of warm complacency while she forgot, for a moment, about the pressing decision she needed to make. To wed or not to wed.

During a pause, while Maybelle checked in the industrial-size oven, Trina made her excuse. "I wanted to take a look around outside before it snows."

"Bundle up, honey. It's colder than it looks."

Trina ran up to her room to grab her jacket, mittens and a red knitted cap, then she went outside. Overhead, the clouds began to mass, but the sky was still blue, and the glare off the snow was brilliant.

Reaching into her parka pocket, she took out the case for her eyeglasses and stuck the prescription sunglasses on her nose. About a hundred yards down the road, she closed her eyes, then whipped around. Her eyelids lifted. With corrected vision, she took in the sharp details of the crazy-quilt house that had been built one room at a time. The building stood amid several tall spruce at the foot of a rising slope. The porch was up five steps from the snow-covered ground. The exterior of the first floor was of stripped, polished logs. The second was clapboard siding. Just below the high, peaked roof was an Alaskan decoration, carved and painted in red, black and greenish blue. The design showed two huge, unblinking eyes, elaborately outlined. In the corners of the eaves were smaller ravens, wolves and bears, peering down like Alaskan gargoyles. The cheerful trim around the windows glistened with bright red paint.

Trina felt herself smiling. It was a strange, exotic-looking house, but she liked it. Would this be her home?

She turned to her left and walked past the other large structure. The two-story lodge had obviously been constructed in a more planned, professional manner. The siding was all log, and the trim was also red. An eight-foot-tall totem pole, depicting a squatting bear, beavers and a soaring eagle, stood in front.

Back toward the house, past the garage and several mysterious outbuildings, she saw the barn. And David. He sat astride a chestnut mare, looking every inch the cowboy with his Levi's and his down vest, his broad shoulders and his black Stetson hat.

The moment Trina recognized him, her heart leapt up in her throat. Immediately, she gulped hard. This response was *not* a good sign! She needed to think of Ivan—his letters, his sensitivity, his generosity. Instead, she felt like singing, like laughing and running toward David with her arms outstretched. Too easily, she imagined him pulling her onto the saddle and galloping off over the snow-covered fields into the primeval forests.

"Oh, damn." This was all wrong. With her little red mittens, she covered the lower half of her face. What was she going to do? *Go back to the kitchen. Forget you ever saw him.* These outrageous yearnings couldn't lead to anything but trouble. If she had an ounce of sense, she would run away while she still could.

Instead, she stepped forward and waved. "David!"

His chiseled features relaxed in a smile when he recognized her, and he eased his mount forward. "Do you like to ride, Trina?"

"I haven't done much riding."

"Today's a good day to learn. Before the snowfall." He swung off his horse and stood beside her. "Let's go to the barn."

He hitched his horse outside, and they entered a large structure with a high flat ceiling, several empty stalls and a tack room. The floor was wood, scattered with hay and very clean. The whole barn smelled pleasantly of leather and hay. "Six horses and two cows," David said, "as I mentioned before, no more pigs or chickens."

"Too succulent," she remembered.

She followed him to the rear door that opened onto a large corralled area where the horses were kept. David whistled two low notes, and a dappled gray horse plodded toward them. In moments, the mare was saddled and David helped Trina swing her leg astride. He adjusted her stirrups. "How's that?"

"Feels tall," she said. She inhaled deeply, struggling to stifle the heart-pounding excitement that arose unbidden at David's proximity.

He mounted his own horse. "Just stick with me."

"What do I do with the reins? How do I make her turn?"

"Basically, you do nothing. This is Myrtle, the original old gray mare. She'll follow the lead horse. But if you want to turn, pull in the direction you want to go. Pull back, like on a hand brake, to stop. We'll just take a short jog."

As they rode slowly away from the barn, the whole day took on a new, beautiful aspect. Despite her sunglasses, the world seemed rose-colored, soft and beautiful.

"Do you like it?" he asked.

"I love it." Why was the snow prettier here than in Denver? Only a week ago, she'd been dragging herself to work in an office in downtown Denver. Today, she was riding on horseback into the Alaskan landscape. She wanted this to be her life-style. How could she ever go back?

When they had gone a ways from the barn, David picked up the pace to a canter. Trina's horse followed suit.

Bouncing up and down in the saddle, Trina said, "What are you doing?"

"Giving the horses some exercise. If we have a blizzard, they'll be inside for a couple of days."

David glanced over his shoulder at her and grinned. He almost laughed out loud. Trina was pretty damn cute, he thought. She was hanging on tight, jostling up and down in the saddle like a yo-yo. Her little red cap bobbled wildly.

"We're going faster," he warned. "You'll like this better. Not so much bouncing."

"G-g-good."

He guided his chestnut mare in a slow gallop across the snowfields. There was another set of tracks in front of them, from that couple who were staying at the lodge, the Winkles, and David purposely turned in another direction. At the edge of the forest, he halted so Trina could catch her breath. Trina's mount pulled up beside him.

"Isn't this where they found the body?" she asked.

"No, it's farther toward the road. North of here." The new pace he set was slow and comfortable.

"David? When we were talking by the fireplace, you said you had a solution to my problems."

"Did I?"

"I'd like to hear it. I'm really confused and maybe you have an idea I haven't considered."

He scrunched down his eyebrows, made a pretense of thinking, then shook his head. "Mustn't have been very useful," he said, "because I already forgot what it was."

But he hadn't. Yesterday, he had almost proposed to her himself. Almost asked her to make Alaska her home, and to make him her husband. But that moment had passed, and David was damn glad he'd not mentioned that idea. He'd been married once already and hadn't been too good at it.

Besides, he thought, he couldn't give Trina all she deserved. David wasn't a rich man. Sure, he had a little nest egg. But no land. Ivan had seen to that.

In spite of his precautions in turning the opposite direction, he spied the Winkles, Phyllis and Bradley, threading through the forest and coming right toward them.

"Hold it right there," Bradley called. He raised the lens of his .35 millimeter camera to his eye, aimed and shot their picture. "Wow! Great shot! This is incredible country."

David performed the introductions. He wasn't impressed with these two environmentalists from Boulder, Colorado, who worked for some kind of weirdo magazine. Bradley was the photographer, and Phyllis was the writer. They'd supposedly come to do a piece on the hunting preserve, but David suspected they were looking for violations of hunting restrictions regarding endangered species.

"That's so Gothic," Phyllis said to Trina. "You're a mail-order bride? How could you give up everything for a man?"

"There wasn't much to give up," Trina murmured.

"But how did you know it was right? Did you have a special feeling? Maybe you knew him in another life...."

"Another life?"

"You know, like karma."

"Don't tell her anything," David warned. "She's a writer."

"Stop it, David! I'm also a human being, and I'm totally sympathetic to Trina." While she spoke, she stroked her horse's neck. "Bradley and I have only been married for six months, so I'm familiar with the problems of newlyweds."

"What problems?" Bradley said.

"You know."

"No, Phyllis, I have no idea what you're talking about."

Phyllis leaned toward Trina. "Sometimes, Bradley is a regular green-eyed monster. Jealous, you know."

"Really," Trina said, glancing at Phyllis who was blond and extremely thin. "Maybe he had a reason to be jealous. In another life."

"We did know each other in past lives," Phyllis said with a completely straight face. "In Atlantis."

"Did you?" Trina nodded. What a wacko! "How did you two happen to come way up here from Boulder?"

"A friend told us about this place. He lives in Juneau."

"A very dear friend of Phyllis's," Bradley said. "A former lover, in fact. You see, I can say that kind of thing because I'm not at all jealous. I'm secure in our relationship of mutual respect and—"

"Nobody wants to hear it," Phyllis interrupted. "Come on, I'll race you back to the barn. And don't worry, David, we'll put the saddles away and curry the horses."

She took off in a graceful canter, riding as if she were part of the horse, and Bradley followed. He was far less competent in his riding and his camera banged against his chest.

As Trina watched them ride away, she couldn't help but comment, "There go a couple of new-age neurotics."

"Radical environmentalists," he said. "We call them greenies."

"Now, David. Their goals are for the good."

"Don't get me wrong, I'm all in favor of conservation and nonpollution and saving the rain forests, but if those greenies had their way, we'd all be wearing loincloths and eating berries. Meat is what people live on up here. It's always been that way. The natural way." He nudged his heels against his mare. "We should be getting back."

"I guess so." The ride hadn't brought Trina any closer to making her decision. All she knew was that she didn't want to leave this place. She intended to make every effort to understand Ivan, to find the sensitive man who had written those letters within the gruff old bear.

STILL EXHILIARATED from her ride, Trina peeled off her parka, hat and mittens and left them in the mudroom behind the kitchen. Though it was only eleven o'clock and Maybelle had said that the guests wouldn't arrive until noon, there were several voices coming from the kitchen.

Feeling like an outsider, Trina could hear them laughing, talking, sharing gossip. She caught a couple of phrases about the dead man who had been found on Ivan's property, then Maybelle's voice drowned out the others. "None of that. I won't have my potlatch ruined by a murder."

"But it's so exciting" came a high-pitched rejoinder. "They say he was shot in the back. In cold blood."

"And I say, no more." Maybelle was firm. "Now, who brought these pickled mushrooms?"

Trina slipped through the kitchen as unobtrusively as possible and went down the hall to Ivan's office. She raised her hand to knock, though the study door was slightly ajar. Hearing an angry voice from within, she hesitated.

"What kind of a sheriff are you, Reuben?" That was Ivan. "The kids who found the dead man were on my land, and I call that trespassing. If you won't prosecute, I'll take the law into my own hands and sue their parents."

"Take the law into your hands?" She could hear Sheriff Rueben Kittridge sputtering. "Listen here, Ivan. We're not talking about the kids. We're talking about the dead man. We haven't even identified this guy."

"I don't know him." In contrast with Reuben, Ivan sounded smooth and in control.

"How do you know? Dammit, Ivan, are you going to let me see your guest book for people who are booked at the lodge?"

"No, sir, I am not. None of your business."

"Were you expecting anybody?"

"Maybe I was, and maybe I wasn't."

"We're not playing games, Ivan. This is murder."

"Are you accusing me of doing it? Just because the guy got himself killed on my property? Probably a damn poacher." Ivan's voice lowered dangerously. "Like you, Reuben."

"What are you saying?"

Trina knocked. She didn't want to hear any more of these angry accusations.

"What?" Ivan shouted.

Trying not to appear timid, she peeked inside. Without her glasses, she couldn't discern the details of their expressions, but both men appeared dark and glowering.

Reuben nodded. "Good morning, ma'am." Beneath his bushy eyebrows and mustache, his face was bright scarlet. Even the whites of his eyes were bloodshot. "I was just leaving."

"Thanks, Reuben, don't go far." Ivan rose from behind his desk and watched the sheriff lumber out the door. Then he looked at her. His expression was arch and slightly disapproving. "You're not dressed to be married, Trina."

"I'm not sure that a wedding is in order." She studied his face, trying to discern his response, but it was like trying to read a wall of ice. "It might be best if we wait, you know, to find out if we're compatible."

"Perhaps you're right." He came toward her and held out his hand, waiting until she reached out. Then he captured her hand and held it. "You've deceived me."

The flick of her eyes betrayed her guilt. He must be talking about David, about her uncontrollable attraction to him. How did Ivan know? Had he seen them riding? Was her attraction so obvious? Ashamed, she looked down at her boots. "I'm sorry, Ivan. I've been so unfair to you."

"You're not twenty-five," he said.

Startled, she looked up. He was talking about her age! That was nothing compared to her inappropriate feelings for David. Quickly, she said, "I meant to tell you, but then you started writing to me, and I—"

"My heart was in those letters, Trina. My heart and soul. And, all that time, you were lying. I'm hurt."

"Oh, come on, Ivan. We're not living in the eighteen hundreds. I'm healthy and strong enough to bear children, if that's what you're worried about. Is it really so important that I be in my twenties?"

"It's the lying," he said, releasing her hand. "And now, this refusal to go through with the wedding. Still, I can forgive you. I still want you to be my bride. But can I trust you?"

"Give me a chance. We'll get to know each other." What was she saying? How had the conversation turned in this direction? "But, Ivan, I need some time to think about this."

"No, Trina. It would be too humiliating to postpone the wedding. Today, my friends and family have gathered to meet my new bride. It must be today. Or never."

"But I don't know..."

"I meant every word I wrote to you in those letters. Every syllable. When you are my bride, you will be taken care of. Well taken care of, financially."

"And emotionally?"

"Of course. I'll do everything I can to make you happy."

His voice was as smooth as velvet. His eyes shone with the sincerity she'd come to respect in his letters. How could she say no?

"Please," he said. "If it doesn't work out, you can have the marriage annulled. And I guarantee I'll be fair with you."

Her emotions forbade her agreement. It wasn't right. She couldn't marry one man when she was attracted to another. She shook her head.

Before she could speak, he said, "Don't answer too quickly. This will work out between us, Trina. I promise." His voice was gentle and as seductive as his letters. "I promise your long nights in Alaska will never be lonely."

She remembered his letters, the sensations she had when she read them. The feelings came from deep in her heart. The man who had written those letters was a man she could love.

"All right, Ivan, I will marry you. Today."

Chapter Three

The ceremony took less than three minutes. Ivan stepped outside his office and called to Reuben who, in addition to being sheriff, was also a justice of the peace. Apparently, the guests would only be present at the party.

Before Trina had time to reconsider, she'd signed the marriage license and said, "I do."

"And now," Reuben said, "following the time-honored tradition, Ivan, you may kiss the bride."

Ivan caught her in his arms. He pulled her hard against his chest, crushing her breasts. He barely looked at her, then his mouth pressed down so hard that her lip was pinched against her teeth. His physical strength overwhelmed her for a moment. Then, instinctively, she fought him, twisting her head to one side. The more she struggled, the tighter his grasp. Where was the tenderness he'd spoken of? Where was the love? She wrenched away from him, staring in shock. All his lovely promises were erased by the rough brutality of his kiss. "What are you doing?"

"Taking what's mine. You're mine now, Trina."

"No!" She was breathing hard. Her lips were bruised. What had she done? "Don't you remember, Ivan, in your letters. You talked about a partnership."

"Partners?" He considered. "In a way, that's true. You be sure to tell Jake Poynter about that."

"Who? About what?"

"Run upstairs and get changed." He turned away from her dismissively. "I don't want my bride wearing blue jeans."

"In your letters," she insisted. "You talked about the lifetime partnership of a man and a woman."

"Did I? Well, get that notion out of your pretty little head, my bride. You'll take what I give you and be glad for it. But the only way you'll ever own anything around here is when I'm dead and gone."

"Why? Why did you marry me?"

"The usual reasons, I suppose. Plus, my bride, I'll call you my special little insurance policy."

"What does that mean?"

"Change your clothes, Trina. You look like hell, and I don't want you to embarrass me in front of my friends."

Appalled at his coarseness, she ran from the room, fled upstairs into her pink chamber where her simple wedding gown lay spread across the bed. The dress was a mockery. This marriage was a sham. She'd been manipulated into a hateful, loveless relationship. Why? Why would Ivan Stoddard want that? Why did he mention Jake Poynter? What did he mean when he said she was an insurance policy?

There was a knock at the door, and Maybelle entered uninvited. "Trina, honey, it's eleven-thirty and you're still not ready. Let's get you into that pretty little frock of yours."

"Did he send you? Did Ivan send you?"

"Yes, he did. Said you might need some help. And, honey, I've never seen him looking so happy. He announced to that whole room of women in the kitchen that he was now a married man.''

"Happy?" If his kiss was a display of happiness, Trina would hate to see him in a vindictive mood.

"I'm sure you're nervous," Maybelle said. "Perfectly natural for a new bride. Now, let's get you changed into your wedding gown. Relax, Trina. Enjoy yourself. Everybody's dying to meet you."

Numbly, she allowed Maybelle to cajole her into the plain white dress with a touch of lace at the neck and wrists. But Trina felt like she was dressing for an execution instead of a wedding reception. There was only one hope she could cling to. David. She needed to talk with him, to have him soothe her fears. She'd made the wrong decision, she was sure of that. And she needed to get away. She wanted David to take her away from here, to ride off beside her into the magnificent Alaskan snow vistas.

"Come on, now," Maybelle said. "Let's see a smile."

Trina didn't dare smile. If she did, her face would crack. She'd burst into hysterics. The last thing she wanted to do was attend a party and listen to people say, "Many happy returns." Quickly, she finished buttoning her dress. "I'll be right down, Maybelle. As soon as I fix my hair."

"You hurry up. Put a hustle in your bustle. The party's going to start, and I'm afraid it's going to be a short one. A couple of snowflakes have already fallen."

The door closed behind the housekeeper, and Trina yanked out her braid and pulled a brush through her thick, unruly hair. Outside her window, crystals of snow drifted lazily down. *Have you ever caught a snowflake and held it in your hand?* She remembered David saying that. *Oh, David, I need to talk with you. You're my only friend.*

She hurried through hallways and corridors, avoiding everyone until she was downstairs in the large room outside David's office and bedroom. Orange flames crackled in the moss rock fireplace.

Taking a deep breath, she flung open the door to his office. He wasn't there. Nor was he in his bedroom. Where was he? She needed him.

Heartsick, Trina sank down on the ledge beside the fireplace, not caring if the soot marked her wedding gown. It was only a dress. She hadn't even worn it during the three-minute civil ceremony. Like everything else, the dress was a fraud. She wasn't a bride. Ivan had made that quite clear. Trina belonged to him. She was a . . . a possession.

Oh, David, where are you?

It wasn't too late, she told herself. She could still annul the marriage. And that was exactly what she intended to do. There was no way in hell that she would go to bed with Ivan Stoddard.

The door from outside shoved open and David stomped inside. He pulled off his vest and Stetson, then turned and saw her. "Trina? What are you doing here?"

"I need a friend."

"Looks to me like you've got a whole house full of people who want that job. Out front, it looks like a parking lot. And they're all here to meet you."

David's hesitant smile broke her heart. He was being polite, being happy for her when she had no reason for joy.

Trina wished she was confident enough to wear her eyeglasses so she could clearly see every detail of David's features. She was glad when he came closer, within her field of clear vision. He sat beside her on the wide stone ledge beside the hearth. His voice was gentle and his words were sweet. "You're a beautiful bride. I don't believe I've ever seen a sight so pretty as you, sitting here, straight and proud, with firelight dancing in your hair."

Not thinking, she reached out and touched his cheek, still cold from being outside. He wore a cowboy's version of dress-up clothing, a navy blue shirt with fancy buttons and black trousers. She realized with a shock that she wished he could have been her groom.

"Ivan's a lucky man," he said. "So, when's the ceremony?"

"It's over."

The stillness in the room became thick and palpable, filled with the weight of her regret. She saw the question in David's eyes as he took her hand and held it. He whispered, "Why, Trina?"

"It happened so fast. Reuben was right there, pronouncing us man and wife before I had a chance to think." She turned toward the fire. "No, that's not true. I agreed to marry him of my own free will. Nobody forced me to sign the marriage license. I did it because Ivan and I were alone for a moment, and he reminded me of the man who wrote those letters. Those damn letters. I was fool enough to believe every word he'd written." She turned to him. "David, I fell in love before I even came to Alaska. I fell in love with words on a page. I know that's crazy."

"Not crazy at all."

"But the words were lies." She had wanted so badly to be in love that she'd fallen for a con job, a crude scam. "I was blind. I was so gullible."

"If it was a mistake, Trina, it can be fixed."

"But I can never trust my feelings again. Never."

"It's not that bad."

"I was a fool. Ivan used those letters to make me think he was someone else, someone sensitive and caring. He's not the same man as the one who wrote to me about waterfalls and migrating birds and lonely Alaskan nights. I can't explain it. Do you understand what I mean?"

"Yes."

David understood only too well. For David had written those letters.

He gazed into her eyes, regretting her pain and wishing there were some easy cure for her aching heart. He had never meant to hurt her. His stumble into deception had begun innocently enough.

When Ivan placed his advertisement for a mail-order bride in a nationally distributed magazine, the response was astounding. Over a hundred women replied, sending along photos and brief letters. Since it was David's job to hire and fire new employees, the letters ended up on his desk. He composed a standard response for the eighty or so that Ivan rejected based solely on their photographs. To the others, David wrote a discouraging letter about the hardships of living in Alaska. Only five responded a second time. Among them was Trina.

He still remembered her letter, which was intelligent, witty and full of hope. She'd spoken of companionship, not passion. And her yearning for adventure rang true. He rejected the other four and started their month-long correspondence. Every night, before going to bed, he composed a letter on his word processor and signed it with Ivan's name. As he grew more fond of her, his letters took an intimate turn. Writing to her and reading her responses became his favorite time of day.

In the back of his mind, he knew that he was signing Ivan's name, but he avoided thinking ahead to the time when she would actually be here. She would never be his. She belonged to Ivan, a wealthy and powerful man. Desperately, he had tried not to care too much.

When he met her at the airport, he should have told her. Yesterday, when they sat in this room, he should have explained. He cursed his cowardice, damn every word and phrase he had written. Right this moment, as he gazed into her pure blue eyes, he should tell her.

"David? Have you ever been in love?"

"I was married once."

"So was I," she said wryly. "I am now. But that's not what I asked."

"I loved my wife when I met her. I was going to school in northern California, and we settled there. I don't know what happened. Maybe we were too young. Anyway, we grew apart." He winced at the memory. "We had two small children, a boy and a girl. Not a day passes when I don't think of them."

"Are they still in California?"

He nodded. "I couldn't stand to be in the same state and not be with them. I came back here, home to Alaska, and buried myself in work for Ivan. Needless to say, he was only too glad to have a foreman who wanted to put in twenty-four-hour workdays and have no other life."

"Seems like a lot of people come to Alaska for that reason . . . to run away from something." She paused, twisted the engagement ring on her finger. "I thought I was running toward something. But it's not here." She rose to her feet. "I can't stay here. I'm going upstairs to change clothes. Will you drive me to town, David? I'll find my way from there."

"You're leaving?" A shock went through him as he stood beside her. He didn't want her to go. Even if she was married to Ivan, he wanted to be near her.

"I can't stay. I don't love Ivan, and I doubt that I ever will." She bit her lower lip. "I mean, look at me, dressed like a bride when I have no love in my heart. I dislike Ivan. In time, I might learn to despise him."

"But, Trina—"

"No. If I stay, I'm as big a liar as he is. Maybe I already am. I didn't tell the truth in my letters, you know. I'm not twenty-five, I'm ten years older. Old enough to know better than to make plans based on promises and dreams."

"Never give up on your dreams, Trina."

She looked into his eyes. "But they'll have to be dreams, deferred. Maybe someday I'll be able to do this right."

"Don't go." He held her chin in his hand. "I'd miss you too much."

"That's kind for you to say. But you hardly know me."

"I know you better than you think. Don't leave. Not yet."

"But I can't stay. I can't...."

She watched as he gently came closer. At the last second, her eyelids closed, and she tasted his lips in a firm but gentle kiss. A tremor went through her. She felt lighter than air, ephemeral as a snowflake.

Of their own volition, her arms reached for him. Without opening her eyes, she clung to him. His second kiss wakened the sweetest sensations. Sheer pleasure blossomed within her. This was the way a kiss should be, a prelude to desire.

The door to the room pitched open. "Hey, David. Get on out here, the party's going and—"

David turned, tried to shield her from the intruder's view. "I'll be right there."

"Oh, dang." It was the voice of Sheriff Reuben Kittridge. "I'm real sorry. I didn't mean to interrupt. . . . Is that you, Trina? Oh, dang."

She heard the door bang shut. She probably should have been embarrassed, but Trina was beyond humiliation. "Now I'm really in trouble, huh? I feel like I'm in grade school, and I just got caught by the principal."

"Are you going to be all right, Trina?"

"I'll survive. But I'm not much in the mood for a party. I guess I need to talk to Ivan before I leave the lodge." She plucked the diamond from her finger. "And I need to return this."

"I'll come with you," David said.

"That's all right. All I need is for you to drive me into town after I talk to Ivan."

"Trina." David stilled her protests by placing his finger crosswise on her lips. "I will be with you when you talk to Ivan."

A sudden warmth coursed through her veins. She felt safer and stronger than any other time during this Alaska sojourn. "Thank you, David. I would appreciate that."

"Ivan's a smooth talker. I know from experience."

They made their way to the kitchen. David advised her to hold back while he called Maybelle to one side. "Where's Ivan?"

"Well, it's the silliest thing I've ever seen. He comes in here, blabs to the world that he's a married man, says I should check on Trina, then tells me he'll be in his study and is not to be disturbed. I've knocked a couple of times, but he doesn't answer.''

"How long has he been in there?"

"Well, gosh, it was about eleven-thirty when he came into the kitchen. And now it's almost twelve-thirty. Everybody's here. They all want to meet Trina and offer their congratulations before this little confetti snow turns into a blizzard."

David grabbed Trina's hand and whisked her past the clusters of guests down the hallway and to the office door. He tried to turn the knob. It was locked. He tapped, then called Ivan's name. Under his breath, he muttered, "I don't know what kind of game he's playing. Wait here, I'll get a key."

Trina stood uncomfortably, trying to look inconspicuous in her wedding gown. It didn't help when Maybelle grabbed her by the arm and pulled her through the living room to the dining room to show her the two long tables on which gifts and flowers were displayed. Near the gifts was a three-tiered, fancy white cake with a tiny statue of a bride and groom on top. Maybelle continued toward the guests.

"Please, Maybelle. Not now."

"Okay, honey. You say when."

Trina returned to the entryway outside the office door. After a moment, the guests began to appear nearby. It seemed to Trina that they were closing in like wolves for the kill.

One man separated from the others. Like her, he was dressed all in white. His snowy turtleneck was tucked into white flannel slacks. His belt and boots were a pale leather. In contrast, his hair was coal black and his complexion was darkly tanned. Though he dressed like a dandy, he exuded an aggressive, masculine strength. "I'm Jacob Poynter."

She remembered Maybelle's description. "You're the Olympic champion."

"That was a long time ago." He gave a practiced, self-deprecating grin. "And you must be the bride-to-be. It's Trina, isn't it?"

"Yes." She shifted her weight uncomfortably from foot to foot, wishing she could fade into the wainscoting. *Where was David?*

"Will we be treated to a wedding ceremony?" Jake asked. "I didn't know that Ivan was religious."

"No ceremony, actually. It's already taken place." She bit her tongue. Why had she said anything? The last thing she wanted was a string of phony congratulations. "Please don't mention this to anyone."

"Are you saying that you and Ivan are already married?"

"We signed a license and said 'I do.' He kissed me." She shuddered. "I don't know if that means anything."

He downed his drink in one gulp. It was white wine, of course, to match his outfit. "Congratulations, Trina. You're a wealthy woman now."

"Thanks." She might be wealthy now, but not for long. Whatever had occurred between herself and Ivan—and Trina didn't consider that brief civil ceremony to be anything like a true marriage—was over and done with. She might be throwing away a fortune, but she felt free. Leaving was the right thing to do.

David returned with the key. Maybelle was right behind him. "When?" Maybelle demanded. As soon as she spotted Trina, she said, "When do we make the announcement?"

David opened the door to the study and flicked on the overhead light. The room looked like an avalanche had rolled through it. File drawers were yanked open and the contents strewn. The fax machine had been torn open and gutted. The computer and modem were similarly disabled. Ivan was nowhere in sight.

David pulled the door shut. "Maybelle, you'd better find Reuben. He ought to see this."

BEHIND THE CLOSED DOOR of the ransacked study, Maybelle, Reuben, Trina and David gathered to discuss the next logical step.

"First, we clean," Maybelle said. She bent down, scooped up a handful of papers and placed them on the desk.

"Don't do that," Reuben said. His walrus mustache twitched from side to side. "Geez, Maybelle, don't you know? That's evidence. Don't you go touching anything."

"Well, if you think I'm going to leave the place like this, you've got another thing coming, Sheriff."

"Lock the door. Nobody's coming in here until I get a look around." He glared at the housekeeper. "I can't believe you didn't hear anything. Somebody was in here, throwing stuff around. Breaking things."

"The office is soundproofed, Reuben. You know that. And we've had a mob of people coming and going. Heck, somebody could have set off a twenty-one-gun salute, and I probably wouldn't have blinked twice."

"I'll have to question everybody." Reuben inhaled and held his breath, self-importantly puffing out his barrel-size chest. "One of them must have seen somebody enter or exit the office."

"Excuse me," Trina said, "but what's the crime? Making a mess?"

"She's right," Maybelle said. "We can clean this up. And there's really no harm done. And I'll tell you this, Reuben, I don't want you wrecking my potlatch by getting all official."

"Ladies, please." Reuben cleared his throat. "You're missing something here."

"Ivan," David said. "We're missing Ivan. And the way the snow's picking up out there, we'd best start looking for him."

"Right." Reuben snapped his fingers, coming to a decision. "We need a search party. We can pair up everybody here and search."

"We most certainly will not," Maybelle said. "I'm not having the entire town of Osprey poking through this house. These folks are nosy enough without giving them permission to roam. I'll organize the searchers."

David said, "I'll check the barn and the garage and make sure Ivan's Jeep is still there."

Maybelle gave the rest of the orders. "Trina, you take Victor and search the upstairs of the house. I'll have Jake search in the lodge. You can go with him, Reuben."

PAIRED WITH the unpleasant Victor Stoddard, Trina climbed to the second floor where both their bedrooms were located.

Victor lounged on the landing while she poked into all four second-floor bedrooms, glancing in closets and peeking under the beds. Victor's room had a stale odor, possibly emanating from the half-empty mugs on the bedside table. But she found no sign of Ivan.

In her own room, Trina found her glasses and stuck them on her nose. Appearances didn't matter now. She meant to cancel this ridiculous marriage, and she didn't care who might know she was thirty-five years old.

Back on the landing, Victor greeted her with, "Isn't that cute. You wear glasses. Bad eyes or age?"

"None of your business." She asked, "Where do we go next? You're more familiar with this house than I am."

"But it's your house, isn't it? You and Ivan are already married."

"Let's get this over with, shall we?"

"You're a regular gold digger, aren't you? Came to Alaska and struck it rich. Was that your plan?"

"Ask Ivan when we find him."

"Why should I put myself through the ordeal of talking to my uncle? I've got you right here."

Something in his words, an undercurrent of barely suppressed bitterness, sent a shiver down her spine.

He continued, "This is a dangerous country. You know that, don't you, Trina? Just yesterday, the sheriff found a dead man in the fields."

"The *land* didn't kill him," Trina said. "He was shot in the back."

"Did I fail to mention that the *people* here are dangerous?" Quick as a striking rattlesnake, his hand shot out and grasped her forearm. He held tight, gripping her painfully. "The midnight sun drives men mad. And women, too."

"Let go of me, Victor."

"You're very pretty, in spite of the glasses. Maybe, when Ivan's done with you, I'll marry you myself."

"Let go or I'll scream."

"Fine." He released her and laughed. "Don't be upset, Auntie Trina. I was only joking."

Like heck he was joking. She'd seen the dark cruelty in his eyes, sensed the unwarranted hatred. "What have I ever done to you?"

"Scammed me out of my rightful inheritance."

"Why would you think I'd cheat you?"

"Oh, please, Trina. Don't pretend that you're an innocent twenty-five-year-old girl. You're a grown woman, smart enough to know exactly what you were doing here. What did you do for my uncle to convince him to marry you?"

Before she could retort, he went on. "Ivan's got quite a reputation with the ladies. Well deserved, I might add. What did you do to make him decide to settle down?"

"Nothing."

"That's a laugh." Victor started for the stairs. "I'm done with this search. No doubt, Ivan's up to something. He'll show himself when he's good and ready."

Trina didn't stop him from heading down the stairs to the front room where the party was still under way. Were any of the guests beginning to suspect that things weren't moving smoothly? Was anyone aware that Ivan had vanished? Though Trina was unfamiliar with the house, she continued searching alone. Solitude was definitely better than being accompanied by Victor. He was even more despicable than his uncle. Ivan, at least, appeared to be intelligent. She thought Victor probably embodied the worst of traits—meanness coupled with stupidity.

As she ascended another flight of stairs, the sounds of the party grew distant. Though this house had been constructed piece by piece, it was a solid structure, well insulated from the cold. On the top floor, under the

eaves of the house, there were only two doors. One led
to a bathroom, which was far more lavishly appointed
than the one on the second floor. It was empty. Trina
knocked on the other door and entered hesitantly, feeling suddenly fearful of what she might find inside.

It was a large bedroom. Ivan's room, she assumed.
The bed was king-size, with ornately carved posts that
resembled totem poles. Facing the bed was a wide-screen
television and an open cabinet that displayed a library of
videotapes. At the far end, beneath a window, was a
huge rolltop desk, a couple of file cabinets and several
shelves of books. She had the sense that Ivan could hole
up in here and be entertained for several days.

She checked the walk-in closet, which was neatly hung
with clothes. On the floor, a row of boots had been lined
up with the toes exactly even. The whole room was tidy.
The only disarray came from discarded clothing tossed
over the back of a chair. Trina took a closer look and
discovered that the clothes were the ones Ivan had been
wearing in the study when they signed the marriage license.

He had come up here to change clothes. But, of
course, he would dress differently for a party where all
of his friends had gathered. He would want to wear
something more formal than corduroy trousers and a
flannel shirt.

She left the room, closing the door behind her. Were
there other places she should search?

IN THE BARN, David called out Ivan's name. He climbed
a ladder and glanced in the hayloft, then returned to the
stalls where he had curried and bedded the horses down
for the night. Ivan's favorite mount, a palomino stal-
lion named Sol, whinnied, and David came closer to the

horse. The mane was still slightly damp. Sol had been ridden recently, after the snow had begun to fall. Why would Ivan come out here for a ride? It didn't make a damn bit of sense.

David sighed. As if anything Ivan did made sense. He was an unbelievably difficult man to understand. Though David hated him for what he'd done to Trina, he knew that Ivan wasn't all bad. They had a grudging friendship. They both loved this land; they gloried in the magnificent landscapes. They had hunted side by side.

There were times when David felt closer to Ivan than to his own father. Not surprising because David's father had been absent for most of his life and had died when David was only twelve.

Many people had said Ivan played a part in that death. David's father had sold his land, which included four hundred acres of Ivan's hunting preserve, for far less than it was worth, and he had invested in a wildcat oil well that came up dry. Disappointment, said some, drove him crazy. But he was killed in a kayak accident. His boat overturned. Within sight of a ferry full of tourists, he'd slipped beneath the icy waters in Glacier Bay. David never blamed that act of nature on Ivan.

He did not, in fact, blame Ivan at all. David's father had been irresponsible from the start. Sure, it would have been great to inherit four hundred acres, but David didn't want to waste his life on fruitless revenge.

He left the barn. The snowfall had picked up force. Heavy flakes pelted down, as if the heavens had overturned and dumped a bowl full of wet white snow.

At the front of the house, cars and trucks were already leaving, and David hoped the guests would make it back to Osprey before the blizzard picked up wind and became impassable. He checked in the huge garage that was large enough to hold six vehicles and found Ivan's Jeep unmoved. There were several other outbuildings—sheds and a hot tub and a gazebo—but David decided to return to the house before searching further.

In the area between the house and the lodge, he spotted Reuben and Jake heading to the house. "Hey," David called out. "Did you find him?"

"Not a trace," Reuben responded. "And you?"

"Not in the barn or the garage. Ivan's horse has been ridden, but he's back in his stall. Ivan's car's still in the garage."

Snow plummeted around them. Heavy flakes clung to Reuben's mustache and eyebrows. "Everybody's leaving," he said. "If they saw anything, I'll never know."

"Come on, Reuben, you can talk to them later. It's not like any of these people are strangers."

"I don't like this," Jake said. "What if something's happened to Ivan?"

"After we go back to the house and make sure nobody's found Ivan there, I'll check the rest of the outbuildings," David said.

But darkness came early in February. By five o'clock it would be night. The temperature was already below zero and dropping fast. Though some of the outbuildings, like the barn and garage, were heated, it made no sense whatsoever for Ivan to be outside. What could he be doing? Hiding? Why? That wasn't Ivan Stoddard's style, David thought. Ivan had never run away from anything.

If he was here, in one of the sheds, he must have been hurt in an accident. Or something worse.

Chapter Four

At the house, Maybelle offered friendly farewells to the departing, disappointed guests who had neither witnessed a wedding nor tasted the ornate, three-tiered cake.

"We'll do it again real soon," she promised two elderly women who left arm in arm, propping each other up against the growing force of the wind and snow.

"Do it again?" David murmured behind her back. "Another wedding?"

Maybelle wheeled around and snapped at him. "I'll see you in the kitchen, young man."

David followed her to the kitchen where Reuben was waiting.

"Well?" she demanded. "Did you find him?"

"No luck," David said.

"Men!" Her pronouncement of the single syllable was so vehement that it sounded like cursing. "And isn't this a fine howdy-do. I knock myself out to put together a wedding reception, and the groom doesn't even bother to show up. I'm going to have words with Ivan. You can count on that."

"Me first." Trina stepped into the kitchen. She'd changed out of her wedding gown into jeans and a flannel shirt over a turtleneck. Unabashedly, she wore her gold-framed eyeglasses; there seemed to be no point in engaging in a search if she couldn't see clearly. "I get the first crack at Ivan when he shows himself."

"You poor baby." Maybelle embraced her and patted her shoulder. "Now, Trina, you haven't actually been left at the altar. Because you did the deed. You got yourself married. But this is no way to start."

"Maybe it's the way to end," she said.

"Oh, honey, you don't mean that."

Another lady from Osprey stuck her head into the kitchen. "Sorry, Maybelle. We've got to hit the road. It's turning nasty out there. But I guess we're due for a blizzard. Haven't had much snow this winter."

"Thanks for coming." Maybelle left the kitchen, turning back for one last remark. "You tell Ivan Stoddard that when he shows up, he's a dead man."

"I sure as hell hope not," said Reuben. "Sorry, Trina, I hate to say this, but I'm worried. I'm afraid something bad might have happened."

Something bad already had happened, she thought. Several rotten, lousy, negative experiences. Still, she knew her marriage wasn't what Reuben was talking about. No matter how much she resented and disliked Ivan, she didn't wish for him to come to physical harm. "What else can we do?"

"There are still the outbuildings to search," David said. "I'll go now."

"I'll come with you," Trina said.

"It's cold out there," he said. "Damn cold and getting worse."

"I want to come."

She trailed David into the mudroom behind the kitchen and donned her parka and mittens. She was already wearing her warmest boots. How cold could it be? She could handle it. Trina was from Denver, where the snow swept down from the front range of the Rockies.

Still, when she stepped outside behind David, she was unprepared for the chill that permeated her every pore. The metal frames on her glasses burned her face. Her breath froze. When she inhaled, it was like swallowing ice cubes.

Though it was only two o'clock in the afternoon, the snowy skies were as dark as dusk. They had only gone a few steps when they heard someone calling to them. It was Phyllis Winkle. She stood in the doorway to the mudroom, hopping from one foot to the other.

"Ignore her," David advised.

"Sorry, Phyllis," Trina called back. "We'll talk later."

"Can we help?" she called out. "Bradley and I could help. We've both done mountain rescue work."

"No," David yelled back. "Go inside."

When Phyllis disappeared into the house, he muttered under his breath. "That's all I need. A couple of do-gooders getting lost in the storm."

"Why do you dislike them so much? Is it because they're involved with environmental causes?"

"Not really. I wouldn't mind seeing this acreage converted to a game preserve with limited hunting. It's just that Phyllis and Bradley are so damn sunny and bright eyed. They're sticky, like a mouthful of sugar, and there's only so much optimism I can stand."

"Have you always been so dark and foul tempered?" she teased.

"Nobody's ever called me perky." He stared into her eyes. "By the way, Trina, I like your glasses."

"You do?"

"They suit you, make you look smart."

"Oh." She assumed he was just being nice. "Like a spinsterish schoolmarm."

"Take the compliment, Trina. You look good."

They began searching behind the barn, poking into a storage shed that was filled with parts and pieces of machinery with which Trina was unfamiliar. Then there was a smokehouse where venison was processed into jerky during the summer months. David even looked into an outhouse that was no longer used.

"Now where?" Trina asked. She was beginning to regret her willingness to tag along. Her jeans were damp from the snow and coldly clinging, chafing her legs.

"Behind the lodge," he said. "There's another garage. Nothing in it but a backhoe."

"Why do you have all this farm machinery?"

"We grow some summer wheat. And we do a lot of construction work." He gestured toward the ghostly shape of a gazebo with fancy latticework that contrasted with the rugged surroundings. "It's like that thing. We don't *need* equipment. Mostly, we have the equipment because Ivan can afford it. Eventually, these things find a use."

As they followed a path that was rapidly being obliterated by blowing snow, Trina pointed to a small octagonal structure that was built up on seven steps and surrounded by a walkway. It stood between the house and the lodge, separate from each but not far from either. A small stand of pine trees surrounded the odd-looking building. "What's that?"

"I call it Stoddard's folly," David said. "It was one of Ivan's more fanciful projects a couple of summers ago. A hot tub."

"Really? Who ever heard of an outdoor hot tub in Alaskan back country?"

"That's exactly what I told Ivan. It's enclosed, but the damn thing takes forever to heat up, and we've got to keep electricity going to it all the time or the water will freeze."

"Have you used it?"

"Once or twice. And I've got to admit that when you ease into that steamy water, it's a luxury well worth indulging. Ivan loves it. On any given day, he'll strip down and run out here. Usually with some . . ."

"Some woman." She supplied the word he had hesitated to say. Trina couldn't have cared less if Ivan bathed with the entire Dallas Cowboys cheerleading squad, but there was something in David's statement that made her think.

"You said he'd strip down," she repeated. "David, when I was searching in the house, I found Ivan's clothes discarded in his bedroom. Everything else was extremely tidy, but the clothes were carelessly tossed over a chair, like he was in a hurry. Maybe he stripped and came out here."

"Let's check it out." David hurried along the snow-covered path leading to the small building that stood between the main house and the lodge. It appeared to be deserted. Latched shutters covered every window. David went up the stairs.

A small branch from a spruce tree was wedged into the hasp. "That's weird," he said. "Somebody used a twig to keep this shut. I don't see the padlock anywhere."

He removed the twig before trying the doorknob. "It's locked," he said. "From the inside."

He hammered on the door. "Ivan! Are you in there?"

There was no response.

Trina had climbed up beside him and stood on the three-foot-wide ledge that encircled the building. "Have you got a key for the door?"

"Not with me. Back at the house." David went to the nearest shuttered window and unfastened the latch. "We can peek inside from here. Step back so I can open this."

When she'd moved a few paces out of the way, David pulled the wooden shutters apart. The four-paned window was jagged and broken. "What the hell?" David said.

Inside, through clouds of steam, he saw Ivan curled in a ball on the floor. The octagonal room was splotched with dark bloodstains. "My God, there he is."

When Trina moved toward the window, he held her back. "Don't look."

"Why? What's wrong? Oh, my God, is he dead?"

"I don't know." But David feared the worst.

"Should I go back to the house and get the key?"

"No time. We might be able to help him." David went to the door. He braced himself for maximum force and kicked hard at the lock. It held.

"David, what should I do?"

"Get help. Blankets."

"An ambulance? Do we need an ambulance?"

"Yes. Hurry." But David sensed that it was already too late. He kicked again and felt the latch loosen. One more kick and the door sprang open. "Trina, go!"

She was waving to someone.

Jake Poynter charged toward them as Trina raced down the stairs and ran toward the house.

"What is it?" Jake called.

David was already inside. He tore off his gloves and knelt. Ivan's body had twisted into a fetal position, probably to maintain as much warmth as possible, though the room wasn't freezing and the water in the hot tub steamed.

Ivan's arms were folded limply over his chest. David grasped his wrist, felt at his throat for a pulse. But there was no life in Ivan's body. There was a terrible, bloody wound in his chest.

Jake hovered behind David. "Is he dead?"

David nodded and rose to his feet. There was nothing he could do for Ivan Stoddard now.

When Reuben strode into the room and took over, David gladly left the hot tub and returned to the house where Trina, Maybelle and Phyllis were waiting.

"He's dead," David said.

Though Maybelle was undoubtedly the closest to Ivan, she appeared to have the least reaction. Her jaw locked. Her eyebrows scowled. And she was uncharacteristically silent.

Phyllis broke into tears. Her thin hands covered her face and her shoulders hunched as she wept loudly. "I'm sorry." She spoke in gasps. "It's just that—" Another sob. "I have to let my feelings out."

As for Trina, David thought he had never seen a more miserable picture. She sat on a tall stool beside the counter in the kitchen with her fingers laced in a tense knot. The usual warm blush faded from her cheeks, and her complexion was as white as a marble statue. But she wasn't made of stone; she was trembling. Behind her little gold-framed eyeglasses, her blue eyes popped wide. And, he thought, she looked frightened.

More than anything, David wanted to hold her, to comfort her and assure her that things would be all right.

But he couldn't lie. The situation couldn't be more wrong. Ivan was dead. Murdered. And Trina had one heck of a motive for killing him. By a quirk of fate, she was now Ivan Stoddard's widow. Which meant she'd probably just become very, very rich.

BY THE TIME they moved Ivan's body into the house, the snowstorm had become a blizzard. Trina stood by the window in the front room, looking out through a heavy curtain of white. Several inches of snow had already accumulated on the ground, blanketing the tire tracks of the many visitors who had headed back to Osprey. The only people left were the Winkles, Jake Poynter, Victor Stoddard, Maybelle, Reuben and David.

They were all gathered here, in this large room, wainscoted in dark oak. The white upper half was hung with framed photographs and painted landscapes of springtime green. The upholstery of the sturdy furniture, early American in style, picked up the forest green tones in the paintings, and the hardwood floor was liberally scattered with woven rag rugs. A fire crackled cheerfully on the hearth. If the circumstances had been different, Trina would have thought the front room had a pleasant, homey feeling. But the atmosphere was fraught with tension as they overheard snatches of Reuben's telephone conversation with the sheriff's office in Osprey. He stood on the other side of a wooden arch that led to the dining room, talking in low tones.

Trina glanced away but heard him say, "Homicide...all right. Small entry wound, probably a .22 caliber..."

There was a loud, heaving sob from Phyllis, and she buried her face on her husband's shoulder.

"That's right, naked," Reuben continued. "The dang fool was taking a hot tub bath."

Trina glanced into the dining room again, where the three-tiered wedding cake was still on display. The creamy icing was untouched. She couldn't imagine eating it now. The sweetness would choke her.

"Right...David's here." Reuben paused, then said, "You can bet I'll be talking to him."

David? Trina glanced toward him. Was he a suspect? He sat near the fire in a heavy rocking chair. His long legs were stretched out in front of him, and his arms were folded across his chest. He had changed from his dressy wedding clothes into Levi's and a blue work shirt over white thermal underwear. The top buttons were unfastened, revealing the beginning of dark hair on his chest. When her eyes met his, she saw him looking back at her, calm and strong.

He couldn't be a suspect, she thought. David was solid and steady, possibly the most sane person in this room. Herself included. She'd known him only a brief time, but she knew he was a good man. Certainly, he was not the type to commit murder.

Besides, David had been with her before they found the ransacked study, which, she figured, provided him with an alibi. Except that he had come into the house from outside. Where had he been? Was that the time when Ivan was killed?

Reuben completed his call and joined the silent circle in the front room. "I guess I don't need to tell you people not to go anywhere," he said. "Nobody and nothing is moving in this blizzard."

Jake Poynter swore under his breath. "Are the roads closed?"

"Those that aren't will be soon. Were you going somewhere?"

"I had planned to leave today. Yesterday, actually. I stuck around for the wedding."

"I hope everyone got back to town all right," Maybelle said.

"My men are checking," Reuben assured her. "But it seems that the returning guests formed a convoy of sorts and rode in a line. The roads weren't bad until just a little while ago."

"Who cares about them?" Victor said.

His self-satisfied smirk twitched slightly, and Trina wondered if he had spared even a moment of sorrow for the death of his uncle. Victor, like Jake, had been drinking steadily since they came into this room. "I want to know what happened to my uncle," Victor demanded.

"Murder," the sheriff said, "that's what happened."

"Who killed him?"

Phyllis continued to whimper softly, and Bradley patted her shoulder. "Does it matter?" she asked. "He's dead. Oh, I feel so awful."

"May I take her to our room?" Bradley inquired. "She needs to rest."

"Why's she so upset?" Victor said impatiently. "You people didn't even know my uncle."

"Awful," Phyllis wailed. "I feel awful."

Though Trina hated to agree with Victor, he did have a point. As far as she knew, the Winkles were only slightly acquainted with Ivan. They were visitors at the lodge. Phyllis's display of grief seemed out of proportion.

"Bradley, how well did you and your wife know the deceased?" Reuben asked.

"Time is unimportant. He was a human being," Bradley said indignantly. "The death of one man diminishes us all, does it not? 'Ask not for whom the bell tolls—'"

"Spare us the eulogy," Reuben said. "How well did you know Ivan Stoddard?"

"Not well," Bradley returned.

"Why are you and your wife up here, anyway? I know you're not hunters."

"We're writing an article," he said. "We work for a magazine based in Boulder called *Environment Now!* and we wanted to do a story on the Alaskan wilderness. I take the photographs, and Phyllis does the actual writing that accompanies them."

"The piece I just finished," Phyllis said between hiccupping sobs, "was not flattering to Ivan."

"I see." Rueben nodded. "You put together a nasty article about Ivan, and now that he's dead, you feel bad about it."

Phyllis wept out her affirmative response.

Though Trina could understand why Phyllis would be upset, she still thought the woman was overreacting— unless there was some other connection with Ivan, something that neither Phyllis nor Bradley had mentioned.

Victor said, "Maybe she's crying because she killed him."

"What? How could you say that?" Bradley maintained his self-righteous demeanor. "Neither Phyllis nor I would ever harm another living thing. And as for murder? Well, it's impossible. I demand an apology."

"Maybe you helped her," Victor suggested. "I know how you save-the-world greenies think. You probably thought you were doing the environment a favor by killing off Ivan."

"Take that back, you son of a—" Bradley tried to shake free of Phyllis, but she clung even tighter.

"Calm down," Reuben ordered. "Both of you."

Maybelle rose majestically to her feet. "Listen, Reuben, I can't just sit here and do nothing. There's work to do. This food needs to be put away and the house needs tidying. Do you have anything else to say?"

"Yes, ma'am, I do." Reuben hitched up his trousers and frowned. "I want you all to stay here, close by, until I have a chance to get your statements recorded. I'm considering Ivan's death to be murder."

"Why not suicide?" Jake Poynter put in. "From what David told us, the door to the tub house was locked from the inside."

David spoke up. "Doesn't mean much. It was one of those locks that you can set when you leave. Plus, somebody had stuck a twig in the outside lock. That would have trapped Ivan inside."

"Maybe," Jake conceded.

"And the window was broken," David said.

"And he was shot in the chest," Reuben added. "I'm not saying that a man can't shoot himself, but there was no gun in the tub house."

"How about this," Jake theorized. At the portable wooden liquor cart in the front room, he poured himself another drink. He had graduated from white wine to vodka. "Ivan could have shot himself, then broken the window and thrown the gun away. Maybe it's somewhere out there, buried in the snow."

"Won't work," David explained. "The shutter was latched from the outside."

"Also," Reuben continued, "shards of glass from the broken window were inside the tub house, indicating that it was broken from the outside, not the inside."

"So what?" Victor almost shouted. "What does that mean?"

Reuben's frown extended to his bushy eyebrows. His whole countenance reflected stern disapproval. "I'm not inclined to share my opinions. This is an official investigation."

"I'll explain," David said. "In simpleminded terms that even you can understand, Victor, here's what might have happened. Ivan was in the tub house, waiting for the water to heat up. He'd locked the door. The murderer opened the shutter, broke the window and shot Ivan, then closed and latched the shutter."

"If you're so smart," Victor said, "why did they bother to lock the door from the outside with a twig? And I was there, David, I helped move him up to his room. Why was he naked?"

"Why did he go to the hot tub in the first place?" Jake questioned. He smiled into his drink. "Seems like strange behavior for a man who had just been married. Perhaps he and his new bride planned to consummate their vows in the hot tub before they greeted their guests."

Everyone turned and stared at Trina. The varying degrees of hostility in their gazes made her uncomfortable, but she refused to squirm. She had nothing to hide. Sure, she'd made a mistake by marrying Ivan, but it was an error that could be corrected by annulling the marriage. "I was with Maybelle," she said, "dressing."

"That's right," Maybelle said. "And I don't care what the rest of you are doing, but I'm going to tidy up. Poor old Ivan won't be here to sign my paycheck, but I won't quit my responsibilities until Trina is ready to take over."

"Wait a minute," Trina said, "I have no intention of taking over anything. As soon as the weather clears, I'm getting out of here."

"Sure," Victor sneered. "The little gold digger's got what she came for. A signed marriage license and a claim on Ivan's estate."

"That's enough," David said. "Knock it off, Victor."

"Protecting her?" Victor's laugh wheezed like a gate hinge in need of oil. "Something going on between you two?"

Trina could see the anger simmering in David. His shoulders tensed. His eyes glittered like dark embers. He looked dangerous. But Victor didn't know when to quit.

"Come to think of it," Victor continued, "you've got a pretty good motive for killing Ivan, David. Everybody knows that you're bitter. Ivan took advantage of your father. Ivan took his land. And, up here, a man's nothing without his property. Did you do it, David? You must have hated him. When was that land scam? Twenty years ago. Have you hated him for twenty years? Did you finally kill him?"

"Stop it!" Maybelle said. "Let's have no bickering. Have you forgotten that a man has died? He was your uncle, Victor. Your employer, David. I won't have any fighting in this house."

"But murder is okay," Victor said. "Come off it, Maybelle. It's a little late to be worrying about proper behavior."

"Listen here, young man—"

"No, you listen to me. All of you." Victor uncoiled from the armchair where he had been sitting. "This is my inheritance we're talking about, and I'm not going to have it taken away because some mail-order bride comes up here and weds my uncle the second before he happens to die."

He paced across the room. "And I'm not going to have the estate go to David, either. That's why he's romancing this woman. He knows she'll get the money, then he has his chance to grab back the land Ivan took from his father."

The viciousness of his accusations cut deeply into Trina's heart. Of course, she knew Victor was sounding off, making unfounded statements. But was there a grain of truth? Was David interested in her because she might inherit?

But David hadn't known Ivan was dead this morning when he kissed her. Or had he?

She watched Victor stride to the dining room. His movements were jerky and disjointed. Though he hadn't been drinking anywhere near as much as Jake, Victor staggered. He whirled to face them as he stood beside the wedding cake, forming a perfect contrast. The cake was white, pure and lovely. It should have been eaten to celebrate the happy union of a bride and groom. Victor Stoddard was dark and horrible and mean.

"Damned cake," he said.

"Don't you touch that," Maybelle warned.

"Why? You planning to save it in case Ivan comes back from the dead?"

"I'll find a use for it."

"He's dead, Maybelle. Nobody's going to eat the wedding cake of a dead man." Victor picked up the silver serving knife that lay ready and waiting beside the cake. He used the knife to point at the traditional bride and groom statuettes that stood on the top layer. "Or maybe Trina wants this as a souvenir."

Maybelle said firmly, "You settle down."

"You're right." Victor eyed the icing decorations. "I shouldn't cut the cake."

He flipped the knife back onto the table. "I should kill it."

From his back pocket, he produced a handgun. Before any of them could react, he'd fired into the top layer of the wedding cake, splattering frosting against the wall behind it.

Before he could make another move, David was on top of him. He wrenched the gun from Victor's hand and passed it to Reuben.

"It's not the murder weapon," Victor said as he pushed David away from him. "My gun's a .45 caliber. I heard you say on the phone that Ivan was shot with a .22."

Reuben's mustache twitched furiously. "I'll have no more of this, Victor. Pull another stunt like that, and I'll arrest you."

"Yeah, sure. Big deal."

The resounding explosion of the gun had silenced Phyllis's sobs and galvanized Maybelle into the action she kept insisting she needed to take. Using napkins, she daubed at the wall, cleaning up after Victor.

Trina went to help her. In the dining room, she found a large chunk of cake on the floor and placed it on the formerly pristine white tablecloth. Beneath the cake, she found the miniature bride and groom statuettes.

As Trina held the tiny figures in her hand, a dark sense of foreboding went through her. The bride's head had been shot off.

"I'm going upstairs," Victor announced. He grabbed the whiskey bottle off the liquor cart. "To my room."

"Do you really want to do that?" Bradley asked. His tone had returned to the very essence of mellow. "I mean, do you really want to be alone?"

"None of you people are good company," Victor returned.

"Think about it," Bradley Winkle advised. "No one else around. A dead man upstairs on the third floor, laid out in his bedroom. Do you want to be alone? You've got to be thinking, as I am, that it was probably one of us who killed Ivan."

Chapter Five

One of them was a murderer.

Ever since they'd found Ivan's body, Trina had feared that possibility. One of them, a person in this room, had held a gun and fired point-blank into Ivan's chest.

She looked at the tiny figurines she held in her hand— a wedding cake groom and a shattered bride. Would the murderer strike again? Would she be next? She wrapped the bride and groom in a napkin and slipped them into the pocket of her Levi's. She would keep them as a re-minder to herself. *Be careful. Be alert.*

With a new sense of urgency, she studied each face, listened to the nuance of inflection in each voice. Who was it? Who, among them, had committed murder?

Maybe Bradley was the killer. Maybe he'd spoken out to divert suspicion from himself or from his clinging, weeping wife. Phyllis? Though she seemed fragile, there was a wiry, athletic strength in her slender limbs. She was an expert horsewoman. Perhaps she was equally good with guns. Heaven knew, the couple was opposed to the hunting carried on by most lodge guests.

Or could it be Victor? Trina had never before met anyone who had such an obvious vindictive streak. He was certainly capable of killing Ivan, especially since he stood to inherit.

Jacob Poynter held himself aloof from the others. Did he think he was godlike, so much better than everyone else that he could kill with impunity? Though Jacob didn't seem to have a motive, she didn't know him well.

Even Maybelle and Sheriff Reuben had reason to dislike Ivan. Had their hostility overtaken their good intentions?

"Okay, everybody," Reuben announced, "here's what I'm going to do. I'm setting up shop in David's office, back in the northeast corner of the house. I'll talk with each of you, one at a time. Be thinking of where you were and what you were doing from eleven-thirty this morning until two this afternoon. I want details. I want every minute accounted for. If you saw or heard something suspicious, I want to hear it."

"Suspicious?" Bradley questioned. "And what, exactly, constitutes suspicious behavior?"

"Unusual," Reuben tried to explain. "You know, if you saw someone where they weren't supposed to be."

"How would we know?" Bradley's voice was peevish. "We're from Boulder."

"He's right," Phyllis chimed on an identical whining note. "I don't know what most of these people do."

"We just watched Victor kill a wedding cake," Bradley said. "If you're looking for unusual, go no further."

"Stop it!" Jake Poynter threw back his drink and glared at the Winkles disdainfully. "I'm out of patience with you two greenies. You know what the sheriff means. Suspicious. Like if you saw someone dripping with blood or discharging a handgun." He turned toward Reuben. "It was a .22, right?"

Reuben sighed heavily. His mustache was drooping. "I'm no forensic specialist, but I've seen enough gunshot wounds to guess. The wound looks like it was made by a .22 caliber handgun."

"Got that?" Jake sneered at the Winkles. "If you saw someone hiding a gun, that would be suspicious."

"Now, Jake," Maybelle said, with as much good nature as she could muster, "there's no need to be rude."

As Trina listened to the bickering ebb and flow, she leaned her back against the wall and closed her eyes. She'd come to Alaska seeking adventure and a new life, filled with promise and love. Instead, she'd found murder.

A hand slipped into her own. The palm was callused, rough and somehow familiar. When his fingers linked with hers and gently squeezed, his touch magically soothed her rising fears. She heard David's whisper, "It's going to be all right, Trina. This will all be over soon."

Her eyelids opened and she beheld his handsome, chiseled features. His dark gaze embraced her with a warmth and tenderness that should have been reassuring, but she couldn't help wondering. Was David the murderer?

Her heart ached to even consider such a possibility. David had been so sweet, so understanding. He seemed to be her only friend in this cold land. Moreover, when he kissed her, she had instinctively reacted with a passion that felt like truth. He wasn't a murderer. Her emotions couldn't be wrong. David wouldn't lie to her. She had to trust him.

And yet... Trina turned her gaze away from him. Hadn't she just learned that she couldn't trust her own feelings? Hadn't her emotions directed her into Ivan's embrace? She hated her suspicions, but she would be a fool to ignore them. Never again, she vowed, never again would she heed the illogic of her heart. Victor, though almost too repulsive to be believed, had said that David had a motive to kill Ivan, to avenge a land scam that had taken place many years ago.

"Trina," David repeated, "we're going to be all right."

"I hope so." But she refused to meet his gaze. She couldn't allow him to see suspicion in her eyes. If he did, she might be the next victim.

DAVID LED REUBEN down the corridor to his office in the room beside the fireplace. Before he turned on the light, he gazed through the window at the pelting snowfall. "I guess the blizzard everybody's been predicting is here," David said. "Picked a hell of a day to come."

"You can say that again."

David flicked on the lights. "I'll get you set up in here, then I'd better go out and check on the livestock. And I might as well make my first run with the snowplow before it's too deep."

He showed Reuben how to work the tape recorder so he could begin working on their statements. "There you go," David said. "You're all set up, and there are extra cassettes in the drawer."

Reuben sat behind the desk, his fingers spread wide on the desktop blotter. His heavy shoulders hunched. When he looked up, his eyes were hard. "I've known you a long time, David. We get along pretty well, but I'm not here today as your friend. Here's where our paths separate. I'm on the one marked sheriff. You're a suspect. This is an official investigation."

"Sure, Reuben. I understand that."

"Did you kill him?"

"No."

"Did you want to? Did you ever want to?"

"Ever? That's a long time."

In David's experience, nothing had been forever. Not his childhood. Not his marriage. Not his chance to father his son and daughter. But those regrets were his alone; he didn't need to tell Reuben about his private sorrows. "Once or twice," he said, "I might have been angry enough to kill Ivan Stoddard. But not today."

His anger today was directed at himself. Ever since this morning, when he'd seen Trina close to tears, he'd cursed himself for deceiving her.

"I'm going to start with you, David. Your statement. I know you want to get out to the barn and get busy, but the livestock is going to have to wait," Reuben said. He flicked the switch to record and watched the wheels in the tape recorder begin to rotate.

David nodded and took a seat on the opposite side of his desk. It was backward to be sitting here, in this position, but he was willing to acknowledge that Sheriff Reuben Kittridge was in charge.

"Say your name and the date," Reuben instructed. "Then tell me what happened today from eleven-thirty onward."

"It's the second time you've mentioned eleven-thirty. Why then?"

"Because that's the last time I saw Ivan alive. And, if you don't mind, David, *I'll* be asking the questions."

David complied, starting with eleven-thirty, when he was out in the barn, checking the horses and making sure that Phyllis had taken proper care of her mount. "I didn't need to worry," he said. "That Phyllis is one strange woman, but she knows horses and is good with them." David continued, reluctantly reliving the time when he'd come back into the house and found Trina dressed in her wedding gown.

"Is that when I caught you kissing?" Reuben asked.

"Does that have to go into my statement?"

"Afraid so, David." He leaned forward. "What, exactly, is your relationship with Trina Martin?"

"I only met her yesterday. There's no relationship to speak of."

The lie was spoken and it echoed within him. Of course, there was a relationship. He had corresponded with Trina for a month, using Ivan's name on the letters. But he hadn't told her, and he sure as hell didn't want to tell Reuben and have her find out that way. The initial deception was bad enough. He didn't need to make it worse.

"What else?" Reuben said.

"Nothing." He wasn't good at lying, not practiced. He couldn't even manage one of those little white lies, like, "I'm busy on Friday." Couldn't even tell the preacher that he meant to come to church when he'd been planning all week to watch football. David knew that he looked suspicious. "Should I tell you what happened after that?"

Reuben nodded.

David ran through the rest, mentioning that Ivan's horse, Sol, appeared to have been ridden and detailing the search of the outbuildings. "Then Trina and I went to the tub house, found the doors locked inside and out. I unlatched the shutters, looked inside and saw Ivan."

"Why was the tub house the last place you looked?"

"We were actually headed toward the garage behind the lodge but we never got there."

"Why didn't you go to the tub house first? It's the closest building to the lodge and the house."

David shook his head. "It didn't occur to me. I guess, with a blizzard coming and people arriving, I didn't think Ivan would take time out to splash around in the hot tub."

"Did you happen to notice any footprints leading up to it?"

"Let me think." David concentrated on his memory of that scene. The trees. The tub house. The falling snow. The steps leading up to it with snow piled evenly on each stair. "No footprints."

"Are you sure?"

"Positive. Whoever went up there with Ivan did it before the snow began to accumulate. That would have been early. Probably before noon."

Reuben pressed the stop button on the tape recorder. "Thanks, David. That's all for now. Why don't you send Jake Poynter in here next? With the way he's hitting the vodka, I don't expect he'll be coherent much longer."

David returned to the kitchen where a flurry of activity was underway. Maybelle had finally gotten her wish, and the cleanup was in progress. Trina, Phyllis and Bradley discarded paper plates and washed dishes while Maybelle concentrated on fitting the containers of leftover food into the already full fridge.

David peered over her shoulder into the jam-packed refrigerator shelves. "You've got enough in there to feed a small army. At least, we won't starve if the blizzard goes on."

"Honey, it would take forty days and forty nights for our little crew to go through this stuff."

The only person who wasn't helping with cleanup was Jake, who sat at the kitchen table, sucking clear liquid from a tumbler. His pristine white clothing contrasted with the sullen expression on his face.

"Jake," David said, "Reuben wants to talk to you. To record your statement."

"He's back in your office?"

"That's right."

When he stood, Jake wobbled unsteadily, but just for an instant. He made his way out the door without betraying a trace of intoxication. Though David hadn't been counting, he guessed that Jake had polished off enough vodka to put most men into a coma. Maybe Jake's athletic training gave him drinking abilities beyond those of mere mortals. Was the man drinking to forget? Was he responsible for Ivan's death?

David eased up beside Trina. "Can I help?"

"I guess so." It seemed like she was trying not to look at him directly, keeping her hands busy. She shook open a large black plastic trash bag. "Come into the dining room with me and we'll dispose of that cake."

"Good idea," Maybelle said. "Though it seems a waste, I don't much care for the taste of gunpowder on my food."

In the dining room, Trina tried to dismantle what was left of the cake in large chunks, but it crumbled in her hands. "Yuck!"

"Couldn't have said it better myself," David said.

Trina scooped up a handful of the gooey white mess and disposed of it in the bag. "This seems symbolic," she said. "Dump the cake and dump the marriage."

"Are you all right?"

"Who wouldn't be?" She was mindful of the bad example set by Phyllis Winkle. Trina was determined not to gnash her teeth or moan or indulge in a flood of self-pitying tears. "In the course of one short day, I've been single, married and widowed. Jake referred to me a couple of times as the Widow Stoddard. Does that sound strange or what?''

''Jake is a little strange.'' David took a glob of cake and shoved it into the bag. ''But he's a fearless hunter and an excellent marksman.''

''He's not much on politeness. We just had a little chat that turned my stomach.''

''About what?'' David asked.

''It seems that he wants to purchase the lodge and the grounds. He claims to have made some kind of partnership deal with Ivan. He didn't want to waste any time, so he talked to me as the possible heir.''

''He wants to buy this place?''

''So he says. And, if I inherit anything, he wants me to sell it to him.''

''You're right. That's cold. Ivan's body isn't even in the ground, and Jake—who was supposed to be his best friend—is already trying to do business. What did you tell him?''

She shrugged. The conversation with the man dressed in white, the Olympic athlete, had felt horribly inappropriate. Not only was Jake supposedly Ivan's friend, but she was supposedly his wife. She should have been in mourning. She should have, at the very least, experienced a sense of abiding sadness. Instead, Trina felt ... relief.

''I don't want any part of this place,'' she said. ''If I'm an heir, I fully intend to step out of the picture.'' She dropped more cake into the bag, where it landed with a sticky plop. ''I wasn't married to Ivan. Not in any real sense of the word. I wouldn't feel right about taking a piece of his estate.''

"Do you mean that?" Disbelieving, he pressed, "Why? Why would you return a huge sum of money that got dropped in your lap? It's like winning the lottery."

"Winning the lottery is good fortune. Ivan's murder is—well, I wouldn't want to think of it as a stroke of luck. That's probably old-fashioned, but I believe that nothing good ever came from another person's misfortune."

"You had to be considering money when you answered Ivan's ad. Ivan was pretty clear about the fact that he was wealthy."

"So what?" Trina returned, feeling a flicker of irritation. This seemed to be the main sore spot in her friendship with David. "You know, David, I'm real tired of you hinting that I agreed to be a mail-order bride because I wanted Ivan's money. You sound like Victor calling me a gold digger."

"That's not what I mean."

"It sure is. I don't want money. All I want is to leave Alaska as soon as the weather permits."

"I'm sorry, Trina."

"It's okay. Forget it."

"I'm wondering," he said, "if there's anything I could say or do to change your mind?"

"About what?"

"Leaving."

She glanced up sharply. "Do you want me to stay?"

"I'm fond of you." He dropped another piece of cake into the bag and licked his finger. "This frosting isn't bad."

"You're fond of me?" Her voice was raised. Her temper was fully engaged. How could he be so arrogant? "Let me get this straight. You'd like for me to stick around in a place where people are getting killed. And other people, like Victor, think nothing of yanking a gun out of their back pocket and blasting away. You'd want me to stay because you're *fond?*"

"Okay, it's more than that," he admitted. "I'm attracted to you."

"Listen here, David. You might have the wrong impression because I came here without meeting Ivan. You might think that all a man has to do is snap his fingers, and I'll come running. But I had a monthlong correspondence with Ivan. I thought I knew him, thought I cared about him." She bent her knees to pick up a glob of wedding cake that had fallen on the rug. "I was wrong. But I'm going to learn from my error. It'll be a hot day in Skagway before I trust my intuitions again."

"Damn, Trina. All I said was that I liked you."

"Well, why don't you find someone else to be fond of." She straightened her back and glared at him. "I might be thirty-five years old with no prospects of a lasting relationship and no job and no assets to speak of, but I'm not desperate."

It felt good to say those words. Her self-esteem, which was never terrifically strong, had taken a beating in the last day and a half. But she hadn't given up on herself. She wasn't ready to grasp at the nearest passing male and hurl herself at his feet. "If you want me to stay, it's going to take more than fond. At least Ivan offered marriage."

"Is that what you want? Marriage?"

Was he going to propose? Stunned by the thought, she nodded her head, then shook it, waving her hands to erase the yes. "I don't know."

"Here." David held out a bit of wedding cake toward her. "You never got to do this part of the ceremony.

Take a bite and let's consider it a kind of promise between us."

"What?" This was crazy! Eating a bite of a cake that had been shot? As a vow?

"Why not?" he asked.

"It's unconventional."

"You accuse me of being weird? Hey, Trina, you're the one who agreed to be a mail-order bride."

"And what does sharing a bit of wedding cake make you, David? My groom?"

"Could be."

"Oh, David. This is silly."

"When you got off the plane, you looked like Alice entering Wonderland. You were so curious and bright. And when I saw you in the firelight, in your wedding gown, I knew you were the most beautiful woman on earth."

Trina was surprised by the warmth she felt growing deep within her. Her annoyance with him faded too quickly, and she wondered if maybe she was an easy mark, after all. All he needed to do was toss a few compliments her way, and she melted.

But it was difficult to stay mad at David. Especially when he was standing next to the demolished cake, holding a piece out to her and smiling, as if he was cajoling a wild animal to eat from his hand.

He continued, "I don't deserve your trust, but maybe you'll be forgiving enough to give it. Trust me, Trina. Be my Alice. Take hold of adventure, as she did. Let me show you Wonderland." He held out the cake.

She opened her mouth and he placed the tiny piece of cake between her lips. The sweetness tingled on the tip of her tongue.

Picking among the fragments of cake on the table, she gave a piece to him, accidentally leaving a smudge of frosting on his lips, which he licked off.

"I now pronounce us," he said, "mail-order bride and wedding-cake groom."

Without thinking, she said, "Kiss the bride."

He didn't need another invitation. Gingerly, he stepped around the full trash bag to stand near her. He removed the gold-framed glasses and set them on the table. Though his kiss was chaste and respectful, the taste of him left her yearning for more.

"Oh, David, I wish things could be different. I wish I'd come here to meet you instead of Ivan."

"So do I."

With a wistful sigh, she stuck her glasses back on her nose. The lenses were blurred with sticky cake and frosting. Together, they carried the heavy trash bag into the kitchen for disposal.

They walked right into an argument. Reuben had left the office with Jake and was speaking to Phyllis. "I need to take your statement alone. Without your husband."

"No!" she shouted. "I won't go anywhere without Bradley."

Jake snickered and returned to his seat at the kitchen table while Reuben looked at Bradley for assistance. "Can you talk some sense into her?"

Bradley Winkle shrugged. "Frankly, I don't see the problem. We were together all day. Our statements are going to be identical."

"That's not proper procedure. I take statements one person at a time." Reuben rubbed his forehead, above the thick eyebrows. He looked angry enough to tear out a thatch of his own hair and stuff it down the combined Winkles' throats. "When are you people going to get it through your heads that this is an official investigation? A man has been murdered, dammit, and we're going to do this right."

"I won't talk by myself," Phyllis retorted. "I want Bradley."

"Why? If your statements are going to be just alike, what difference does it make?"

"That's how it's going to be."

"Work it out with her," Reuben told Bradley, "or, I swear, I'll arrest the both of you for obstructing justice when we get out of here."

"I'm not afraid of jail," Phyllis said. She struck a Joan of Arc pose that might have been heroic if her cause had not been so childish. "I've been arrested before."

"Have you?" Reuben was interested. "You have a criminal record? What were the charges?"

"Malicious mischief. I was arrested in a protest against the use of fur for personal adornment."

Jake hooted with laughter, and Reuben looked away, disgusted. He pointed to Trina. "You're next."

Without comment, she followed him down the hall to David's rooms. In the outer room, the fire seemed low, and she said, "Wait just a minute, Reuben."

His huge shoulders stiffened. He looked as big as an irate bear. "You don't have a problem talking to me, do you?"

"No."

"What's wrong with that Phyllis, anyway? You'd think I was asking her to strip naked and dance the hootchy-kooch."

"She's high-strung," Trina said. It was an understatement, but Trina decided to be generous. "I'll be right there. I just wanted to do this." She added another log to the fire before entering the office. The simple task made her feel as if she belonged here.

Taking a chair on the opposite side of the desk from where Reuben was standing, she said, "I'm ready."

"Before I start with this statement, Trina, I want to take the opportunity to offer you an apology. After you signed that marriage license, Ivan was rough with you. I witnessed it, and I felt like I should have stopped him." He came around the desk and stood behind her, placing both his large hands on her shoulders. "Can you forgive me?"

"Sure." Behind her glasses, her eyes darted. What was going on here?

"I wasn't thinking." Reuben continued to massage her neck. "You needed help, but I was too caught up in my own problems to pay attention. I don't want you to think I don't care about you."

"It's all right," she said.

If she'd had any doubt about the fact that the sheriff was flirting with her, it vanished when he stepped in front of her, easing his large body between the chair and the desk. He was too close for comfort. "I like you, Trina. You're a very attractive woman."

"Thanks." She swallowed hard. This was unbelievable! In Denver, Trina had only two dates in the past year, both of which turned out to be duds. But here, in the Alaskan back country, she'd had two eligible men telling her how pretty she was within the space of fifteen minutes. Amazing! And she was even wearing her glasses. Welcome to Alaska!

"I guess I need your statement," Rueben said.

When he returned to his official demeanor, it seemed to her that his interest wasn't in her own whereabouts, but in where David had been. How long, Reuben wanted to know, had she been waiting in her wedding gown before David came in from the yard? While they were searching, did David purposely avoid the tub house? Who suggested looking in there? "Did you?" he asked.

"Not really. We both went there." She felt compelled to add, "David was shocked when he opened the shutters and saw Ivan."

"Why that particular set of shutters?" Reuben wondered aloud. "Was the window broken when David opened the shutters?"

"Yes," she said. But she seriously considered Reuben's point. Why had David gone to that set of shutters? It was almost as if he'd known that would be the broken window. But it must have been coincidence. "They were closest," she said. "Just to the left of the door."

"And did you go inside with him?"

"No." David had warned her not to. She'd thought he was protecting her. "I don't deal well with death. Yesterday, after we ran into you and your men hauling away the body of the dead man you'd found, I was kind of queasy and upset. David probably thought I couldn't handle seeing Ivan.... Jake was passing by, on his way back to the lodge. I called to him, and he went into the room with David."

"Was David alone with Ivan's body at any time?"

"I guess so. For a couple of seconds."

Reuben didn't need to tell her that David had enough time alone with Ivan to dispose of incriminating evidence. She'd already drawn that conclusion. Her suspicions of him, again aroused, were more painful this time. She didn't want to suspect him, didn't want a suspect groom.

Chapter Six

Later that night, the snow was still falling and Trina's mind still churned with doubts. She wanted to believe in David's innocence, wanted to trust him. But her heart had already proven to be unwise. The very fact that she was attracted to him ought to warn her that there was something wrong with the guy. But, oh, when he kissed her, she was thrilled from the roots of her hair to her toes. Could she feel like that about a murderer?

"That's my libido," she muttered, "not a lie detector."

Dressed in her red flannel nightgown instead of the slinky white satin she'd bought for her wedding night, Trina prepared for bed. She'd washed her face, brushed her teeth, brushed her hair and fastened it in a long plait down her back.

There was an immediate problem to consider. Her bedroom was all wrong. In addition to the ghastly pink decor, there was lack of security. Her door had a keyhole, but no key with which to lock it.

She hauled a pink-painted wooden chair to the door and tried to brace the back—which was decorated with fancy white cherubs—under the doorknob. But the chair was too tall. Instead, she placed the chair flush against the door and piled her two empty suitcases on top of it. This makeshift barricade wouldn't stop anyone who wanted to get into the room, but it would make enough racket that Trina would wake up, and she was within easy screaming distance of help. Maybelle, Reuben and Victor all had bedrooms on this floor. David, unfortunately, was off in his own bedroom at the far northeast corner of the house.

Too easily, her mind conjured up a picture of him in that cozy, cedar-paneled room that was so different from this excessively fluffy pinkness. She imagined that he would be naked under the blankets and sheets. One arm would rest across his chest. A muscular arm, she thought. And it was simple, in her imagining, to add herself to that picture, snuggling against him.

Even if she was suspicious, Trina would have felt much safer if he'd been close. Safety? She smiled and shook her head. *Be honest, Trina. Safety isn't the primary reason you want to be close to David.* There was something sexy about the man that enticed her. Yes, indeed, she'd like to be close—as close as a woman could get to a man.

There was a tap on the door, and she heard his voice in a whisper. "Trina? Can I come in?"

"Just a minute." She tried to move the suitcases without making too much noise, but dropped one. The chair fell over when she moved it.

"What are you doing?"

She yanked open the door. "Rearranging furniture."

He stepped around the suitcases as he entered, and he closed the door. "I wanted to check on you." He kept his voice low, in deference to the other people who might be sleeping. "To make sure you were all right."

"So far, so good," she said brightly. Too brightly, she thought, as if the pinkness of her room had transformed her into a perky gal, full of beaming smiles and flirtatious dimples. Though she'd imagined being with him in bed, the fact that he was actually here made her tense.

"I'll tuck you in," he offered.

His low voice sounded husky, and she wanted to ask him to join her beneath the covers, but they weren't really alone. There were too many other people on the second floor, sleeping or listening.

Trina climbed into bed. She took off her glasses and put them in their case by a bedside table that was covered with a pink chiffon skirt. In her out-of-focus vision, the pinkness of the room seemed even more overwhelming, and David—standing in the middle of it—made a handsome masculine contrast.

When he pulled the covers up to her chin and sat beside her on the bed, she closed her eyes, waiting to feel the gentle pressure of his lips against hers. But he kissed her forehead instead. His hand stroked her jawline. His thumb traced the outline of her lips. "Trina, if anything scares you in the night, come get me. Don't hesitate. Don't stop and think, just come and get me."

"What could happen?" She looked up at him. Should she be afraid of him? "Do you think there's still danger?"

"I don't want to scare you."

She thought of the wedding-cake figurine, the beheaded bride. But no one had attacked her. No one had threatened her. "What are you trying to tell me?"

"I don't know." His smile was hesitant. "Good night, Trina."

"Wait!" She didn't want him to leave. She wriggled her arms free from the blankets and propped herself up on the pillows. "I was thinking."

"About what?"

"This room. You redecorated it, didn't you? According to Maybelle's specifications."

"That's right."

"It's awful. All this froufrou and pink."

"Agreed. And your point is . . ."

"The rest of the house is very pleasant, so this doesn't reflect Maybelle's taste. I think she did this girlish pinkness as a statement of hostility. I think Maybelle hated the idea of Ivan's marriage."

"Possibly. But why should it matter? She's leaving at the end of the month."

"Do you think. . ." Trina wasn't exactly sure where she was going with this logic, but she knew there was a rationale somewhere. "Do you think Maybelle was in love with Ivan?"

David tilted his head back, considering. "If so, she kept it well hidden. But I'll concede the possibility. Where does that lead?"

"If Maybelle loved Ivan, she must have been heartbroken when he decided to marry another woman. A mail-order bride would have been even worse, because it meant he preferred a woman he hadn't even seen. His decision to marry was an insult to her. She might have lashed out at him."

It was a far stretch to imagine the practical, commonsense housekeeper as a woman scorned, so vengeful that she had murdered Ivan in the tub house, and Trina felt like a traitor for even suggesting it. Maybelle had been unfailingly kind to her.

There was a tap on the bedroom door. "Trina, honey, it's me, Maybelle."

Uninvited, she strolled right in. When she saw David sitting beside Trina on the bed, Maybelle chuckled. "Well, well, I thought you might be a little nervous in the night, Trina. But I see that you've arranged your own protection."

"I was just leaving," David said.

"Don't go on my account." She reached into the pocket of her plaid wool bathrobe. "I was just bringing Trina the key to this room. Thought she might want to lock herself in."

"Thank you. Yes, I would."

"This old house has a lot of creaks and groans. Right, David? And, when the wind picks up, it screeches around the corners like a freight train. And, of course, there are the wolves. They can howl up a storm."

"Wolves?" Trina shuddered, thinking of the body Reuben had found yesterday. The man had been torn apart by wolves. But he'd already been dead, shot in the back. The real danger wasn't from the wildlife. The threat, if it came, would emanate from a two-legged creature, someone who was staying here at the house or at the lodge where the Winkles and Jake Poynter were sleeping. Had the same person who killed the man killed Ivan?

"You won't hear wolves tonight," Maybelle said. "The snow's still coming down. How deep would you say it is, David?"

"Two feet, at least. By morning, it could be three or even four."

"At least we've got food," Maybelle said. "And heat. Are you warm enough in here, Trina?"

"I'm fine."

"Good, because I've been playing with the thermostats. Turned off the whole third floor." A pained expression flickered across her face, pulling at the corners of her lips. "That's where we put Ivan. In his own bed."

She didn't need to add that the dead man had no use for the benefits of central heating. The mental picture was vivid in Trina's mind. She glanced at the ceiling of her room. Ivan was up there, on the third floor. His tidy bedroom was a death chamber where he lay in state until Reuben could arrange to transport his body.

Hoping to erase that grotesque image, Trina said, "I had a question about this room, Maybelle. What were you thinking when you chose the decor?"

She grinned widely. "It's wild, isn't it?"

"That wasn't the first word that came to my mind."

"Tacky?" Maybelle suggested with a wink. "I'm sorry, Trina, but Ivan kept insisting on feminine, and I went a little overboard in giving him what he wanted. It was kind of fun. Like playing with dolls when I was a little girl." She looked around. "The final result is pretty awful, isn't it?"

Trina shrugged, satisfied with Maybelle's explanation. The decor wasn't chosen because of anger, and she was glad. She didn't want to suspect Maybelle any more than she wanted to think that David had anything to do with the murder.

He said, "I'll be going now. Sleep well, Trina."

"Here's the key." Maybelle held it up and placed it on the dresser. "You get some rest now. Good night."

They left together.

Trina leapt from the bed, locked the door and turned out the lights. In her overly pink bedroom, she was utterly alone. But safe, she thought, with the door locked.

Now, the trick would be to fall asleep. Though she was tired, her eyelids felt like they were stuck open by toothpicks. Her back and tailbone were a little sore from the morning's horseback ride, and her brain was racing, considering and discarding theories about the murder. If she could solve this crime, she could quit suspecting David. And if she quit suspecting him of murder, she might be able to think of him in another way.

She breathed deep and concentrated on relaxing her muscles. Sleep would come. It always did. Eventually, the night would overtake her and she would rest.

TRINA MUST HAVE BEEN sleeping, because she was suddenly aware of being awake. Drawn from a deep, unconscious rest, her senses prickled. Not yet alert, she listened. There was a sound. Not the creaking of the house, but something else, something that was very near.

Her body tensed beneath the covers. In her sleep-fogged state, she didn't know whether to scream or peer through the dark or ignore the slight rustling. It might be only her imagination. Her door was locked. Logically, she knew that no one could be here.

And yet, when she peeked over her shoulder, she saw a crack of light from the landing. Her door—her locked door!—was slightly ajar. As she watched, a figure went out through the door and closed it with a click.

My God! Someone had been in here! She yanked the covers over her head. *No, I can't hide. They might come back.*

Cautiously, she crept from the bed. In the darkness, her toe stubbed against her suitcase that was lying on the floor. She returned to her bedside table and flicked on the light. Her bedroom appeared to be undisturbed. The only things out of place were the chair and the suitcases that she had moved herself. It didn't look as if anyone had been in here. Did she dream the intruder?

Trina snatched her glasses and put them on. If she'd been wearing them in her sleep, she might have recognized the person who went out the door. But all she had seen was the shadowy outline of shoulders.

She stuck her feet into slippers and wrapped her white terry cloth bathrobe around her. Not knowing what she might find on the other side of her bedroom door, she hesitated with her hand on the knob. It turned easily in her hand. Unlocked.

Yanking open the door, she stared onto an empty landing. The only light was the faint glow of a night-light near the bathroom. Whoever had been here was gone now.

She went back into her room and closed the door. No point in locking it. Apparently, there was more than one key. Maybelle should have told her. Pacing the perimeter of her room, she tried to figure out what to do. Someone had been in here. The door was unlocked. That proved it. But why?

Or perhaps she'd been dreaming....

Pausing by the window, she eased the curtain aside and pressed her nose up close to the glass. Outside, the snowfall continued steadily. Light from the porch showed billowy white drifts sweeping against the side of the garage. The road leading to the house had vanished. The snow had almost covered a truck. Reuben's official vehicle, she thought. Should she wake him? And tell him what? That she thought someone might have been in her room?

Trina flung herself on her rumpled bed and glanced at her digital clock. It was thirteen minutes after one o'clock. Too early to be awake and too late not to be sleeping.

With a sigh, she scanned the room and noticed that her closet door wasn't quite closed. A sudden fear rushed through her. The intruder might still be here, hiding in the closet, waiting for her to turn out the light. But she'd seen the person leave, hadn't she?

Her heart beat faster as she stared at the closet door. She was certain that she'd closed it all the way when she went to bed because she wanted to minimize the heat loss. The hinges couldn't have sprung open by themselves while she slept.

Was someone in there? She had to know. She couldn't lie back and wait until they attacked her.

Summoning every ounce of courage she possessed, Trina raced across the floor, whipped the door open and jumped back. There was nothing inside the narrow closet except for her clothing. She ducked her head down, checking to see that no one was hiding behind her few dresses and shirts. Nothing. No one. But the closet didn't look right. She pawed through the hangers.

Her wedding gown was missing.

Trina felt certain that the missing dress was meant as a threat. Someone wanted to frighten her. And had succeeded. Fear quaked through her. She was plenty scared. She needed help. David, she thought. David had said to come to him if something happened. And this qualified.

Trina opened her door and eased onto the landing. Allowing her eyes to become accustomed to the shadows, she moved silently to the stairs. Each step creaked as she descended, and she was afraid to turn and look back, afraid that she might see a dark figure, poised at the top of the stairs.

On the main floor, Maybelle had left enough night-lights scattered through the rooms to give some illumination, but Trina was hurrying, moving too fast. She bumped against a chair, and the noise sounded loud as cannon fire. Pausing, she listened. The old house groaned in the freezing night. It seemed to be complaining, as if it were alive, waiting to swallow her whole. As quickly as she could manage, she made her way, dodging furniture. Through the kitchen, she bolted into the corridor that led to David's rooms. In the large outer room, the last embers glowed in the moss rock fireplace. She ran to his bedroom door and knocked. "David! It's me."

She heard his muffled response. What if something had happened to him?

She dashed into the room and ran to his bed. "Are you all right?"

"Trina?" He turned on the bedside lamp, fell back on the pillows and squinted at her. "What's the matter?"

"You told me to come here if something happened."

When he sat up, she realized she'd been correct in her imaginings. David's chest was bare. Despite her fear and panic, she was extremely aware of the intense desires he sparked within her. Somehow, she felt that if she lay beside him, everything would be all right.

But that was a lie told by her heart. She had reason to suspect David. He had no alibi for what seemed to be the crucial time period right after Ivan had left the study. And during their search, he'd avoided the tub house until the very last.

She edged toward his door. Coming here might have been a huge mistake. She might have run to the arms of a murderer. But that wasn't how she felt. Should she listen to her heart?

"What happened?" he asked.

After she'd told him, he shook his head. "Your wedding dress? Why?"

"I don't know."

"Okay, Trina. Let's go up and take a look." His hands grasped the covers. "Do you want to leave while I get dressed?"

"Go back out there by myself?" Into the moaning, breathing house with the shadowed corners and furniture that seemed to leap into her path? "I'll just turn my back."

She stood facing his door, listening to the scratchy noise of his bedsprings as he arose. Was he nude? The temptation to twirl around was absolutely overwhelming. She braced her hand against the soft, smooth cedar boards of the paneled wall to ground herself. She heard a drawer open and close, the rustle of cloth, the sound of a zipper.

David turned off the light, and her breath caught in her throat. The darkness introduced a new level of intimacy, enhancing her hearing even more. She could sense him moving toward her.

Then he said, "What the hell is that? Trina, come here."

She turned to see him, fully dressed, staring through the uncurtained window behind his bed.

He pointed outside through the driving snow. "Do you see that? It looks like a lantern. Somebody's going into the barn." He glanced at her. "I'd better check it out."

"I'll come with you."

"You're not dressed to go outside."

"I'm not staying here by myself," she said firmly. Facing whatever was outside was better than remaining inside alone with an unknown threat. "Give me something to wear."

"Come on, Trina. It's better if you stay here. You can lock my door."

"Locked doors don't mean much in this house."

He could have stood his ground and argued with her, but time was passing, and he could tell by the determined expression on her face that argument was futile. Grumbling, David went to his dresser and pulled out a pair of Levi's and thermal underwear that would be at least four sizes too big for her.

He tossed her the clothes. "There are boots and jackets in the mudroom that might fit you. Hurry! And don't turn on the lights. We don't need to let them know we're awake."

He stepped into the other room and went to the window. The light he'd seen had vanished. He hated to think of someone messing around in the barn. There was a lot of damage that could be done in just a few minutes. A fire, even in this snow, would be disastrous.

David went into his office. Behind his desk was a wooden file cabinet. He opened the top drawer. In the back, behind the files, he found his Colt .45 revolver. He'd meant to return this weapon to the gun cabinet by the kitchen pantry but hadn't gotten around to it. Now, he was glad. He checked to make sure it was loaded and went out by the dying fire.

Swathed in his overly large clothes, Trina rushed out of the bedroom and joined him. For a minute, he forgot his urgency and just stared at her. She looked pretty damn spunky. Her long braid bounced behind her. Her glasses slid down on the tip of her nose. As she ran, she hitched up his Levi's, like a kid in hand-me-downs that were too big.

"Stick with me," he said.

"You're taking a gun?" she questioned. Behind her glasses, her eyes were wide.

"We might need it," he said.

"I can't believe this. Does everybody up here have a gun?"

"This is a hunting lodge," he pointed out. "We use guns to hunt."

He led the way into the kitchen and to the mudroom where they found parkas, hats, gloves and boots. This was taking forever, David thought. But they'd be crazy to race out in the snow without proper gear. The barn wasn't all that far from the house, but slogging through the snow would be tough.

As he opened the door, he wished they could turn on the yard lights. But that flash of illumination, more than anything, would alert whoever was in the barn.

David braced himself against the cold and the freezing wetness. The wind had increased to gale force, blasting so furiously from the north that the snow was no longer falling from above. Rather, it seemed to be thrown in his face in lashing waves of bitter cold. Behind him, he heard Trina gasp.

"It's so damn cold," she said.

"Probably thirty below. Let's keep moving."

Earlier, he'd gone over the area with the snowplow, digging paths from the house to the barn and to the lodge, but the drifting snow had all but obliterated his work. The accumulated inches of frozen crystals rose above his knees. David put his head down and charged forward, breaking the way for Trina to follow.

When they neared the barn, his efforts were rewarded. He pointed to the ground that was sheltered by the buildings. "Footprints."

Near the side door, it was clearer that someone had entered. Or two people walking single file as he and Trina had. But hurtling winds made it impossible to tell if the intruders had gone or which direction they had taken.

David grasped her hand and pulled her into the barn. Inside, the relative warmth and stillness provided dangerous relief from the maelstrom. Their breathing sounded loud. So much for the element of surprise, David thought. He pulled off a heavy glove and took his revolver from his parka pocket.

Though he kept a few light bulbs burning in the barn all night, the interior was brighter than it should have been. He stepped forward slowly, holding his weapon ready. Nothing seemed odd or out of place until he neared the horses' stalls and saw a Coleman lantern set on a stool.

"Trina," he called out. "Turn on the lights."

She flipped switches near the door until the barn was fully lit. The horses nickered, seeming annoyed at the disturbance.

David searched quickly. Since he was familiar with every corner and cubbyhole, he was satisfied that he hadn't overlooked anything. He pocketed his gun. "Nothing."

Trina waddled toward him in her bulky, ill-fitting snow gear. "I can't believe we came out here for nothing."

"I'm afraid so. Somebody was here, all right, and left a lantern behind." He picked it up and turned it off. "I wonder why."

"You didn't happen to find my wedding dress, did you?"

"Didn't see it." He grinned. "The horses aren't wearing anything but their usual drab blankets."

She went to the horses' stalls and patted the nose of the gray mare named Myrtle she'd ridden this morning. "Too bad. This old lady might like a fancy gown."

"But it wouldn't look as good on Myrtle as it did on you."

"Gosh, David, thanks a lot. It's nice to know that I look better than a horse in a dress."

Her smile seemed a little shaky, and he knew that she was joking to cover darker emotions, feelings of fear. He wished, with all his heart, that she didn't have to go through this. It wasn't fair. She'd come here full of hope, and every one of her sweet dreams had been dashed. If he could, David would make it up to her. Somehow, he would make things right for Trina.

"So now what we do?" she asked. "Go back to the house and see who's been outside?"

"And what do we accuse them of? Sleepwalking? Coming to the barn?"

"It's suspicious," she said. "Reuben wants to know about suspicious stuff."

"Did you tell him about your wedding dress?"

"I kind of didn't," she said sheepishly. "It seemed too weird."

"Like this," he said. "Why did somebody come out here? What did they do?" He pulled up the hood on his parka. "Let's get back to the house before we're too comfortable in here to want to move."

"By all means," she muttered, "we should make sure that we're as cold, miserable and uncomfortable as possible."

When he looked into her face, he had to smile. "You're a funny person, Trina."

"Funny? No way! I'm miserable. My glasses are fogged. My hair is tangled. And I'm wet and cold."

"When we get back to the house . . ."

"Yes?"

He wondered if she knew what he was thinking. That when they got back, he'd like to haul her into his bedroom and show her the best way to get warm. But he said, "I'll make you hot chocolate."

"Gosh, David, that's so exotic."

"Did you have something else in mind?"

"Isn't there some special Alaskan drink? Moose milk? Caribou tea?" She bobbed her head. "Actually, hot anything sounds wonderful."

They staggered through the driving snow again, moving more easily now since the wind was at their backs. In the mudroom, they discarded the wet, cold clothes. When Trina peeled off the Levi's she'd borrowed from David, she still had her nightgown on underneath.

Shivering in the kitchen, David filled the teakettle and set it on the burner. "Instant hot chocolate. Is that okay?"

"Fine with me." She glanced down at his wet jeans. "Why don't you take those off before you freeze?"

"Sure." He peeled off the denim. Underneath, he wore two-piece thermal underwear that had stayed relatively dry.

Trina smiled. She'd always thought that long red underwear was the silliest outfit a man could wear. It was something akin to footed pajamas with a flap in the back. However, on David, it looked good. The thermal cotton clung to his muscular thighs and slim torso. His shoulders were broad. When he turned away from her to check on the teakettle, she noticed that the tail of the shirt didn't cover the sag of the underwear at his bottom.

She chuckled, and he turned his head to look at her. "What are you laughing at?"

"Your baggy drawers."

"This is the Alaskan version of a cover model." He struck a ridiculous muscle-man pose with his biceps flexed. "Beats California all to heck, doesn't it?"

"Oh, yeah, those tiny little Speedo bathing suits are nothing compared to long red underwear."

"A real man doesn't wear a Speedo." He glanced warmly at her. "And a real woman doesn't wear a long flannel nightgown."

"I hadn't planned to. Upstairs in my room I have—" She stopped herself from saying more. There would never be a use for the slinky white satin gown she'd purchased for the occasion of her wedding night. She shook her head. "Forget it."

"But we can't seem to forget, can we?" The teakettle whistled, and he moved it to another burner. "For your sake, Trina, I wish none of this had happened."

"So do I."

"Still," he said, "if it hadn't happened, I never would have met you. And I wouldn't trade that for anything." He held his arms wide in invitation, and she gladly stepped into his embrace.

Perhaps she should have been frightened, should have been thinking of all the reasons to suspect him. But her mind went blank as she glided her arms around him and tilted her head, waiting for the kiss she knew would come.

He removed her glasses and she blinked.

Finally, they were alone, and he took his time in tasting her lips. The gentle pressure of his mouth against hers wakened all the yearning she'd felt since her arrival in Alaska. More than that, his kiss touched deeper emotions, lifelong desires.

His hands caressed her back. He held her tightly, and his virile strength melted her fears. The storm was within her now, blanketing any suspicions she might have known. But the raging in her heart wasn't cold like the snowfall. She was burning for him.

Her lips softly parted, and she welcomed his tongue into her mouth. When he withdrew, she heard herself moan with desire for him. Nothing in her life had ever felt so right.

She gazed up at him, at the rugged planes of his face, stared deep into his dark eyes that glowed with a reflection of her own passion.

He spoke the words she'd been longing to hear. "I want you in my bed, Trina."

"Yes."

Ignoring the promise of hot chocolate, they walked hand in hand down the hallway to his rooms. As soon as they stepped inside the outer room, she felt his hand tighten in hers.

"Damn it," he said.

Dropping her hand, he went to the moss rock fireplace. The embers had become a raging flame. The wood was stacked high. And there was a strange odor, different from the fragrance of burning cedar or pine.

Using the poker, David retrieved a wad of wet, partially burned material and a charred bit of leather.

"What is it?" she asked.

"I'm not sure, but I'd guess this was a piece of a terry cloth robe. And the sole of slippers." He looked at her and frowned. "This must have been what Ivan was wearing when he went to the tub house."

"Oh." Trina took a deep breath, stifling the passion that still flamed within her. "I guess we should tell Reuben."

"This can't wait until morning."

"Of course not," Trina said.

That would be too suspicious.

Chapter Seven

As it turned out, they didn't need to hurry. Sheriff Reuben, who'd slept in his long johns and wrapped a plaid blanket around his shoulders, was stolid as a totem pole figure. He alternated mutters of disbelief with cavernous yawns.

Sprawled at the kitchen table, he rubbed the sleep from his eyes and swigged his hot chocolate. "So, you're telling me that somebody went creeping into Trina's room and stole her wedding dress. Then they burned a bathrobe and slippers in David's fireplace."

"That's right." David nodded.

"Excuse me, but that's just plain old rubbish."

"It does seem strange," Trina agreed. "This person sounds like somebody who's got a thing for clothes. Maybe we've got some kind of homicidal dress designer on the loose."

Reuben lowered his eyebrows and glared across the table at them. "What's going on with the two of you?" he demanded. "You keep telling me there's no relationship, but here you are together in the middle of the night."

"I've already explained," Trina said. "I was frightened. Somebody was in my room."

"But I'm sleeping right next door to you," Reuben pointed out. "Why'd you come all the way downstairs to David?"

"I don't know. I wasn't thinking clearly."

"Damn right, you weren't."

He gave her a searching look, and she remembered how Rueben had been flirting with her. "I'm sorry," she said, hoping that he would catch the double meaning. She was sorry that she hadn't done the logical thing. Also, she was apologizing for not being interested in him.

"You trust me, don't you?" Reuben peered deeply into her eyes. "I surely do hope that you don't suspect me. You know, of murder."

"No." The thought hadn't seriously crossed her mind. Though she'd heard Reuben arguing with Ivan when she first entered the study, she hadn't thought much of it. It had seemed to her that they were both strong-willed men with a difference of opinion.

"Ivan made some comment," Reuben said. "You might have heard it. About poaching."

"I remember that," she said.

"Well, it wasn't about breaking the law and poaching. I know his boundaries, and I wouldn't hunt on his land." When Reuben tossed his large head, she was reminded of an angry walrus. He glowered at David. "You know I don't poach."

"It's none of my business. I don't have a problem with people from town coming on the hunting preserve as long as they're not greedy. In fact, I'd like to get some hunters out here to go after the wolves if I can get some of the greenie restrictions lifted."

"Yeah?" A grin spread beneath Reuben's mustache. "Well, I think a wolf hunt could be arranged."

"But no helicopters," David said.

"Aerial hunting is no fun, anyway."

"Excuse me," Trina said. Hadn't they been talking about the murder? Men were so easily diverted. Show them a rifle or a football, and their minds went blank. "If you two are finished making your hunting plans, I'd like to know what Ivan was talking about when he accused Reuben of poaching."

"Oh, that. He was talking about a gal. Blond hair, green eyes. Five foot three. Lives in Osprey." It sounded like Reuben was describing a suspect until he added, "Very pretty. Anyway, Ivan took a fancy to her, but then she decided she liked me better." He chuckled. "It wasn't often that Ivan lost a woman," he continued, as if momentarily forgetting that Trina had been Ivan's wife.

"I find that hard to believe," Trina said. "I've met few men in my life who were as offensive as Ivan Stoddard."

"That so? Then why'd you marry him?"

Reuben's point was well-taken. "Well, he did seem charming at first." And there were all those beautiful letters. "I guess I got taken in."

She wondered if that was typical of Ivan's behavior. He might have been one of those men who got a thrill out of the chase, like a hunter stalking his prey. Then, when he had the woman under his thumb and the chase was over, he would lose interest.

"Ivan was good at that," Reuben said. He scratched his ear and yawned. "Taking people in. Am I right, David?"

"I hate to say it, but you're right."

"Ivan Stoddard was a born con man who didn't need to work any scams because he was richer than Midas."

But Trina was still thinking about the women, and Ivan's reputation as a ladies' man. She remembered the phone call he'd taken in the office after she'd first met him. Trina had sensed that the caller was another woman. Maybe Ivan had set up a rendezvous with her at the tub house, and maybe she'd been angry enough to strike back at him when he told her he was married. "Do you think he went to the hot tub to meet another woman?"

"There's a good possibility of that."

Trina continued, "And she shot him?"

"Possible," Reuben conceded.

David pointed out, "There were lots of people starting to arrive for the party. He could have been killed by someone from town."

"Hold it," Reuben said, raising his hands. "You can't have it both ways. If he was killed by someone from town, who's sneaking around the barn and stealing wedding gowns?"

Neither Trina nor David had an immediate answer to that question. But she thought for a moment. "What if the woman was Phyllis Winkle? What did she and Bradley say in their statement?"

"They were together all the time. Every minute of every day, they are together." Reuben pushed away from the table and rose heavily to his feet. "I'm going to try to get some sleep. Trina, would you trust me to escort you upstairs to your room?"

She glanced longingly at David, then quickly looked away. Tonight would not be theirs to share. "I guess that would be wise."

THOUGH REUBEN HAD SLEPT with his door open to hear any intruders and she had stacked the chair and suitcases against her locked bedroom door, Trina didn't get much sleep. She faded in and out of consciousness. Snatches of her dreams alternated between panic and desire.

At eight o'clock in the morning, she finally gave up on restful sleep and climbed out of bed. Through her window, she saw that the snow continued to fall steadily, but the force of the storm had passed. The view across the meadow was a dramatic vista of stark white and dark shadow. Though it wasn't clear enough to see the mountains beyond, she could feel their icy chill. This vision of Alaska was glacial and cold, and she wished that her antidote might be a cozy fireplace and snuggling with David.

"Right," she murmured to herself. "Just as soon as we solve these nasty little murders."

At least, her suspicions of David had proved to be unfounded. He couldn't possibly have been the person in the barn because she was with him. Nor did he burn Ivan's robe and slippers.

Grateful for that small relief, she dressed and went downstairs where Maybelle had set a breakfast buffet of muffins and cereal.

The coming of morning always made everything better, Trina thought. Reuben smiled pleasantly at her. Maybelle bustled. Though Victor and Jake were deep in conversation, they looked up and nodded when she came into the room. Coming from those two, a nod could be interpreted as an exuberant dance of joy.

In the kitchen, Trina filled a mug with coffee and grabbed a muffin. She asked Maybelle, "Is David up?"

"He's already out working with the snowplow. Looks like we've got the worst of the blizzard out of the way. About three and a half feet of snow, and the radio says we can expect another six inches. It'll take until tomorrow for people to dig themselves out and get things back to normal."

That was a relief. Trina thought of Ivan. Tomorrow, she thought, he would be gone. And, possibly, so would she.

Though she was terrifically attracted to David, there was nothing permanent between them. Nor should there be anything. She didn't need to have her heart broken twice in one week. When she considered the emotional consequences, she was glad that they hadn't gone to bed together last night. It was far more sensible not to be involved with him. Far more sane.

Then he walked through the door from the mudroom. The instant she saw him, sanity fled.

His face was ruddy from the cold, and his dark eyes glowed. When he smiled at her, her careful logic skewed and her pulse accelerated. She could barely keep the husky tones of desire from her voice when she said, "Good morning, David. Did you sleep well?"

"Not well at all." He came close and lowered his voice to a husky murmur that only she could hear. "Something was missing from my bed."

"Something or someone?" As she gazed up at him, her glasses began to fog.

"I think you know what I mean, Trina."

From the dining room, they heard the loud nasal whining that signaled the entrance of the Winkles.

Predictably, moments later Reuben was in the kitchen, escaping as quickly as he could from Phyllis and Bradley. "Hey, you two. I need your help this morning."

"With what?" David said.

"I want to go through Ivan's study. Somebody tore that place apart, and I want to know why. Now, I know it's unorthodox to enlist the aid of a couple of suspects..."

David and Trina exchanged a glance. Just how serious was Reuben when he said he suspected them?

"However," Reuben continued. "I was in there earlier, and I don't have a clue about where to start. I know you did a lot of the office work for him, David."

He nodded. "That's right."

"I want you to give me a hand."

"And what should I do?" Trina asked.

"Until I hear otherwise, I'm operating under the assumption that you are Ivan's widow, therefore his legal heir. You should be there."

As Bradley and Phyllis surged into the kitchen, exclaiming about the pristine, primeval wonders of the blizzard, Reuben exited toward the office. "Join me when you're ready."

Phyllis descended on David. "How are the horses? Last night was so terribly cold that I worried about them. I couldn't sleep for trying to remember if I'd settled them down nice and cozy."

"They're fine," David said.

Her head was in the refrigerator. "I'm going to run out to the barn right now, Bradley. I'll take some carrots. Maybe some apples, too."

"Good morning," Trina said.

"Oh, hi." Phyllis waved, totally disinterested in human contact when she was thinking about her equine pals.

"Last night," Trina said, "you didn't actually go out to the barn, did you?"

"In that cold?" Phyllis gave an exaggerated shiver. "Brrr."

David hooked his arm through Trina's and escorted her from the kitchen and into the office where Reuben sat in Ivan's chair behind the desk, shaking his head and shuffling papers. "I don't know what any of this stuff is," he muttered. "Stocks. Taxes. Investments. Gains and losses. Property. Ivan sure had his fingers in a lot of pies. How'd he keep it all straight?"

"He used a secretarial service based in Juneau," David said. "Mostly, they'd just fax documents back and forth or use the computer modem. But a clerk comes out once a week to do all the filing and take care of the paperwork details."

"Got a name for this service?"

"Elite, I think. Or High Tech." David shrugged. "We can check with Ivan's lawyer, Darien Greenlee. He's in Juneau, too."

"Where do we start?" Reuben spread his big hands to encompass the whole room. "I don't know which end is up."

"I have a suggestion," Trina said. She'd worked as a secretary for years, and the procedures didn't vary all that much from one place to the next. "If Ivan had clerical help, I would assume the files were well labeled and in order so that he could easily find any document he needed to put his hands on."

"Correct," David said.

"Let's assume the person who searched in here was looking for a document. He or she could probably find the file they needed without too much trouble." She looked at the two men. "Yes?"

"Keep going," Reuben said.

"And the rest of this clutter is a cover-up so that no one will know what they were looking for."

NOT ACTUAL SIZE

*This lovely necklace will add glamour to your most elegant outfit! Its cobra-link chain is a generous 18" long, and its lustrous simulated cultured pearl is mounted in an attractive pendant! Best of all, it's **absolutely free**, just for accepting our no-risk offer!*

HARLEQUIN'S

With a coin — scratch off the silver card and check below to see what we have for you.

181 CIH AWFZ (U-H-I-07/95)

YES! I have scratched off the silver card. Please send me the free books and gift for which I qualify. I understand that I am under no obligation to purchase any books, as explained on the back and on the opposite page.

NAME _____

ADDRESS _____ APT. ____

CITY _____ STATE _____ ZIP ____

Twenty-one gets you 4 free books, and a free simulated pearl drop necklace

Twenty gets you 4 free books

Nineteen gets you 3 free books

Eighteen gets you 2 free books

All orders subject to approval. Offer limited to one per household and not valid to current Harlequin Intrigue® subscribers.

© 1991 HARLEQUIN ENTERPRISES LIMITED. **PRINTED IN U.S.A.**

DETACH AND MAIL CARD TODAY

THE HARLEQUIN READER SERVICE®: HERE'S HOW IT WORKS

Accepting free books places you under no obligation to buy anything. You may keep the books and gift and return the shipping statement marked "cancel". If you do not cancel, about a month later we'll send you 4 additional novels, and bill you just $2.44 each plus 25¢ delivery and applicable sales tax, if any.* That's the complete price—and compared to cover prices of $3.50 each—quite a bargain! You may cancel at any time, but if you choose to continue, every month we'll send you 4 more books, which you may either purchase at the discount price ... or return at our expense and cancel your subscription.

*Terms and prices subject to change without notice. Sales tax applicable in N.Y.

If offer card is missing, write to: Harlequin Reader Service, 3010 Walden Ave., P.O. Box 1867, Buffalo, NY 14269-1867

BUSINESS REPLY MAIL
FIRST CLASS MAIL   PERMIT NO. 717   BUFFALO, NY

POSTAGE WILL BE PAID BY ADDRESSEE

HARLEQUIN READER SERVICE
3010 WALDEN AVE
PO BOX 1867
BUFFALO NY 14240-9952

NO POSTAGE
NECESSARY
IF MAILED
IN THE
UNITED STATES

"How do you explain the computer damage and the busted fax machine?"

"Same thing. To destroy files." She stepped around the desk and regarded the computer. The screen was broken, and the hard drive was smashed. "What happened to the disks?"

"These?" Reuben pointed to a stack of small plastic disks that looked like they'd been whacked with a hammer.

She frowned. "Maybe an expert could reconstruct this information. But it seems to me that Ivan's computer files are pretty much wiped out. As for the fax, well, maybe Ivan was expecting a fax communication that the person who created this mess didn't want him to receive."

"This all sounds reasonable," David said, "but I'm not sure how it's going to help us find what's missing."

"Assume that the searcher found the file right away without any trouble. Then created the rest of this mess. The important file will be near the bottom of the pile . . . unless he or she removed it."

She stepped over the dumped trash basket and stood in front of the file drawers. Picking through the stacks, she selected three files and read the labels. "Ermine. Environment. And Quilting."

She placed a file in each of their hands, giving the smaller files—Ermine and Quilting—to David and Reuben. She kept the thick Environment for herself, assuming that since she had been trained as a secretary and was accustomed to shuffling papers, she'd be more likely to pick out oddities.

"What are we looking for?" Reuben asked.

"Anything that's out of order."

Trina sat cross-legged on the floor and began to scan the correspondence and documents. The filing system was, indeed, simple, with the most recent dates nearest the front of the folder. "Anything over six months old," she said, "isn't relevant."

"Then I'm already done," Reuben said. "This is about a quilting bee that some charity group wanted to hold here at the hunting lodge. They wanted Ivan to discount their rooms. He told them to stuff it."

Trina instructed, "Put that one somewhere so we know it's been read. Then get yourself another file."

When she glanced over at David, she realized he was studying her closely. She lowered her gaze. Her cheeks grew warm, and she felt a trembling in her stomach, like the flutter of butterfly wings.

"You were a secretary," he said.

"Yes. Still am, I guess."

"I'd forgotten."

"Oh." *How had he known in the first place?* Trina didn't think she'd mentioned her occupation. Though she enjoyed the people she worked with, her actual job was fairly uninteresting, and she seldom talked about the surveying offices where she'd worked for the past five years.

When she looked at David, his head was down, reading his file. She shrugged and did the same.

Her file was extremely interesting. An environmentalist group called COPA, which stood for Conserve Our Protected Animals, accused Ivan and Stoddard Lodge of violations to environmental protection statutes concerning endangered wildlife. They raged about the cold-blooded murder of a breed of ferret she'd never heard of. According to this group, Ivan had thrown the entire ecosystem of southeastern Alaska out of whack.

Ivan's lawyer, Darien Greenlee, had gotten involved. Strangely, his correspondence often chided Ivan and backed the environmentalists. In one of his letters, he told Ivan that COPA was definitely going to sue. At the close of that letter, he referred to an unrelated topic, a title search on Ivan's land and an indication that the lodge might have been used as collateral in several loans.

She passed the letter to David and said, "I thought Ivan was wealthy. Why would he use the lodge as collateral?"

"He wouldn't. Ivan wouldn't risk this land for anything." He stared at the page and shook his head. "Several loans?"

"That doesn't make sense," Trina said. "Even if Ivan had taken a loan, why wouldn't he arrange it through one source? Unless he was somehow getting around interest rates."

"In this letter, it says details will be forthcoming. And this letter is dated February tenth. Maybe we can find the other letter. I'll dig through his legal correspondence."

Trina set the puzzling letter aside and moved on to another file folder.

As she read Ivan's letters, she tried to pick up a thread of the charm he'd exuded in his correspondence with her. But that gentle sincerity was totally absent in his abrupt, businesslike comments. She ran her finger across his signature, as she'd done so many times after reading his letters. Something about it was different. The slant. The shape of the letters. When he'd written to her, he'd been a totally different man.

After half an hour, they had read three stacks of folders. Each stack was a foot high, and they were beginning to see floor beneath the papers.

David reached for another file, labeled with Victor Stoddard's name. "What a nasty piece of work. Victor and Ivan, going at each other like a couple of bull elk in rutting season."

Trina said, "I guess Victor has a motive for murder."

"He's pretty direct about it." David's eyes skimmed the file's contents. "He wanted a fifty-thousand-dollar loan, and Ivan told him no. Here's what Victor says. 'My father, who was your brother, would turn over in his grave if he knew how you treat me. Don't you know, Uncle Ivan, I'm all you got. I'm your only family. You'd better treat me right. Or else, when you're dying, remember me and listen hard because you'll hear me laughing.' "

Trina tried to swallow the nasty taste that Victor's threat left in her mouth. His sheer meanness disgusted her.

"He had motive," David said. "But those two have been sending each other hate mail for years. Why would Victor kill Ivan now?"

Softly, Trina said, "Because Ivan was getting married. Victor would lose his claim on Ivan's estate to his bride. To me."

The idea that she was the only thing standing between Victor and his uncle's money was not a pleasant one. If he'd killed Ivan, he wouldn't hesitate to get her out of the way.

"Aha!" Reuben said, picking up a file that had been under the desk. "Here's what I was looking for. "Last will and testament. A fairly standard form."

As he settled down to read, both Trina and David watched him, waited for him to share the information. But Reuben said nothing. He looked up once, frowning at David. "Did you know the contents of this document?"

"No."

He closed the file. "I think it's time we put in a call to Ivan's lawyer." He pushed the phone across the desk to David. "Would you get him on the phone for me?"

David flipped through the Rolodex until he located the phone numbers for Darien Greenlee in Juneau. "I'll try him at home first because it's Saturday."

David got an answering machine and left a message. Then he called the offices. The phone rang several times before he got a receptionist and asked for Mr. Greenlee.

As Trina watched him speak into the telephone, she saw his expression change. A shadow crossed his face. When he hung up, he said, "Darien Greenlee has been out of town since last weekend and isn't expected back until Monday."

"So?" Reuben demanded. "Where can we reach him?"

"Here," David said. "He was going to a conference in Skagway, then coming here for a week of hunting with Ivan."

But he never arrived. Trina thought of the man's body in the field. He'd been dressed in expensive clothing, shot in the back and torn apart by wolves. Now that dead man might have a name. Darien Greenlee.

Reuben's large paw descended to the telephone. The easy jocularity vanished from his manner as he slipped into his official sheriff persona. "Thank you both for your help. I won't be needing you anymore. Please don't repeat anything we've said in this office to anyone else."

Trina and David stepped outside the office and stood in the entryway of the house. From the dining room, they could hear the mumble of people talking. Maybelle's laughter. A low growl that had certainly come from Jake Poynter. Though the entryway was spacious and high ceilinged with stairs leading up and a door leading out, Trina felt claustrophobic and trapped. There were too many people in the house. She could feel their presence all around her, closing in.

"David? Did you know the lawyer?"

"A little." He laid one finger across his lips, indicating silence. "Let's go back to my rooms."

They passed through the kitchen, exchanged small talk with Maybelle and Bradley who seemed to be deeply engrossed in a discussion of the merits of fresh ground coffee versus vacuum sealed, and slipped down the hall to David's large outer room.

While she sat on the plaid-upholstered sofa, he stoked his fire.

"There's something I don't understand," David said.

"Only one thing?" Trina's head whirled with so many confusing implications and contradictions that she couldn't begin to sort them out.

"If Greenlee was coming here for a week, he surely must have told Ivan, and Ivan would have told me. When we have guests, I generally handle the arrangements, like making certain the bedroom is freshly cleaned and letting Maybelle know so she can set another plate at the dinner table. But Ivan didn't say a word."

"It hardly seems likely that his attorney would come all the way from Juneau, planning to spend a week, without telling anyone."

"Maybe he did," David said. "Maybe someone else intercepted the communication."

"Let's figure out the timing," she said. "Greenlee was coming here from Juneau and probably left on Saturday. He must have called at least a day before that. So, who was staying here last Thursday and Friday?''

"Jake and the Winkles. And, of course, Maybelle and me.''

"Not Victor?"

"He didn't arrive until day before yesterday."

Trina was disappointed because Victor was really her suspect of choice. He was such an unpleasant person, and he obviously resented his uncle. But this tidbit of evidence did not implicate Victor at all.

"I would assume that Greenlee called Ivan directly or left a message on his answering machine," she said. "How could the Winkles have access to Ivan's private phone? Why would they?"

"They wouldn't." David sat on the sofa beside her. "The most likely person to have known about Greenlee's planned visit was me."

Once again, the clue pointed to David. "But why would you kill Greenlee? You have no motive."

"There was something in the will," David said. "You saw the way Reuben looked at me after he read it. Ivan must have been planning to leave me something. And there was that stuff about loans against the land. I wish I could have found the letter that was referenced."

"I'm sure it's on file in Greenlee's office," she said. "It'll turn up."

"Which makes the whole thing about tearing up Ivan's office especially weird," he said. "If they were looking for an official document, it had to be somewhere on file. Or on disk."

Maybelle poked her head through the door. "David and Trina, come out to the front room. Reuben has some kind of announcement he wants to make."

They followed her out and took a seat in the front room where everyone else was waiting expectantly. Reuben started talking as soon as they joined the group.

"I've just spoken to my office," he said, "and there has been a preliminary work-up on the man who was killed out in the field near Hunter's Creek. He was shot in the back three times. The bullets are from a .45. I will need to confiscate all .45 caliber handguns from you people for ballistics tests."

Victor said, "You already have mine. You took it last night."

"Who else has a .45?"

Jake Poynter raised his hand. "I own one, but I usually only use rifles up here."

Reuben looked directly at David. "And you?"

"I have a .45 revolver in my office."

"I thought you might." Reuben's voice was grave. "I will also need statements from everyone who was here last Saturday."

"Why?" Bradley demanded. "Do you have an identity for the man who was shot?"

"I believe so. We don't have a formal identification of the body yet, but from preliminaries based on fingerprints, I can tell you that we believe the dead man was Ivan's attorney from Juneau. His name was Darien Greenlee."

If Reuben had hoped for a reaction, he got one. In fact, Trina noted, he got several.

"Damn," said Jake Poynter.

"Greenlee, huh? He was a self-righteous prig," said Victor, maintaining his track record for hating everyone. "The last time he informed me that Uncle Ivan would not consent to a loan, Darien Greenlee suggested that I get a job."

But Bradley Winkle seemed the most shocked. Over and over, he repeated the phrase, "No, that can't be."

Reuben asked, "Did you know the man?"

"Hell, yes. Darien Greenlee was the man who suggested we come here. He's dead? I can't believe it."

Beside him, on the sofa, Phyllis had stiffened. Gradually, like the receding tide, the color drained from her complexion. She was whiter than the sheets of snow. Instead of the copious weeping she'd done when she heard of Ivan's death, she made only a tiny peep. Then she fainted dead away.

Chapter Eight

After Phyllis had calmed and Rueben had, once again, set up shop in David's office to take statements, the guests and residents of Stoddard Lodge gathered in the living room, arrayed on the sofas and rocking chairs around the fireplace. All except for David, who was, again, selected as the first to give a statement.

Outside, the snows continued. In the house, a thick silence descended. Without David, Trina felt even more trapped, closed off from the real world and contained in this small environment, inside an Alaskan bell jar. A web of intricate design meshed around these people, interconnecting them in ways that confounded her. Moments ago, she didn't even know the name Darien Greenlee, and now he was thoroughly entwined.

Jake Poynter rose to his feet. "This is one hell of an inconvenience."

"Why?" Trina asked. This was the most emotion she'd seen from Jake. "I mean, other than the fact that murders are never terribly convenient."

"Greenlee was my attorney, too. If he's dead, I'm left midstream in a number of deals."

What kind of deals? Trina had no idea of what Jake did for a living, besides rest on his Olympic laurels. "What business are you in, Jake?"

"Realty." He turned toward Maybelle. "I'm going back over to the lodge so I can have some privacy to use the phone."

"Why tell me?" Maybelle said. "Reuben's the one who needs to talk with you."

"I'll be back."

Victor popped to his feet. "Should I come with you, Jake?"

Though the two of them had seemed engrossed in each other's company since breakfast, Jake was terse. "No. I said I'd be back."

The moment he left the room, Victor took his own peevish stance. "Well, if he doesn't have to stay here, neither do I. Maybelle, I'll be in my room."

"I'm not your social secretary," she snapped. "And I'm not your mother, either. You don't have to tell me where you're going."

But she followed their example and headed out toward the kitchen.

That left Trina with the Winkles. Phyllis had stretched out on the sofa with her head in Bradley's lap. He stroked her hair gently, and when she looked up at him, Trina saw the genuine affection between them. For the first time, the Winkles looked like newlyweds. It seemed a shame to drag them through a murder investigation. And yet, they were involved as closely as anyone else. Darien Greenlee had been a friend to Bradley Winkle, and who knows what to his wife. A lover? If so, how jealous was Bradley? Jealous enough to kill?

Trina realized that she was staring at the couple. "Excuse me," she whispered and went up to her room and closed the door.

Though now they had scattered, she still felt the presence of the other people who were trapped in this desolate lodge. Someone here was a murderer. But who?

She flashed through the suspects like playing cards in a game of Clue, and paused on the one that identified David St. John. Though he seemed to be just as entangled as the others, she didn't want to believe he was guilty.

And yet, there were the facts. He had no alibi for the time between when Ivan left the office and when David joined Trina beside the fireplace. He had reason to hate Ivan because of a land scam in which David's father was the victim. It was likely that he had taken the call from Greenlee, who was now dead. David owned a .45 caliber revolver. There was something in Ivan's will that implicated David.

But then, last night, someone else had gone to the barn. Someone else had burned Ivan's clothes in David's fireplace. There was no way David could have done that. She'd been with him every minute.

She sat on a straight-backed chair, staring out the window at the unending snow. The skies were no longer white, but a solid, endless gray that hid the rest of the world and isolated her in this house.

Her body was tense and stiff, itching for action, for escape. It felt as if she'd been carved of wood. So tired of thinking. Trina felt paralyzed and helpless to stop the driving course of fate, even if it meant David had committed murder.

"No," she whispered, and the spoken syllable freed her from her heavy reverie.

Breaking away from the chair, she paced through the pinkness of her room. She wanted to leave this place, to run to a far corner of the earth where the snow never fell and the wolves never howled and danger was a million miles away.

But wasn't that how she'd gotten here in the first place? Running away? She'd been so desperate to escape her boring little life that she'd hurtled into the Alaskan back country without thinking. Acting on her emotions, she had believed herself to be in love. Wretchedly, she realized that she was in danger of making the same mistake with David.

Moments later, when she heard him knock on her door and call her name, her brain flashed a warning. Tell him to go away. Don't trust him.

But her hand was on the doorknob, pulling it open. And when he stepped into her room, she wrapped her arms around him. For a long moment, they stayed that way. Drawing warmth from each other, they huddled together, seeking respite from the oppressive cover of snow.

"I don't know what to do," she said. "It feels so helpless to just wait. David, I think we should try to figure this out, even though that's Reuben's job."

"He's already decided who murdered Ivan." David inhaled, and she felt his chest expand against her. "In fact, he thinks I killed both Greenlee and Ivan."

A harsh, discordant screech sounded deep within her brain. The sound was a warning.

"When I gave him my gun," David said, "he held it like a murder weapon. Of course, it's not. When they do ballistics tests, they'll know it's not. And Ivan was killed with a .22. I don't even think we've got a small-caliber gun like that on the premises. It's a toy, not a hunting weapon."

"Deadly toy," she said, separating from their embrace. It didn't seem right to be clinging to each other while they casually chatted about murder weapons. "Did you learn anything else about the connection between the Winkles and Greenlee? It seems that when we met them, riding, Phyllis mentioned a friend who directed them to Alaska. And Bradley made his nineties guy comment about how he wasn't jealous of the friend who had been his new wife's lover."

David nodded. "That's the way I remember it, too."

"Her lover," Trina repeated.

"At the time, I didn't think much about it."

"Do you think Ivan liked Phyllis? Or lusted after her? Do you think Phyllis Winkle was his type?"

"Ivan liked anything female. But let's not talk about that, Trina."

"Ivan's love life?" She went to the bed and sat on the edge. "Don't worry about my feelings, David. I wasn't in love with him. I was in love with a man who didn't really exist, a man I only knew through his letters."

"I don't know whether to hate those letters or to be grateful for them. They brought you here...."

"It's just possible that Phyllis was the woman Ivan intended to meet at the hot tub," Trina interjected.

"Possible," he said. "But it's hard to believe that she could tear herself away from Bradley long enough to have an affair with Ivan. During the time they've been here, I don't think I've ever seen them apart."

"Then who was he going to meet?"

David shrugged. "Maybe he was going to the hot tub alone."

Trina ignored the comment. "If it's not Phyllis, then it had to be some woman from Osprey who had a .22 in her purse."

"Hold it right there," David said. "If this supposed woman killed Ivan because she was a woman scorned, why did she go after Greenlee, too?"

"Phyllis might have a motive. If he was her former lover, she..." Another thought was forming in the back of Trina's mind. "COPA," she said.

"Cabana," he said. "Copacabana?"

"I mean COPA, the environmentalist group that intended to sue Ivan. Remember that letter we couldn't find in the office?"

"The one about the title search and the loans?"

"It also talked about the environmentalists. That's why I had a copy in the file I went through. Maybe there's something in that letter."

"Maybe," he said. "We need to contact Greenlee's office. They'll have that correspondence on file."

"But it will have to wait until Monday." Today was Saturday, and Sunday stretched ahead of them like an eternity.

"In the meantime," he said, "Maybelle sent me up here to tell you that lunch is ready."

Trina laid a hand on her stomach. The last thing on her mind was food, but lunch might be a chance to find another clue and untangle another strand of the web.

Unfortunately, the meal was sullen and uneventful. The Winkles nibbled their sandwiches quietly, like a couple of EPA-protected otters, refusing to speak except in whispers to each other. Apparently, Jake had finished his business with Greenlee's office because he'd returned. He and Victor opted to drink lunch and were sitting silently in the front room. As soon as David finished his soup and sandwich, he headed out to the barn.

The only useful bit of information that Trina picked up came when she was cleaning up in the kitchen with Maybelle.

"You think Reuben's done in the study?" the housekeeper asked. "I'd like to straighten up that mess."

"Put it out of your mind for a few days," Trina advised. "There's a ton of stuff in there, and it's going to take a major investigation to sort it out."

"Waste of time. But I don't dare go against what Reuben says. He thinks he's so important, such a big deal. I'll tell you, honey, the sheriff's head is as puffed up as a balloon in the Macey's Thanksgiving parade. He's..."

It occurred to Trina that in her perusal of the files, she hadn't seen anything about herself. Not a file or a letter or a note. And she'd been through a file dedicated to advertisements. Surely, Ivan would have kept his own ad for a mail-order bride, as well as related information.

Perhaps, she thought with a rising sense of dread, he had even saved the letters she'd written to him. "Maybelle? Is there anyplace, beside the office, where Ivan might have kept his files?"

"Sure. In the rolltop desk in his room. He'd take work up there to read at night."

"I guess we ought to tell Reuben."

"I'll do that," Maybelle promised. "As soon as he deflates a little. Maybe tomorrow."

Good, Trina thought, because she'd like to investigate on her own first. It would be horribly embarrassing for Reuben to find her sentimental, romantic letters to Ivan. She'd spilled her heart to him, told him her fondest, silliest imaginings.

Finishing in the kitchen, Trina went up to her room to plot her strategy for this brief investigation. It shouldn't be difficult. All she needed to do was go upstairs to Ivan's room, open the rolltop desk she'd seen on the west wall and search for her letters. It shouldn't take more than a few minutes. But how could she go up there? Ivan's corpse was laid out on his bed in the cold room.

Maybe she should wait for David to accompany her on this foray. Great idea! She scoffed at herself. She'd be absolutely humiliated if David perused those letters and saw for himself what a besotted idiot she'd been.

If she dared to go up there, it would have to be alone.

Cautiously, she ventured out of her room and onto the landing. The narrow stairway to the third floor stretched before her. At the top was a landing, then Ivan's room. It was dark up there. Maybe she ought to forget it. She turned toward her room. After all she'd been through in Alaska, what was one more embarrassment?

One more? That was one too many!

She pivoted. Before she could change her mind, Trina charged up the stairs, two at a time, and pushed open the door to Ivan's bedroom.

A blast of cold air struck her in the face. The air was frigid. A fetid stench crawled around her, rising in bleak miasma to seep into her pores.

Darkness pervaded the room, enhancing the cold. The only light came from a dim glow that crept around the edges of the heavy, drawn curtains.

He was dead, she told herself. He couldn't hurt her.

With trembling fingers, she flicked on the overhead light. Without looking at the bed, she aimed for the rolltop desk on the far wall. Her hands shook with such a terrified frenzy that she could hardly open the drawers. The hairs on the back of her neck prickled.

This was no good. She'd have to look at him, to confront her fears. He couldn't possibly look worse than in her imagination.

She swung around, took two steps toward the bed and forced herself to stare.

Ivan was dressed in a black suit with a white shirt. His eyes were closed. His cheeks were sunk in. His skin was gray. Beside him, on the king-size bed, she saw her wedding dress, laid out, nice and neat. A knife handle protruded from the bodice, right where her heart would be.

Trina stopped breathing. Her heartbeat echoed in her ears.

And she ran.

Out of the room, onto the landing. She raced down the stairs.

Leaning against the doorframe of her room, with his arms folded across his scrawny chest, was Victor. His hate-filled gaze bored into her. And he laughed. "Scared, Trina?"

She gasped for breath. Terrified, she groped toward the wall. Dizzy. Panicked. Her knees weak. The only thing that kept her standing was a stubborn will.

"What's the matter, Auntie Trina? Cat got your tongue? What were you looking for in Ivan's room?"

"Why?" She struggled to pull herself together. "Why are you trying to scare me?"

"Trying? From the looks of you, Trina, I'd say someone succeeded in terrifying you."

"Why did you do this?"

"Because you deserve it." His tone was oily and vicious. "You think you can come in here for one day, marry the old sod and inherit a fortune. I'm going to make it my business, Auntie dear, to see that doesn't happen."

"I don't want your money."

"So you say." He peeled himself away from the wall.

When he came toward her, Trina cringed. She wanted to run, but her legs felt too weak. Staggering, she moved back.

"You disgust me," Victor said. "How could you sell yourself to him?"

"I didn't."

"You married him!"

His words echoed. He came closer, backing her up toward the stairs.

"No!" She couldn't go up there again. Fear gave her strength. She shoved Victor and ran for the stairs that led to the main floor. Clutching at the handrail, she stumbled down the staircase. She ran blindly, not knowing where she was headed but sure she needed to escape. In the kitchen, she flung herself into a chair at the table.

Maybelle and David stood near the counter. They stared at her.

"What's the matter, honey?" Maybelle said. "You look like you've been chased by the devil himself."

Maybe she had been.

David came to her. He was all concern and kindness as he knelt by her chair, took her hand in his and began to massage her ice-cold fingers. "What's wrong? Can you tell me what happened?"

Maybelle brought her a glass of water. She started to take a seat on the opposite side of the table when Reuben's deep voice resonated from down the hall. "I could use some coffee in here, Maybelle."

She muttered, "Yes, your highness." Then, she patted Trina's shoulder. "You'll be okay, honey. We're all stressed."

After the housekeeper had bustled from the room, David repeated, "Tell me what happened."

"I was searching. Looking for that letter. Ivan had a rolltop desk in his room."

"You went up to the third floor?"

She nodded.

"You knew he was up there. Dead. Cold." His hand, holding hers, tightened. "Why didn't you come and get me, Trina? It's about the dumbest thing I've ever heard of to do, but I would have come with you."

"It wasn't dumb."

"I'm not saying you're dumb. Hell, I'd never say that. You're smart and sensitive and clever and beautiful. But, damn, Trina." He searched her face, looking for an answer. "Sneaking around in a room with a corpse is a pretty sure way to scare the jeepers out of yourself."

Archly, she said, "I had my reasons for going there. Alone."

David opened his mouth to tell her that she was almost as crazy as Phyllis, then he closed it again. Maybe she'd been rash, but she looked so miserable that he didn't have the heart to berate her.

"I wanted to find something," she said. Behind her glasses, her wide blue eyes were liquid, near to tears. "It was the letters I wrote to him, David. They're very personal, and I want them back."

A sharp twinge of guilt prickled through him.

"I feel like such a dope," she continued. "Ivan was a terrible person, but I didn't know that. In his letters, he was different. When I wrote to him, I never imagined it would turn out this way."

"It's okay, Trina. I understand."

He needed to tell her. David *knew* that he needed to tell her about the letters. It was unconscionable to let her think she was a fool. He was a liar. He was the jerk. When he wrote to her and signed Ivan's name, he'd committed a deception. That was why he said nothing to her. She might not forgive him.

In a way, he was as spooked as she was, scared that she'd hate him when she knew the truth. "You're safe now," he said, still kneeling beside her chair. "No matter what happened before, you're all right now."

"Am I?"

When she told him about bolting up the stairs to the third floor, shaking like an aspen leaf and scared to death, he listened in silence. When she told him what she'd seen on the bed, he was angry. A knife through the bodice of her wedding dress? "What kind of sick mind would think to do that?"

"There's more," she said.

As she described her confrontation with Victor Stoddard, David felt a rage burning within him. It was a sudden flame, a conflagration that spread with unbelievable speed. He was sweating. Rising to his feet, he stalked the floor in the kitchen. "That bastard."

"David, please calm down."

"I'm fine." But he needed to take some kind of action or he would erupt. It was a damn good thing that Victor wasn't in the room, because David didn't trust himself not to lash out. If he saw Victor right now, he would rip the smirk off his ugly face.

"David? Are you—"

"I'm mad," he said. He hated bullies. He despised the sheer evil intentions of Victor's prank. "I'd like to wring Victor Stoddard's neck."

Immediately, he regretted his words because Trina pulled away from him. She was quiet. Her lips were closed tight. Her arms were folded beneath her breasts. Withdrawn.

He assured her, "But I won't. I won't hurt him." *Not unless he give me a reason....*

"There's been enough violence, David."

"I know. I know." He swallowed his rage, forced himself to smile at her. "Tell you what, Trina. I'll promise not to break both of Victor's skinny arms if you promise that you'll never take off by yourself like that again."

"Don't worry," she said. "I won't be here long enough to get into any more trouble. Maybelle said the roads would be open by tomorrow, and I intend to be on my way."

"You can't leave now." Not before he had a chance to explain about the letters.

"I can't stay," she said.

He heard Maybelle returning to the kitchen. For a house that was as big as this one, it was almost impossible to get any privacy. He stood beside her. "Grab your coat. We're going to the barn."

"David, it's freezing out there."

"I need to talk to you, alone."

When Maybelle entered the kitchen, she frowned at both of them. "What's going on here?"

"What do you mean?" Trina countered.

"The tips of David's ears are beet red, which is a sure sign he's angry. And you, Trina, your hands are trembling."

"Stress?" Trina suggested.

"Perfectly natural if we'd been snowed in for a week, but it's only been a day. It's too early to be getting shack-nasty."

"Shack-nasty?" Trina questioned.

"That's what I call it when we're all closed in. Trapped in the house. And no matter how big the house is, it seems like a little shack, you know. Shack-nasty. It's like cabin fever."

"I've got a cure," David said. "We're going outside."

Maybelle pulled aside the kitchen curtain and looked out. "Well, the snow's letting up. It's only sputtering now. But there's a good three or four feet out there, more in the drifts. You dress warm."

He grinned at her. "Sure thing, Mom."

In the mudroom, David made sure that Trina was bundled up warmly. This time, before going outside, they put on water-resistant snow pants and tucked the inner layers down into their boots.

When he wrapped a wool scarf around her neck, she protested, "That's enough. I won't be able to move if I put on any more clothes."

"You look real cuddly," he said.

"Oh, yes. I've always considered the Pillsbury Doughboy to be a major sex symbol."

"I didn't say you looked sexy," He flicked the fringed end of the scarf against her nose. "Sexy is when I imagine what's under all those clothes."

Dryly, she said, "You must have an extremely active imagination."

"Want me to show you?"

"Show me what?"

"This."

He pushed aside the scarf and kissed her on the lips. He lingered there, allowing his imagination to soar. Her softness enticed him and soothed the anger he'd felt only a few moments ago. In her arms, there could be nothing but sweet pleasure. Though her long hair was tucked into her cap, he could remember what it looked like flowing around her shoulders. He imagined bare shoulders, smooth as alabaster beneath her silky hair. Underneath the parka, her sweater and turtleneck, he visualized her breasts, perfectly fitted to his hands.

As he kissed her again, David felt himself growing warmer. This sensation was nothing like the heat of rage. Instead, he felt a glow, an arousal.

When he ended the kiss and stepped away from her, his mind was full of incredibly sensual images. Though she was swathed in layers of clothing, he said, "You're a very sexy woman."

"You're sexy, too."

Though he would have liked nothing better than to take her to his bed and peel off all those clothes and make love to her for hours, Reuben was in his office. There wasn't any privacy in the house. "Okay, let's go."

"Do we have to? I'm really not excited about going to the barn and talking to the animals."

"Want to ski?" He pointed to a rack of cross-country skis and outdoor equipment. "Or walk around on snowshoes?"

"I don't want to play," she said. "I want these murders solved. I want all my suspicions and fears put to rest."

"You want to investigate."

"That's right."

Though he hadn't planned to play sleuth, he understood exactly what she meant. "Okay, let's investigate. Outside. Let's go."

The light snowfall felt bracing. Icy cold, but somehow clean and pure. David's plowing had opened a large area between the barn and the house. He'd also cut a path to the lodge, and that was the direction Trina wanted to go.

Though the path was wide enough for them to walk side by side, they went single file. On either side of them, the snow piled up almost as high as Trina's chin. There was less accumulation among the trees.

She pointed. "There. I think we should check in the tub house for clues."

"I doubt we'll find anything. Rueben, Jake and I made tracks inside while we were moving Ivan's body."

"But aren't those fresh footprints leading to the stairs?" Trina asked.

With the blowing, drifting snow, it was hard to tell. David nodded. "I think you're right. It's hard to tell exactly when, but it looks like somebody went in there today. Maybe we should get Reuben before we go inside."

"You mean go back to the house, take off all these clothes, find Reuben, convince him to come with us, get dressed and come back." Her lips puffed a wisp of snow breath. "No. We'll just be careful not to step where the other person did."

Tromping a path beside the other prints, David climbed the stairs. Before the snowfall, there were seven steps leading to the door of the tub house. Now, four of them were buried.

David reached back, held Trina's hand and helped her negotiate the stairs.

The door to the tub house was open, and they went inside. With all the shutters closed, it was dark inside. David turned on the light. He had a bad feeling about this, a sense that they were going to find the clue that would end suspicion and show them the identity of the murderer.

Chapter Nine

In different circumstances, Trina would have found the tub house to be charming. The octagonal shape was about fifteen feet in diameter. The floor was covered wall to wall with heavy beige carpet. The walls were of smooth, polished cedar, and there were built-in benches that followed the angles. In the northwest corner was the tub itself, a huge hot tub with room for eight to sit comfortably. But no bathing beauty would perch on the ledge today, because the water inside was still and cold.

Splattered on the light carpet, Trina saw the dark, rust-colored stains of Ivan's blood. She looked away. Though she'd been eager to investigate, she wasn't quite ready to see the direct evidence of murder. The enclosed room suddenly felt too hot, though she knew the thermostat was set low. There was a foul odor. Or was she imagining it? The air seemed too thin, as if there was not enough oxygen. She gasped, feeling light-headed. ''I'll step outside...''

Standing on the walkway that surrounded the tub house, with her hands grasping the railing, she inhaled deeply. Though Trina had never thought of herself as squeamish, her stomach lurched. She was nauseous.

David stepped up behind her. "Maybe this wasn't such a good idea."

"When I came to Alaska,," she said, "I knew it would be a challenge—very different from living in a city apartment. I wanted to be rough, tough and ready for anything. More like Maybelle."

"Trina." His hand rested on her shoulder. "You're perfect exactly the way you are."

"Perfect? I think not." She shook her head. "I lied as much as Ivan. First, I subtracted ten years from my age. Then, I presented myself as somebody who was ripe for adventure."

"Typical adventures don't include double murders," he said. "Let's go back to the house."

"Nope. I'm going to do this. I'm going to prove that you didn't kill anybody."

"And why are you so sure?"

She wasn't all that positive. But she couldn't tell him that her decision was based on wishful thinking. "Let's just open these windows."

As they opened the shutters of the four windows, her nausea abated. She was going to be fine. She could handle this. When Trina went inside the tub house again, she felt one hundred percent better. With the windows open, she lost the sense of claustrophobia. The cozy paneled interior contrasted with the stark snowfall in the spruce trees.

She gazed at the jagged, broken window, and tried to think like a detective. What happened here yesterday? Had Ivan stood in the middle of the room, waiting for a guest? When had he known he was going to die?

She was aware of David watching her and asked, "What was it like to take a bath here?"

"Real nice," he said. "In the summer after a day of escorting idiot hunters around the hills and making sure they don't accidentally shoot their own toes, it's great to lie around in here with all the shutters open. You can look out at the trees and let the hot water soak all the kinks out of your muscles."

"Is that how Ivan used the hot tub?"

"He generally didn't come out here alone."

Without the slightest hint of rancor, she said, "I can understand why he'd bring women here. This would be a great place for romance. A little music. A little wine. And any woman would melt. Even when the weather outside was snowy."

"Actually, it's seldom used in the winter. It takes too long to heat the water. Because of the windows, it's often not really warm in here."

"And it might be a problem moving from tub to seduction," she said with a nod. "You wouldn't want to make love on this hard floor. And a run through the snow back to the house would put a dent in anyone's passion."

David grinned at her. "A little cynical, aren't you?"

"I'm thirty-five," she said, "not a dewy-eyed, naïve young thing. I'm practical."

"Even about love?"

"Of course." She snooped around the room, looking high and low for a clue. "Especially about love."

"Really," he said.

David knew from reading her letters that Trina didn't feel that way. Her sense of practicality was tempered by a wide streak of wondering, wishing and yearning.

Once he'd sent her two dozen roses, in Ivan's name, and in her thank-you letter, she'd spoken of a beauty that—like the rose petals—folded upon itself. Roses, she'd written, nourished her heart. That didn't sound like a cynical comment to him.

She peered into the hot tub waters. "Help me search, David."

"What exactly are we looking for?"

"I don't know. A scrap of paper. A broken matchstick. A clue." She opened the door to a cabinet. "It looks like this is where towels are kept. But it's empty. Why?"

"Mildew. As Maybelle says, you can't leave damp things lying around in this climate or else they'll grow fur and run off."

He sat on a bench beside the door. "Here's what I don't understand," he said. "Why was Ivan naked?"

"Isn't that the usual attire for bathing?"

"But he had to be dressed to come out here. He couldn't walk through the house nude."

"And there weren't any clothes when you found the body?"

"Not a stitch."

"The murderer took the clothes," she said. Trina was down on her hands and knees. She pulled off her mittens to pluck a tiny piece of lint from the floor. "Then burned them in your fireplace."

"Why? What could be incriminating about a bathrobe and slippers?"

She held the lint up to the light, then discarded it. "I don't know."

"Let's try to reconstruct the crime," he said. "Somebody opened the shutters, broke the window and shot Ivan. And then took his clothes?"

"Maybe they took his clothes first."

"Okay." He went along with her. "Why?"

"Who knows?"

She squinted toward her left. Something beneath the benches attracted her attention, and she crawled toward it, offering him a view of her backside. In the bulky snow pants, she was as roly-poly as a bear cub.

He almost laughed, but when she turned her head and looked at him, his amusement vanished. Her eyes were wide and confused. And fearful, he thought. Afraid of him? "What is it?" He joined her on the floor, wondering what she'd found. After all, Reuben had already searched. Trina scooted away, as if the thing on the floor was a poisonous spider that might bite.

He found the exact spot she'd been searching. There on the carpet, written in the dark rust color of dried blood, were three letters. DSJ. David St. John. His initials.

As always, Ivan had the last word. No doubt, he'd reached out from the grave for one last act of malevolence. "It's a lie," David said. "I don't know why he did it, but it's not true."

"Of course not," she responded. But Trina was on her feet, pulling on her gloves. "Gosh, it's cold out here. Maybe we should go back to the house now."

He could feel her suspicion, and it hurt more than physical pain. "I didn't kill him."

Her fingers rested on the doorknob. "We'd better hurry. Maybelle will be wondering if we've frozen."

"You don't believe me." He stood. When he took a step toward her, she backed away. Frightened? If only he could hold her, reassure her. But he knew, with gut-wrenching certainty, that she wouldn't let him get that close. "I'm being framed. I didn't kill Ivan. Or Darien Greenlee. Don't you believe me?"

"I hardly know you."

"Listen . . ." He called upon the romantic spirit he knew from her letters. Softly, he summoned the woman she'd been to him on those lonely nights when he sat at his computer, writing to her of his dreams and desires. "Listen to your heart, not your head. You know, in your heart, that I'm not a murderer."

Her lips parted, as if to speak, but she said nothing. Her blue eyes, behind her glasses, seemed to gaze inward.

"Search inside yourself," he encouraged. "That's where you'll find the truth."

"In my heart?" She gave a short laugh. "That's where I make mistakes. My heart told me to marry Ivan, sight unseen."

"You can trust me."

"Can I? Would you ever lie to me?"

He longed to tell her that he never would, but he already had. He'd perpetrated a gigantic hoax by writing to her and signing Ivan's name. The only thing he could, in all honesty, say was, "I didn't kill anybody."

"Then there's only one thing to do," she said. "We've got to wash those initials out of the carpet."

"We can't do that."

"The sheriff isn't going to believe you, David. He's going to look at the evidence, and that blood looks like Ivan wrote your initials as his last act on earth."

"I won't alter evidence," he said. "I don't have a damn thing to cover up. I'm innocent."

But he knew how bad it looked. He might as well have Ivan's ghost rising from his deathbed and pointing an accusing finger in his face. If it was Ivan . . .

There were low voices outside, and Trina looked at him with panic in her gaze. "Somebody's coming. They'll see."

"Might as well get this over with," he said.

David went to the tub house door and opened it. Outside at the bottom of the stairs were Victor and Jake.

"Before you come up here," David said, "I want you both to notice one thing. There are two sets of prints leading in here."

"I saw that," said Jake. "One set was from three or four hours ago. Probably only one person. The other is two people. You and Trina?"

"Correct," she said, peeking out from behind David's shoulder.

"Why are you here?" Victor demanded.

"Why are you?"

"Following your tracks." He climbed the stairs, obliterating the separate tracks that David and Trina had been so careful to maintain. As he drew even with them, Victor said, "You better not have messed up anything in here."

David felt his muscles tighten. He'd never liked Victor Stoddard, but because of the way he'd treated Trina, David hated the man. Victor was a bully, a jerk, nothing but mean. He deserved a hard right jab in the middle of his weak chin.

Behind him, Trina whispered, "You promised. No more violence."

David stepped aside to allow Victor and Jake to enter. Keeping his voice low and controlled, David said, "As a matter of fact, Trina and I discovered a piece of evidence."

"What?" Victor sneered.

"That." David pointed to the shadows beneath the bench.

Victor bent down, stared and read aloud. "DSJ. David St. John. And it appears to be written in blood." A huge grin twisted his face, emphasizing the ridged eyebrows and sunken hollows on either side of his cold, red nose. "Well, well, well. So, you killed the old bugger, after all..."

"No, Victor, I did not."

"Well it sure looks as if Ivan wrote your initials in his own blood because he wanted to identify you as the killer."

"The initials don't necessarily prove that he's the killer," Jake said. "There were those other tracks leading out here. Somebody else might have written that. We didn't see it yesterday."

"It's under the damn bench," Victor shouted. "In the shadows. We wouldn't have noticed it yesterday."

"But why would Ivan write it there?" Trina questioned. "If he wanted to accuse David, wouldn't he put the initials in a more obvious place?"

"Good point," Jake said. "And I don't see any other blood around it. No smears. Hardly even a splatter. If Ivan crawled over here, he would have left a trail."

"What's wrong with you?" Victor said. "David did it. The initials are proof."

His tone was purely petulant, and it grated on David's nerves. His gloved hands were aching to reach out and punch Victor's jaw.

"I'm going to tell Reuben," Victor continued. "Then he can stop this stupid nonsense of taking statements and put DSJ under arrest. Where he belongs." He stomped toward the door. "I, for one, am delighted. I'll sleep better tonight."

"Is that so?" Trina snapped. "Does this mean you won't be sneaking into my room and stealing clothes?"

Victor slowly reversed his position, turning away from the door. When he glared at Trina, his eyes were mean. "Whatever are you talking about?"

"You know. My wedding dress. You took it, and you mutilated it."

"Do you have any proof for that accusation?"

"Not right now," she admitted. "But there will probably be a forensic investigation as soon as the police can get through the blizzard. Then they'll take fingerprints."

"You have no evidence, Auntie Trina. So I suggest you shut up."

David took one step forward. His blood was boiling. "Here's a little warning for you, Victor. Don't you ever talk to her like that again."

"I don't have to listen to you. You're dirt, David. A murderer. And you're going to spend the rest of your sorry life in a prison cell. The only way this could be better is if you, Auntie Trina, were also implicated."

"Hey," Jake put in, "lighten up, Victor."

"She makes me mad," Victor said. "I wish she was guilty. Then I wouldn't have to fight her for the estate."

"How many times do I have to tell you?" Trina said. "I don't want your money."

"Prove it," he challenged. "I'll draw up a document and you can sign it."

"Don't sign anything," David advised.

"Back off!" Victor pointed his index finger in David's face. "She doesn't need you. The thieving little witch can make her own greedy decisions."

"Excuse me?" David's voice belied the raging fury in his belly. "What did you call Trina?"

"Don't try to protect her, you stupid cowboy. Don't be any dumber than you have to be."

One punch, David thought, wouldn't be enough.

Victor continued. "She came up here and basically sold herself to Ivan."

David landed a hard jab to Victor's midsection. The force of the blow was enough to make Victor double over, in spite of his layers of snow clothes.

"Stop it," Trina said. "David, you promised."

"Sorry, I must have slipped." David moved closer to Victor. "Go ahead, pal. If it'll make you feel better, take your best shot."

Victor drew his arm back and delivered a roundhouse right, which David easily dodged. To Trina, David said, "If I hit him back, it's self-defense."

Victor screeched, "Is she your boss, now?"

"What do you say, Trina?"

Jake, settling back on the bench above where David's initials were drawn, added his opinion. "I'd call it self-defense."

In a quiet voice, Trina said, "Don't hurt him."

Victor swung again, clumsily. David blocked the punch then backed Victor up against the wall. In the process David scratched Victor, drawing blood.

David sighed. "Let me tell you something. Victor, old boy, you'd better be damn glad that I'm not a murderer because if I ever felt like killing someone, it would be you."

David let him go, and Victor slumped down on a bench.

From outside, they heard Reuben shouting, "What the hell is going on in there?"

Trina opened the door for him. "We were just—"

"I can't believe this!" Reuben threw up his hands. "When Phyllis Winkle told me something was going on in the tub house, I thought she was crazy. But now I see you're the crazy ones." He looked down at Victor. "What happened to him?"

"He slipped," Jake said with a grin, "and fell down."

"That's right," Trina said. "We were just getting ready to help him back to the house."

"None of you touch me," Victor snapped.

When he raised his arm, she saw that his wrist—between his parka sleeve and his glove—was bleeding. Victor noticed the injury and complained, "I'm hurt."

"You go inside and let Maybelle take care of it," Reuben ordered. "The rest of you get out of here, too! What's the matter with you people? Haven't you ever heard of forensics? Don't you know better than to mess around at a murder scene? If this thing ever gets solved, it'll be a miracle."

"It's solved," Victor said. He pointed to the initials.

With a heavy sigh, Reuben said, "Jake and Trina, both of you go back to the house. David, stay. I need to talk to you."

David sat on one of the benches, his back against the wall, and waited for the worst. Under his parka and thermal underwear, he was perspiring, but not from the fight with Victor. He expected to be arrested. They'd found his initials written in blood at the murder scene. The only more damaging evidence would be a photograph of him standing over the dead body with the smoking gun in his hand.

Without looking up, he said, "It's ironic, Reuben. There was a time, when I first came up here after my divorce, that I wouldn't have cared if you locked me up and threw away the key."

"As I recall," Reuben said, "I did arrest you once. Every time you came into town, you'd get into a fight."

"I was hurting bad. I missed my kids so much that I didn't care what happened to me." He sighed. "But then, I settled in here. I got back to my roots. Working here."

Maybe it hadn't been much of a life—all work and not much time for pleasure—but the schedule suited David's needs. If he kept busy every minute, he didn't have time to think and remember and regret his failed marriage. Maybelle had encouraged him to get involved with someone and start over, but he never wanted to care for a woman again. He couldn't stand the pain of separation when it was over, and he'd vowed never to love again. But that was before he met Trina.

Quietly, he said, "I lied to you, Reuben."

"About what?"

"Trina. You've heard her talk about those letters Ivan wrote to her. Well, the words didn't come from Ivan. I wrote them. For a month, I wrote to her almost every night. And the things she said when she wrote back were food for my soul. I care about her a lot. She's the first woman I've really cared about since my divorce."

"Why are you telling me this?"

He looked down at the bloodstained carpet. "I didn't kill Ivan. And I want a chance to prove it. Right now, for the first time in a lot of years, I have a real reason to live."

A heavy stillness descended as the two men sat silently on benches in the tub house. Reuben's heavy features, even his mustache and eyebrows, seemed to be carved of stern stone, but David could tell that he was considering.

And David dared to hope. His gaze lifted to the open shutters. Outside the snowfall continued, streaking the gray skies with pure white. Though the temperature was subzero with the windchill, the atmosphere felt colder inside the octagonal room where Ivan Stoddard had died. David's world stood still while he waited for Reuben to make up his mind.

"I don't know." The sheriff cleared his throat. "I just don't know. I appreciate your honesty, but the way you feel about Trina gives you another motive to kill the man who married her."

"Just until tomorrow." David didn't want to beg, but if that was what it took, he was willing to abandon his pride and crawl. "The roads won't be open until then, anyway."

"I'm not giving you permission to investigate," Reuben said. "Let's keep that straight. If you find anything, you bring it directly to me."

"Understood."

"By tomorrow, late afternoon, we'll be surrounded by coroners and forensic people and state police. I've been on the phone, and I found out that Darien Greenlee was an important man in Juneau."

Great, David thought. More pressure. More complication.

Reuben continued, "I already took a phone call from a reporter. There's going to be a hell of a stir, and I doubt the city and state officials are going to pay much attention to me, a back-country sheriff."

"You'd like to have the murders solved by then," David said.

"Doggoned right, I would. But I'm not holding my breath." Reuben rose and straightened his broad shoulders. "I'm not going to arrest you now."

David inhaled a breath of freedom.

Reuben continued, "In spite of everything, I don't believe, in my gut, that you killed Ivan. Plus, I've got no easy way to restrain you, apart from handcuffing you to the bumper of my truck." He grinned. "And then, who'd do your chores?"

"Thanks," David said.

"Until tomorrow."

IN THE HOUSE, Trina and Jake were alone in the mudroom, peeling off layers of snow clothing. Jake's outfit was, as usual, white. With the heavy, water-resistant snow pants and hooded parka, he resembled an athletic snowman.

"For hunting in winter," he explained. "In this kind of weather, I need every advantage. In the white, the prey might not see me coming for a few extra seconds. And those seconds make all the difference."

In her mind, white was for Arctic foxes and snow hares with milky fur that made them all but invisible in the snow. "I always thought white in Alaska meant protective coloration."

"I don't need protection."

His swagger, she thought, was so ingrained that it was natural. The undeniably handsome Jake Poynter considered himself a superior specimen, a hunter. Nothing would dare get in his way.

"By the way, Trina, in case you do inherit, my offer stands. I want this lodge. With my contacts, I could make something of it."

"And Ivan didn't?"

"This was a hobby for him. He wasted his time building gazebos and hot tubs because it pleased him. I could turn a profit with this lodge, a hefty profit. Ivan couldn't. He didn't want to. Ivan was getting old and soft."

"Soft?" She had to question that. In her brief acquaintance with Ivan Stoddard, he had seemed anything but soft. "How do you mean?"

"You. A bride," Jake said. "You're proof of how Ivan was changing. All of a sudden, he wanted a wife and kids. In any case," he continued, "I want this place. I'll offer a fair price. You can sell to me and get out of Alaska. That's what you want, isn't it?"

When she said nothing, he left her alone in the mudroom to consider—not that Trina had anything to think about. She had no intention of being involved in the future of the lodge. Unless her efforts could somehow help David.

He looked guilty. Every piece of information they uncovered pointed more directly to him. The timing. The motive. Whatever Reuben had seen in the will. The initials.

And what about the way he'd punched Victor? Not that David had been in a homicidal rage. Not at all. Still, he'd pinned Victor against the wall and threatened him.

On one side, her emotions told her David was innocent, and she wanted to trust her gut feeling. But she'd misjudged Ivan so hugely that she didn't dare ignore logic. And logically David looked like a murderer.

The sounds of weeping and a loud argument drew her from the mudroom into the kitchen. At the sink, Maybelle was taking care of a cut on Victor's forearm that was still bleeding slightly. The loud voices of Bradley and Phyllis Winkle came from the dining room.

Maybelle muttered something under her breath about having a houseful of children, then said, "Trina, would you try to get those two to calm down?"

"What do you suggest?" Trina grinned. "That I turn a hose on them and pull them apart?"

"Just quiet them down," Maybelle said.

"Or shoot them," Victor said. "Oh, but that's your boyfriend's department, isn't it?"

Maybelle yanked his arm and he winced.

In order to avoid responding to Victor, Trina opted for the less despicable alternative. The Winkles. She went through the door from the kitchen.

"Bradley! How could you say that?" Phyllis slapped at the front of her husband's shirt. Her face was contorted, and her eyes were red from crying. "How could you even think I'd be with another man?"

"I forgive you," Bradley said. "Come on, I'm not angry. We can work this out."

"But I didn't do anything."

"Now, Phyllis, honey—"

"Don't call me honey!"

He moved toward her as if to embrace her, but she turned her back on him. Amid her gasping sobs, she said, "I hate you. I hate you for thinking—"

"You don't mean that."

"Would you please stop forgiving me, Bradley?" She stared at Trina. "I'm right, aren't I?"

Trina had to agree with her. All that rational understanding was more than a little cloying. But she really didn't want to take sides.

"Phyllis, dear," Bradley said, "I hardly think we need to ask the advice of a stranger."

Though Trina knew she was intruding on a private moment between newlyweds, she didn't leave. "I could be impartial," she offered. "Maybe if you explained your problem, I could give you another perspective."

Phyllis was only too willing to spill her guts. "For absolutely no reason, Bradley had gotten it into his head that I was involved with—"

"I have a reason," he said.

"Just because I wasn't with you every minute? You call that a reason?" She sobbed again. "Oh, this is so unfair."

"Should I tell Trina?" Bradley asked. There was a threatening note in his voice. "Maybe I should tell the sheriff, too."

"I don't care what you do," Phyllis shouted. "I wasn't having an affair with Ivan."

She turned on her heel and fled from the room.

Chapter Ten

Bradley started to follow his wife into the kitchen, then halted, staring after her with strangely hungry eyes. When he turned toward Trina, his fingers twitched nervously, then drew into fists. He seemed to be angry, but he spoke like a true gentleman of the nineties. "I feel badly about this, Trina. I'm sorry you got drawn into it."

He was good at apologizing, but she wasn't going to let him off the hook so easily. "Why would you think your wife was involved with Ivan?"

"Excuse me?" His supposedly easygoing grin tightened so much that his lips were white.

"I was just wondering," she said, assuming an air of innocent concern, "since I got forced into this discussion, anyway, why you thought Phyllis was having an affair."

Though he probably would have liked to tell her that it was none of her business, Bradley attempted to resume his mellow, passionless attitude. "I must have been mistaken."

"Come on, Bradley. That's a pretty serious accusation. You must have had some reason."

"Phyllis would say that I was being overly jealous." He paused like an actor who had forgotten his lines. He sucked in a couple of deep breaths. When he spoke again, he was calmer. "Perhaps some jealousy is to be expected when an average man like me marries a remarkably beautiful woman like Phyllis. Perhaps I have a primitive, male-driven urge to protect what is mine. Of course, that's not right. I should meditate. I should get in touch with my female side. Of course, there are—"

"Bradley," Trina interrupted. "What actually happened?"

"From the first day we were here, Ivan flirted with her. His manner was so blatant that I considered him comical. But, apparently, Phyllis took him seriously."

"From what I've heard, Ivan was a notorious ladies' man." Trina paused, waiting for Bradley to tell her more, but he clammed up. She prodded. "Like Darien Greenlee. I seem to remember that Phyllis was also—"

"Yes, she was. Past tense. She told me before we came up here that she'd been involved with Darien. But their affair was over. She didn't even like him anymore. You see, Darien was a hunter and Phyllis can't abide the killing of any living thing."

Though Trina couldn't imagine mellow Bradley, the nineties guy and staunch environmentalist, being driven by savage jealousy, there was the coincidence of two men being involved with his new bride. Two men who had been murdered. "What makes you think Phyllis and Ivan went further than harmless flirting?"

"I really can't say."

"Can't or won't?"

"Both. It's all a matter of timing, really." The smile he affixed to his face was practiced and bland. "I suppose I ought to go looking for my wife."

Impulsively, Trina said, "Let me. She might feel more comfortable talking to another woman."

"Oh, I really don't think—"

"Nonsense." She pointed toward the front room. "You stay here. Read a book. Relax. I'll take care of Phyllis."

Trina whipped into the kitchen where Maybelle had finished with Victor and was repacking her first aid kit. Trina asked, "Which way did Phyllis go?"

"Out," Maybelle said. "Unless I miss my guess, she's on her way to the barn. That woman loves the horses."

Out, again. Trina stomped into the mudroom and began dressing. Again. It seemed that her major occupation in Alaska was putting on and taking off parkas and scarves. If she ended up staying here for any extended period, she would have to invest in some really good, full-body, silk thermal underwear. Not that she planned to stay any longer than needed.

Once more, she was out in the cold. She looked up in time to see David heading into the barn. Had he followed Phyllis? For an instant, Trina wondered if Phyllis was also having an affair with David, but she dismissed the thought. David had made it quite clear that he couldn't stand the woman.

Trina charged onward, into the wind. The path to the barn had been plowed and wasn't difficult, but she had to fight through the blasting cold that tore through her clothing and chilled her bones.

Still, she covered the way quickly. Inside the barn, the relative warmth and shelter closed around her, holding her gently like a chamois glove.

She heard the nickering of the horses and above that came David's voice, conversing in a reasonable tone. David, she thought, wasn't like Bradley, who had lost his identity trying to be the kind of man his wife wanted. Nor was David like Jake who could have cared less what anyone thought about him.

David was simply himself, his own man. He wasn't perfect by any means—because a perfect man wouldn't have been drawn into a fight no matter how repulsive Victor had been. Nor would a perfect man have worked for Ivan. If David had been perfect, she thought, he would have stopped her from marrying Ivan and swept her off her feet. When they kissed, she felt like he was the real reason she came to Alaska. Not Ivan. Not this whole ridiculous mail-order-bride business. The fates had brought her here to meet David St. John. And, if he was perfect, he would have known that.

"What else did Ivan tell you?" she heard David ask Phyllis.

"He was just horrid. A liar."

Feeling guilty, Trina crept closer so she could observe their conversation without interrupting. Was David to be trusted or not? She hid behind the wall that separated the tack room from the stalls. The walls were hung with riding equipment. The saddles and bridles exuded a leathery scent.

From where she stood, Trina could see Phyllis by the horses' stalls. She'd removed her gloves and was stroking the neck of the chestnut mare. Her wrists, like the rest of her body, were incredibly slender. Almost delicate. Her attention to the horse seemed loving and natural, unlike the hostility she'd aimed at Bradley.

David sat on a long bench, leaning back against the wall and looking up at Phyllis. The dim light from one of the bare bulbs outlined his profile. "How did Ivan lie to you?"

"Should I tell you?" Her tone was coquettish, and Trina realized that this woman behaved far differently when she thought she was alone with a man. She batted and lowered her eyelashes before she peeked up through them, a trick Trina had never mastered due to her eyeglasses.

"What did Ivan promise you?" David asked.

Phyllis left the horses and came toward him. Squatting in front of him, she rested her hands on his knees and looked at him. "David, I'm going to tell you something that I haven't told anyone, not even Bradley. Okay?"

"Sure. Okay."

"I was the last person to see Ivan alive."

Trina, hiding in the shadows, concentrated on not making a move that might distract Phyllis. A huge excitement built within her. She fought the urge to leap out and yell, "Aha!" The last person to see Ivan alive would have been the person who killed him. Was Phyllis about to confess?

"On the day before the murder, he told me to telephone him in his office," she said. "And I did."

One mystery solved, Trina thought. Phyllis was the unknown caller who had disrupted her first meeting with Ivan.

"And then?" David asked.

"He wanted to see me immediately, but it was impossible for both of us. I asked him to say anything important on phone, but he wouldn't tell me anything. He teased. Then he made an appointment to meet with him at the hot tub at eleven-thirty on the following day."

"Why?" David asked.

Silly question, Trina thought. Obviously, Ivan had been interested in recruiting Phyllis Winkle as his next conquest. That meant that when he'd married her, Ivan had already arranged for his first infidelity.

"He told me," Phyllis said, still gazing intently into David's face, "that he was willing to turn this whole area into a wildlife preserve where the birds and animals would be protected with no hunting allowed. That's exactly what we want at COPA. He was most concerned, as I am, about the endangered eagles and the ptarmigan."

"The eagles," David said.

"Yes." She bobbed her head on her long skinny neck and widened her eyes.

"You are referring to the fifteen thousand birds that have a multitude of protected habitats in this vicinity."

"The majestic eagle. Ivan was concerned about them."

David shifted his weight. He leaned forward, only inches from Phyllis's nose. Distinctly, he said, "Bull."

"I believed him," Phyllis said. "He sounded so sincere. All week we had been discussing the possibility, and he was especially unhappy when I told him I had discovered signs that he wasn't strictly following the game restrictions about hunting."

"How so?"

"He allowed Jake Poynter to hunt alone. I saw him, two or three times, taking off with his rifle."

David sighed heavily. "Jake goes his own way."

"But he's not supposed to. According to the U.S. forestry regulations, he must be accompanied by a registered guide or a resident."

"When you got to the tub house," David said, "what happened?"

"It took me a few extra minutes to get there, because I needed to make an excuse to Bradley so I could sneak away." She fluttered a hand to her breast. "I feel so terrible about lying to him, but it was for the greater good. Saving the wildlife."

"Yeah, right. And what happened?"

"Ivan was already there. He was wearing only a robe and slippers, standing beside the hot tub, waiting for the water to warm up. He told me that we could discuss the wildlife in a leisurely way if I took off my clothes and joined him in the tub. Of course, I knew what he really wanted."

Brilliant deduction, Trina thought. Confronted by a naked man, even Phyllis could guess what he *really* wanted—and it wasn't a bird sanctuary.

"I refused," she said. "He came toward me. And I, well, I kicked and I slapped and I fought. And I...I left him there."

She was leaving something out, Trina thought. Though she could envison Phyllis battling Ivan, Trina had felt Ivan's iron grasp when he held her and forcibly sealed their false wedding vows with a kiss. She had to struggle to break free. The memory brought a shudder of disgust. Though Ivan wasn't a huge man, he had a wiry muscularity that was more than a match for Trina. How had skinny Phyllis been able to escape him? In a small place like the tub house, it would have taken some pretty fancy moves. Was Phyllis capable of pulling it off? Had the slender woman ever been trained in self-defense?

"When you left him," David said, "did you come out here to the barn?"

"Yes." She gasped. "How did you guess?"

"When I was out here a little bit later, I saw that one of the horses had been ridden. Where did you go?"

"Gosh, I'm not even sure," Phyllis said. "I was terribly upset. I just needed to get out, to ride."

"And then?"

"I rode back here, left my horse, found Bradley and went to the party." She pursed her lips in a pink bow. "Do you think I should tell the sheriff about seeing Ivan in the tub house? It doesn't seem important, and nothing happened, and I just know my Bradley will be so annoyed if he hears about how Ivan attacked me."

David plucked her hands off his knees and stood. "Tell Reuben. This isn't a game. It's murder, two murders. Reuben needs to know everything."

Good for you, David. Trina almost cheered.

"Will you come with me?" Phyllis asked in a tiny little voice. "I'd feel so much braver if you were there."

That was enough of Phyllis and her fluttering eyelashes and girlish poses. Trina banged around behind the wall as if she'd just entered the barn. She tramped loudly as she came around the corner.

"Phyllis," she said, "your husband is so upset. Almost distraught. He's sorry for not being more understanding and promises to get in touch with his female side."

"Does he?"

"Absolutely. He's really, really sorry. And I mean that."

"I must go to him," Phyllis said dramatically. She pulled up her hood and stuck her hands into her gloves. Turning to David, she said, "You understand, don't you? Bradley needs me."

"Sure. Go."

"Before you run off," Trina said, "I'd like to ask you a favor. Woman to woman."

"What is it?"

Trina wanted some clarification, and she fabricated her story as she went along. "I think Bradley mentioned that you knew something about self-defense, and I've always been interested in learning about that. With all that's happened, I'd feel more confident if I knew...."

"Every woman should know how to defend herself," Phyllis said adamantly. "Of course, I've taken self-defense classes."

"Could you give me a demonstration?"

"The first thing you do is yell, really loud. Like this." Phyllis threw back her head and issued forth with a booming screech that startled the horses and the cows into silence. Phyllis continued in a chatty manner, "Some instructors suggest that you go for your attacker's face and groin. But I'm far more advanced than that."

"I'm not quite sure that I understand. Maybe you could give me an example." Trina glanced toward David. "You could use David."

David's eyebrow shot upward. "I really don't think we need to do this."

But Phyllis had pivoted and faced him. Her legs were bent at the knees. Her weight was balanced. She beckoned him forward. "Come at me."

"I think not."

"Don't be afraid," she encouraged. "It's important for Trina to know how to do this, and I promise not to hurt you."

"Imagine my relief," he muttered. "So, what do I do?"

"Come at me as if you were going to attack me."

He shook his head in annoyance. Then he made a halfhearted attack, grabbing for Phyllis's arms. But

Phyllis dodged him. She lashed out with a flying kick, which he avoided. While she was bracing for another assault, he caught her hand, spun her around and pulled her against his body.

"How's this?" he asked.

"Let me go," she whined. "You're hurting my arm."

When David complied, she whipped around and unleashed another flying kick, missing him completely and landing hard on her bottom. This time, her loud screech was for real.

"Is that what you did with Ivan?" David asked. "Leapt around and landed on your butt?"

"I had him right where I wanted him." Furious, she bounced to her feet. "He thought he was so smart, but I taught him a lesson."

"How'd you do that?" David asked.

"He thought he could embarrass me." She glanced toward Trina. "You know what I mean, don't you?"

"I'm afraid I do."

"I suspected he might be up to something when he wanted to meet at the hot tub. After all, I'd had a whole day to think about it. So I was ready for him. I turned the tables."

"How?" David said.

"I don't have to tell you. I don't have to tell you anything."

"I think I know," Trina said. If she had Ivan in her power, she knew exactly what she would do. "You took his clothes, didn't you? He was already stripped, and you grabbed his robe and his slippers and left him out there in the tub house stark naked. Then you stuck a twig through the outside latch so he couldn't get out."

"It was a pretty good trick," Phyllis said. "It gave me extreme pleasure to leave him naked with guests arriving."

"But how did you do it?" Trina asked.

"I just grabbed his clothes and ran to—"

"To the barn," David finished. "Then, last night, you came out here and got the clothes and brought them back to the house and burned them in—"

"Leave me alone!" Phyllis snapped. "I didn't do any of that. You're making it all up."

"We need to know everything," Trina said. "Reuben needs to know."

"I'm not talking to the sheriff, and you can't make me. Everything we've said here is supposition. It could all be a pack of lies."

Phyllis turned on her heel and fled from the barn.

Trina turned toward David. Her instinct was to comfort him, to offer him shelter in her arms and to soothe away his troubles. She took a step closer. Tentatively, she reached out for him. "David?"

He caught her outstretched hand and laced his fingers with hers. "I'm glad you were here, Trina. I didn't have the patience to drag all that out of her."

"You know how it is," she said. "Being another woman, I didn't have to put up with her coy routine."

"What do you mean?"

Trina whipped off her glasses and looked up at him in a simpering imitation. Her eyelashes fluttered like hummingbirds on the wing. "Golly gosh, should I tell you my big secret?"

"That's sick." But he smiled. "I guess what I'm trying to say, Trina, is that we make a pretty good team."

He was grateful for her concern and the gentle contact of her grasp. She seemed to know exactly what he needed. As if by magic, she sensed the moments when he needed a lover, and the moments—such as right now—when he needed a friend.

He would have liked nothing better than to forget that he was under suspicion. Though he wanted to spend every second of his possibly limited freedom with Trina, there were two crimes to be solved by tomorrow. And tomorrow was less than twenty-four hours away.

When he left Reuben in the tub house, his plan had been to search the house and the lodge from top to bottom. Then he'd seen Phyllis running to the barn and had thought to follow.

Sticking her glasses onto her nose, Trina asked, "How much of her story do you think is true?"

"It's hard to say. Ivan would never have turned this land into an animal sanctuary. He loved to hunt. And he hated environmentalists with all their restrictions and rules."

"Obviously, that was his excuse to entice her to the hot tub."

"I guess you were right, Trina. You kept saying that Ivan came to the hot tub to meet a woman."

"And now we know why he was naked."

"I'm not sure about that. Phyllis might have stolen his clothes, but I can't believe she pummeled Ivan into submission with her brilliant self-defense skills."

"She's not the karate kid," Trina agreed. "But all it would take is a lucky, well-placed kick to the groin."

"True."

"Somehow, she must have managed it. Because hiding the robe and slippers in the barn sounds exactly like something Phyllis would do." Trina paused for a moment, thinking. "But why would she take the horse? Why would she choose that minute to go for a ride?"

"She said she needed to get away, but maybe she saw something else," he suggested. "There might be one more piece to the puzzle that Phyllis hasn't mentioned."

"The identity of the murderer?"

"Bingo."

Still holding Trina's hand, he tugged her across the barn until they reached a room behind the stalls. A heater blew warming air in a kitchen area with a sink, counter, cabinet, table and chairs. There was a coffeepot, unplugged. "For the horses?" she asked. "They're more civilized than I thought."

"In the spring," he explained, "when we have a crew for construction or doing the fences, Maybelle doesn't like for us to go tracking in and out of the kitchen. So we keep food out here."

"Cozy."

"Right now, it's pretty damn cold. But in the summers, it's mild and pleasant. Temperatures are in the sixties or seventies. You'd like it," he said. "Everything's green."

"Except for the freezing-cold glaciers, of course."

"They're beautiful, Trina. You know. You saw the Mendenhall Glacier down near Juneau."

"It was incredible," she said.

"When you see it from a plane, as you did, the glacier looks like a shimmering piece of the sky that's fallen to earth." He gazed at her. "Like your eyes. I'd like to see it with you, to walk beside the frozen blue."

"Maybe sometime, in the summer, I'll visit you."

Reality came crashing around him again. If David didn't get serious about solving this crime, she'd be scheduling her visits for fifty years in the future, when he finished serving his jail sentence for murder. "Reuben gave me until tomorrow to come up with some answers," he said. "Then he's got to arrest me."

"But he doesn't have any proof."

"Well, it does look as if Ivan wrote my initials in blood. Anyway, tomorrow is when the other investigating officials are going to be able to get through. Forensic teams. State police. I guess Darien Greenlee was an important man in Juneau."

"All we have is today," she said.

"That's about the size of it. One lousy day." He couldn't keep the bitterness from his voice. Though David had done a lot of things in his life that he wasn't proud of, he was totally innocent this time. And it could hardly look worse. "And we don't have much to go on."

"At least we have another solid suspect."

"Phyllis?"

"Actually," Trina said, "I was thinking more of her husband, Bradley."

She told him about the suppressed jealousy she'd seen in Bradley Winkle, who tried as hard as he could to appear calm. Had his newlywed wife flirted with Ivan, then dragged Bradley to Alaska so that she could either meet with Ivan or her former boyfriend, Darien? "Both men are dead," Trina said. "It's kind of a huge coincidence."

"Bradley?" David had seldom seen a man so completely dominated by his wife. He didn't seem to have the makings of a murderer, especially not for a crime of passion. But David was willing to entertain any speculation. "So, what do you think happened?"

"Phyllis made her phone call and arranged to see Ivan," Trina supposed. "But Bradley overheard and followed her to the tub house. After Phyllis fled, he killed Ivan."

David nodded slowly. He liked this theory. "But how do we get proof?"

"The gun."

David returned to his earlier plan. "I'm going to search in the house and the lodge. That pistol has to be somewhere."

"I'll come with you," she said. "And we can also look in Ivan's room for that letter."

"That's my job," he said. "You don't need to go back up there."

"I'd prefer not to," she said. "But you've got to promise me one thing, David. If there's anything personal, you won't read it. Okay?"

"Personal?"

"Like the letters I wrote to Ivan. We never found a folder pertaining to me in his office, and I'm afraid he might have kept all of that paperwork in his room. Promise me, David, you won't read all the stupid things I wrote."

"I promise." But he knew they weren't stupid letters. He had not only read every word, but he'd committed large portions to memory. "But I doubt you need to feel—"

"I was deluded," she snapped. "And I'd rather not talk about it."

Back outside in the blowing snow, they followed the path to the lodge and entered through the back door into a mudroom with pegs for coats and hats. Several sets of cross-country skis and snowshoes were racked along the wall. They stamped the snow off their boots and left their parkas behind.

The kitchen was nowhere near as spacious as the one in the house, but the design was more efficient, and the appliances were relatively new.

David led her through a swinging door, then past a huge dining area that housed two long tables with benches on either side. It looked as if the room could accommodate twenty people, at least. The front area was low ceilinged and long, with a fireplace at one end and a cheerful blaze behind the screen.

"It must cost a fortune to heat this whole place," she said.

"Not cheap," David agreed. "But the rooms are on separate thermostats, as they are at the house. If nobody's staying in them, we don't keep them warm."

He pointed down a hallway with doors that opened on either side. "These are the two best rooms in the lodge. The Winkles are on the right and Jake has his usual room on the left."

"What's upstairs?"

"It's kind of like a dormitory with five rooms on each side of the hallway. There're two bathrooms."

"Okay, David. Where do we start?"

"I'll search the Winkles' room and you search Jake's."

She knocked on the door loudly, then called out Jake's name. Because there was no answer, she tried the knob. "David, it's locked."

"That's weird. Nobody bothers to lock their doors up here. Especially since the keys are hanging in the kitchen, on the wall next to the mudroom."

She hurried to the kitchen, feeling like an intruder, grabbed the key to room number one and returned. As she fitted the key into the lock, she noticed the door to the Winkles' room was standing open and assumed that David was inside.

She unlocked Jake's door, then entered the room and flicked on the overhead light.

A dozen shiny eyes stared back at her.

Chapter Eleven

Heads. Jake's room was a taxidermist's dream come true. There were heads of deer and caribou. A row of magnificently colored salmon and rainbow trout. A giant moose head dominated one wall. Hung from its antler was a red, white and blue ribbon and a beautiful medallion, the Olympic bronze medal.

Trina looked around the room, revolted by what she saw. They give prizes for this? Most pathetic were the smaller animals—a buck-toothed beaver and wolverine. On the bed was a Kodiak bearskin; the bear's eyes stared at her. The mouth was open, displaying teeth that looked as if they could rip a man or woman to shreds. It was the most macabre decor Trina had ever seen.

She couldn't search in here. Trina could barely stand to be in the room while these dead eyes were watching her. When she turned toward the door again, Jake blocked her way.

"Do you like my trophies?"

"They disgust me."

"Most women feel the same way, Phyllis Winkle in particular. No stomach for hunting." Jake strode into the room and stretched out on the bed atop the bearskin. His dark hair was almost the same color as the bear's. Today, he wore a white turtleneck and jeans. His fingers stroked the fur. "This is my prize. A Kodiak bear. The damn thing stood over ten feet tall."

"And you killed it with your gun," Trina said dryly. "How awfully brave."

"Not a gun. Take a closer look. This skin is unmarked. No bullet hole. I wanted a perfect trophy, so I used a crossbow. It took three arrows in the chest to stop this delicious monster. Even that didn't kill him."

If he was trying to turn her stomach, he was doing a mighty good job of it. As Jake continued, offering further details about the hunt, Trina blanked her mind. *I can stand anything for a brief period of time.* "Fascinating," she said, and she even managed to sound relatively sincere. "But I'll be going now."

"Don't rush off," Jake said coolly. He twisted his head to look past her. "Come on in, David. You tell her. Just last month, David and I stalked a bull elk. Fantastic animal."

She remembered that story. Ivan had written to her about it. "And Ivan was with you."

"Not that time," he said, glancing around his room with great satisfaction.

David stepped into the room but said nothing.

"Hunting is the only truly practical sport," Jake continued. "If you win, you eat."

"And if you lose?" Trina asked.

He shrugged. "You die."

"Sorry to disturb you," David said dryly.

"Feel free to search in here," Jake offered. "That's what you're doing, isn't it? Looking for evidence?"

"That's right," David said. "There are a couple of documents missing from the office."

"Really?" Jacob affected an attitude of total disinterest. "And the gun. A .22 caliber, wasn't it?"

"You know damn well what kind of gun it was."

"I don't know much at all. Only what I hear from Reuben. And that doesn't sound good for you, my friend." He frowned at David and shook his head. "If I were you, I'd take a rifle and run for the hills before they lock you up and throw away the key."

"I tried running once before," David said.

When he'd fled from his painful divorce in California, he couldn't escape the sorrow. Running didn't solve problems. This time would be even worse, because he would be pursued. "I won't run."

"I would," Jake said. "If I had the right equipment, nobody would ever find me. I could live off the land for years and years."

"But out there in the wild with only the birds and the berries," Trina said, "there wouldn't be anyone to admire you."

"I don't need admiration. I never had a fan club, never wanted one. Somebody like me who excels, who wins an Olympic bronze in biathalon, doesn't get big money endorsements or television commercials or ticker tape parades. The people who know my name are few and select."

"Did you kill Ivan?" Trina suddenly asked pointblank, hoping to take Jake by surprise. "Where were you when Ivan was killed?"

"The time frame Reuben seems to be suggesting was between eleven-thirty and twelve-thirty. And I, like everyone else, have no solid alibi. I was hunting in the morning, but I'd just gotten back. I really didn't look at a clock. But I joined the party at just about the same time you did, Trina. Remember?"

"Yes," she said. "We were both dressed in white."

"Interesting thought. I hadn't noticed."

David didn't believe that for a minute. He was sure that Jake noticed everything. Not only was he smart, he was also canny, more clever and patient than the animals he stalked. They wouldn't find incriminating evidence in this room. Not unless someone else had hidden it there.

As David and Trina headed toward the kitchen, they ran into the someone who continued to plague David's suspicions. Victor Stoddard. He dropped his two suitcases on the floor and pointed at David. "You keep away from me."

"What are you doing?" Trina asked.

"I'm moving from the house here to the lodge. I'm not going to spend another night under the same roof with you, David. I told Reuben that. I can't believe he hasn't arrested you."

"Come off it, Victor. You know I didn't kill your uncle."

"Then why did he write your initials in blood? Why did you attack me?"

"That wasn't an attack," David said. His voice was low and dangerous. "That was just foolin' around."

"You cut me," Victor whined. "I was bleeding."

"I'm warning you, Victor. Don't push me."

Victor opened his mouth as if to speak, then closed it again and swallowed hard. His insignificant chin withdrew into his neck as he stepped aside so David and Trina could pass.

Pulling on her parka again, Trina said, "You really shouldn't threaten him."

"But it feels so good." David grinned. "Maybe I need to get in touch with my female side."

"Like Bradley? No, that's not you. But you're not a macho man like Jake, either. Or a creep like Victor." Trina rolled her eyes. "Honestly, I've never met such an obnoxious assortment of men. If it wasn't for you and Reuben, I'd think Alaska was a breeding ground for jerks. No wonder there are seven men for every woman."

"Do you need seven?"

"With this sorry selection? Yes."

"I was hoping that one would be enough."

"One man and one woman." She smiled at him. "I guess that depends on the man."

He linked his arm with hers and escorted her through the dusk gray snow to the house. They passed into the kitchen, which was empty but redolent with a simmering pot of stew on the back burner. From the dining room, they heard voices. Suppertime.

David caught hold of her hand and tugged, pulling her down the corridor to his rooms. He peeked into his office. For the moment, Reuben had abandoned his desk.

"We're alone," David said. He pulled her into his bedroom and closed the door. "Privacy. At last."

When he kissed her, David knew he should be doing other things. He should be probing and searching. He needed to find evidence to solve the crimes he was accused of. But his mind went blank as he savored the moment. Holding her was truly luxury.

He pressed against her, subtly leading her toward the bed.

"David, stop. Reuben could be back at any minute."

"We'll lock the door."

"But we need to search."

His arms dropped to his sides, but he did not move away from her. "I'm not going to find anything, Trina.

That letter from the office about COPA and the loans? Since someone went to all the trouble of stealing it, they've surely destroyed it. That means the only proof is the .22 handgun."

"So? We'll find the gun. We'll look everywhere—"

"Won't do any good. Even if we do find it, do you think there'll be fingerprints? Nobody's that dumb."

"What are you saying, David?" Her gaze darted around his room. "You can't just give up."

"I might have only one day left." He raised his hand and traced the curve of her chin. "I want to make one perfect memory. One night with you."

He reached behind her and unfastened the clip that held her braid in place. His fingers stroked through the long, thick texture of her hair, loosening the crimping left by the braid and spreading the shimmering mantle of soft brown waves around her shoulders. He went to his door and locked it.

"A lot of good that will do," she said. "With keys hanging on hooks in the kitchen."

"That's only in the lodge. In the house, there're only two master sets. Maybelle has one, I have the other.

"No extras?"

"None that I know of."

"That can't be right, David." Her eyes flashed, then she looked away from him. "Because that would mean it was you who came into my room last night."

"And stole your wedding dress? You believe that?"

"I don't know what to believe, anymore."

He felt a tightening in his chest, as if a cold knife had sliced through him. And he knew that she still suspected him.

"It wasn't Maybelle's key that opened my door," she said. "Because she gave the key to me."

"Ivan's door was locked before somebody went in and ransacked his office. Maybe I used my key there, too. Is that what you think?"

"Somebody had access," she said. "Maybe that's what we should be looking for. A set of keys."

David went to his dresser drawer and fished around until he found a key ring. Attached was a metal tag that said House. He flipped through until he found the key for Trina's room, then detached it and tossed it to her. "There you go, Trina. Now you have both of the keys." He unlocked his door and opened it. "Sleep well tonight."

"David, you don't understand. I'm not accusing you."

"You don't have any reason to believe me." More than anyone, he was aware of her reasons to distrust him. He had lied about the letters. "I mean that, Trina."

"What are you saying?"

He had deceived her. His absurd falsehood stood between them. If he told her... No, not tonight. He couldn't tell her tonight. He didn't want to hurt her. If he was arrested tomorrow, he didn't want his last memory of her to be the sight of hatred in her clear blue eyes.

She pushed his door closed with a slam. "I'm not going anywhere, David."

"You can't trust me," he said.

"Maybe not." When she whirled around to face him, her hair spread like a fan. "And maybe I don't care. Listen, David, I'm not the same timid creature you picked up from the airplane. A few days ago, I was distraught about the thought of wolves, bedazzled by Alaska, tripping along some kind of snow-covered, primrose path toward a splendid, romantic future with a mysterious man I thought I could love." She stamped her foot. "Things have changed. I have changed."

"I never meant for you to go through all this."

"Life happens, David. Maybe that's the big secret I've been avoiding all my life—settling for a dull, boring job instead of striking out to do something more adventurous. I've been hiding behind my glasses, finding all kinds of reasons I couldn't have a relationship or try another career or take a chance." She felt the power of change pulsing through her body, giving her life, giving her the courage she'd never known she lacked. "Oh, yes. I'm different now."

When she looked at him, she saw approval reflected in his gaze. More than that. She saw his admiration. For her! Little Trina Martin, who always effaced herself and backed away from challenges, fearing she wouldn't succeed.

"In the past two days," she said, "I've been married and widowed and scared half to death a dozen times. I've seen a man shoot a wedding cake with a pistol. I've looked into a dead man's face and seen my gown with a dagger through the heart. I've been insulted and repulsed."

In silence, he stared at her. Trina's cheeks flushed bright red, and he thought she was remarkable. She was the most beautiful woman he'd ever seen.

From her very first letter, he'd seen hints that this strong, proud woman existed. She fascinated him, and he wanted her. He needed to claim her for his own. If only for one night, one miraculous night.

He caught hold of her hand and yanked her into his embrace. Her body against his was pure excitement. "Trina, do you think I'm a murderer?"

"Logic says, yes, it's possible. My instincts say no, but I can't trust them, can I?" If only she hadn't been so very wrong about those letters, Trina might have been free to follow her heart. "Since I've been up here, I've found only one thing I care about. That's you, David St. John."

He smiled broadly. His dark eyes glowed.

She continued, "Nothing is going to rob me of my night with you. Not logic. Not instinct. Not anything." She leaned away from him, reached for the door and turned the key in the lock. "So, what do you say to that?"

"There are no words." He kissed her with the tremendous passion that had been building within him for a month. She was the woman he'd dreamed about, had fantasized about. He wanted to make love to her all night and into the next morning.

When she separated from him, her eyes were dazed and her glasses askew. "One more thing," she said.

"Anything."

She took his hand, led him to the bed and stretched out on it. "Since I've been up here," she said, "I feel like half my time is spent dressing for the cold and undressing after I come in."

"Yes?"

She stretched her arms gracefully above her head on the pillows. "Will you undress me?"

"Oh, yes."

He took his time removing her clothing, layer after layer, and when they both were naked, he joined her under the covers of his bed. Before they made love, he thought once more of his deception and considered telling her about the letters. But the balance was so delicate, so perfect. He would not destroy this sweet, beautiful moment with talk of lies.

LATER THAT NIGHT when the other people in the house had settled in, Trina and David went in search of food. He wore long johns and a robe, while she made do with heavy wool socks and one of his long flannel shirts. She struck a pose and smiled. "Sexy, huh? I look more like an elf than a femme fatale."

David merely winked in response. He was a fantastic lover. Trina had never been so completely fulfilled. Her marriage to Ivan had been a sham. David was the man she was meant to find in Alaska. Though they were not married, she would always think of him as her groom. Her suspect groom.

She shook away thoughts of murder. Right now, there was only room for one appetite—food. She was starving.

When they sneaked into the kitchen like a couple of thieves, she couldn't help chuckling. "I feel like I've been naughty."

"Why? We're a couple of healthy, consenting adults."

"I know. But this doesn't seem proper. Maybe because I feel like a guest, like I don't belong here."

"You're wrong about that, Trina. This is where you belong. Here. With me."

"For tonight," she said. And tomorrow? She didn't want to think about tomorrow and the strong probability that David would be arrested. The impermanence of their relationship was far too scary to contemplate.

In the refrigerator, they found bread and leftover soup Maybelle had prepared for dinner. After the soup had a zap in the microwave, they took their bowls and returned to David's rooms. He stoked the blaze in the moss rock fireplace and they sat in front of it, balancing their food on their laps and sitting in rocking chairs.

She didn't bother with conversation while they ate. It was only after she'd swabbed up the last bit of soup with Maybelle's homemade bread that she leaned back in her rocking chair and propped her heels on the ledge in front of the fire.

"Satisfied?" he asked.

"More than you'll ever know." She sighed contentedly, but she wished this night could be the beginning of a real future with David, instead of an ending. "I don't think Reuben will be able to arrest you—" she said hopefully. "Not after the forensic teams arrive."

"Are you thinking of fingerprints?"

"Not really. It hasn't escaped my attention that we are in a part of the world where people wear gloves most of the time. But there are other bits of evidence."

"Such as?"

"The guns," she said. "They'll run ballistics tests on your Colt .45 and find out that it wasn't used to kill Darien Greenlee. And, of course, there's the mysterious .22 caliber handgun that was used to kill Ivan. It has to be registered to someone."

"Lots of guns aren't registered."

"But this didn't look like a planned killing."

"What about my initials in blood?"

"That's a problem," she conceded with a frown. "It seems so melodramatic, doesn't it?"

"Murder tends to be like that. Melodramatic. Not that I've had a lot of experience."

"That's reasssuring," she said wryly. "I'd hate to think that I'd just been to bed with a killer."

"I'll tell you what's melodramatic," he said. "Your wedding dress with a knife through it."

She shuddered at the memory. "That was horrible. I'll never forget that sight. My dress lying beside Ivan who was all neatly dressed in a suit. Why did they dress him up as if for the funeral? Certainly, there'll be an autopsy."

"Sounds like Maybelle's handiwork. It's her job as housekeeper to keep up appearances, and she takes her job seriously. In her mind, I'm sure, it wouldn't be proper for Ivan to be dressed in anything other than a suit."

"Are we sure Maybelle wasn't in love with Ivan?"

"We're not sure of anything, Trina. So we'll stick to the facts."

"Okay. I know that Victor was responsible for the knife through the wedding dress. He as much as admitted it to me when I ran into him in the hallway. He went to the trouble of setting up that whole disgusting prank to warn me off, to let me know that I didn't belong here."

"That's his style," David said. "Sneaking around and playing sick games. I think he's terrified of direct confrontations. That's why he moved over to the lodge, so he wouldn't be under the same roof as me, a murderer. I'm sure he babbled to Reuben about his fears, using the occasion to emphasize the suspicions against me."

"Do you think he killed Ivan?"

"It's possible. Darien Greenlee was shot in the back. That sounds like Victor. And Ivan would have been helpless, locked in the tub house. He might have done it. But I doubt it."

"Why?"

"Victor's not intelligent enough to pull off a couple of murders. From all I know about him—things that Ivan would say—Victor is one of those guys who sets up elaborate money-making schemes that never work because he's simply not able to figure out the basic details."

"Ivan talked about him?" she questioned.

"Oh, yeah. Victor was a blood relative. If he'd been half a man, Ivan would have been delighted to make Victor his heir. But he couldn't stand the guy."

"So, here are the facts," Trina recapped. "Victor probably wouldn't inherit much because Ivan disliked him. True?"

"I'd say so."

"Victor pulled the knife in the wedding dress stunt."

"True," David said.

"Victor shot the wedding cake with a .45 caliber gun. So, we know he has one."

"True."

"He's not very smart, and he's the king of melodrama."

"Those are opinions," David said.

"But here's another fact." She lit upon it with both feet, knowing that she was onto something. "After your fight with Victor, he had cuts on his arm that Maybelle was dressing in the kitchen. But you didn't cut him with anything."

"I scratched him."

"Barely. What if he'd made those other cuts himself? Earlier today or late last night?" She elaborated. "What if Victor used his own blood to write your initials in the tub house?"

"Why?"

"As a cover-up. A diversion."

David shrugged. "Victor would have to know that as soon as the forensics team did DNA tests on the blood, they'd be able to identify him."

"But maybe, by then, you would have already been arrested, and Victor could have fled. Or gotten what he wanted."

"And there's the problem," David said. "There's the empty hole we have no facts to fill. What does Victor want? If it's the inheritance, you've told him half a dozen times that you won't stand in his way. Besides, it's going to take court battles and probates and all kind of things before he gets his hot little hands on the money. What good would it do Victor to frame me?"

"The will." She bolted from the rocking chair and stood upright, certain in her conclusion. "Ivan's last will and testament. Remember when Reuben read it over in the office? That's when he seriously started suspecting you."

David shook his head. "I assume Ivan may have left me something, but it wouldn't be much."

"But remember the COPA letter we found in the office?" Trina persisted. "It also talked about attachments and loans against the estate. Maybe there was some kind of legal loophole and your father really didn't sign the land over to Ivan. Maybe you own some of this land." She frowned. "But no one could believe they'd cover this up by stealing a letter. All of this information would be on file in Darien Greenlee's office."

"Sure," David said. "That's right."

But his mind was no longer on the investigation. What if he owned this land? He had not expected to be able to purchase any significant piece of property, not for years and years. Not only had the price of land risen near Juneau, but much of the existing acreage was federally protected game preserves. That was why Ivan's hunting lodge was such prime real estate. But if it belonged to David, if some portion of this property was his, he could truly start over. Maybe he could make a settlement with his ex-wife, set up trust funds for his kids and still have money to spare.

Finally, David could envision a future. He could imagine himself being able to afford the life he wanted. Though he didn't dare dream of such a fantastic possibility, he could hope. Someday...

"One thing is certain," she said. "We're going to talk to Victor first thing tomorrow morning. If he pulled that stunt with the blood, we need him to admit it to Reuben." She glanced at him. "David, are you listening to me?"

He had heard enough, more than enough. For the first time in many years, David forgot his regrets. A future!

"Enough talk," he said. His gaze swept over her body. "I think it's time for some action."

"And what did you have in mind?"

"Take off your glasses and get over here."

"Just like that, huh? What makes you think you can order me around?"

"This." When he kissed her, he felt her acquiescence. She almost swooned in his arms. Her supple body molded to his. They belonged together. Gratified, he knew that she wanted him as much as he wanted her. He lifted her off her feet and carried her to his bed.

Chapter Twelve

The next morning, Trina didn't allow herself the pleasure of sleeping late in David's arms. Before first light, she was wide-awake, thinking like mad. Though she and David had raised dozens of questions about the murders, they didn't have answers. And they needed evidence to keep David from being arrested.

Even if forensics solved the murders, even if he was only in jail for one night, she didn't want that to happen. Suspicions, once founded, were difficult to overturn. Even if David was innocent, he could be imprisoned and wrongly brought to trial.

She snuggled against his warm chest, listening to his steady breathing. Of course, he was innocent! He was the most wonderful man she'd ever known, strong and brave and sensitive. Largely because of David, she had survived the past few days and emerged a better person with a brand-new confidence.

Leaning over, she gave him a nip on the neck, a tiny love bite, to waken him.

He brushed with his hand, as if swatting a pesky insect. Then his hand ventured lower, coming to rest upon her naked breast.

Softly, she whispered, "David? Are you awake?"

He made a growling noise in the back of his throat, like a polar bear being roused from hibernation.

She turned on the lamp on the bedside table and slipped on her glasses. "Come on, David. Wake up. We have to go see Victor now."

"Sleepy."

She lay there for a moment, watching him. In repose, the laugh lines around his eyes were smoothed. His cheekbones and strong nose stood out. His dusky blond hair was tousled, and his lips were so inviting.

Longing to stay with him in the cozy nest of his bed, she traced his jawline and ran her thumb along the line of his lips. His eyelids opened, and he smiled.

"Beautiful sunrise," he said.

"But it's still dark."

"You are my sun, Trina." His hand reached up to tangle in her hair and pull her close to him. "My sun. My moon. My stars."

He kissed her lightly. "Have you ever seen the northern lights? They dance in the heavens and turn the skies into a magical show. I'll show them to you. We'll watch them together."

"If that's your plan, we'd better get busy."

"Why?"

"Evidence." She gave him a stern look and pulled away so there was a space between his body and hers. "There are a few pieces we can hunt for before the criminal investigation people get here."

He groaned. "Now? Do we have to do this now?"

"If we don't talk now, we might be communicating through the bars of a jail cell."

"All right." He rubbed his eyes and blinked. "I'm awake."

"Number one," she said. "We're going to have a little chat with Victor. Just a chat, David, no punching. We want to know why he's set out to frame you for Ivan's murder."

"And why he's so dead set against you."

"We know that," she said. "He thinks I'm going to touch his precious inheritance."

"I would." He folded his hands behind his head and stared at the ceiling. "If I had a chance to claim this land as mine, I'd grab it. We need to find out what's in Ivan's will."

"That's number two," she said. "Number three is to find that letter about COPA and the loans against the land. You'll have to search Ivan's bedroom."

"Right. And the gun," he reminded her. "We need to find out everything we can about that .22 caliber gun. And I'm afraid we ought to talk to Miss Phyllis again. There's something about her story that bothers me. Why did she burn Ivan's robe and slippers?"

Trina shrugged. She hadn't thought destroying the clothes was all that strange. It made a certain degree of sense to get rid of evidence that she'd been in the tub house with Ivan. Sooner or later, the clothes would have been found in the barn, and they might have led to Phyllis.

"What if there was blood on the robe?" David's gaze stayed focused above his head on the ceiling. "Blood on the clothes would mean that Ivan had been shot before Phyllis took his robe. Maybe that he'd been shot by Phyllis."

"Or by Bradley."

When David looked at her and their eyes met, a spark ignited. And that flame had nothing to do with investigating and uncovering the truth. Trina did her best to fight the electric current that crackled between them. "We have to get started, David. Right away. It's almost seven o'clock."

"Victor won't be awake for another hour," he said. "We have time."

"Maybelle will be in the kitchen. Now."

"Good for Maybelle." He shifted suddenly. Before she knew what was happening, he rolled her to her back and pinned her with the weight of his body. "We can skip breakfast."

If he kissed her, she wouldn't stop him. Though there was a need for urgent action, there were other needs, as well, physical and emotional needs that only David could fulfill for her. She closed her eyelids and waited for the exquisite pressure of his lips against hers.

AN HOUR LATER, they were showered and dressed for the day. Trina followed David into the kitchen and had filled a mug of coffee from a huge silver urn before Maybelle came bustling in from the dining room.

"More early risers," Maybelle said. Her eyebrows were raised. "I didn't expect to see either of you until much later. Did you both sleep well?"

"Yes, thank you," said Trina, feeling like she was fibbing to her mother about being out past curfew on a date. "Very well. We slept, that is, I slept very soundly."

"Like a rock," David said. "She sleeps like someone in a deep coma."

"I'm sure that's none of my business," Maybelle said.

David sipped his coffee. "Anybody else up?"

"Jake and Bradley. I just served them breakfast— sausage, toast and eggs. Can I get anything for you two?"

"Only coffee for right now," David said.

"Please don't worry about cooking for us," Trina said. "When we're hungry, I can manage."

"Not yet, dear. This is still my kitchen." Maybelle planted her fists on her ample hips. "As long as I'm here, the kitchen will be run the way I see fit."

"Of course," Trina said. "I didn't mean to—"

"There seem to be a lot of things you don't *mean* to do, honey. But they somehow happen, don't they?"

Trina gasped. "What?" *What was she implying?*

"Like you didn't *mean* to marry a man you didn't love, but you somehow did. And you didn't *mean* to go upstairs and disturb Ivan's bedroom, but Victor told me that he saw you coming down the stairs. And now there's something going on between you and David. I don't suppose that was *meant* to happen, either."

"I meant for it to happen," David said. "And I'm damn glad that it did."

Maybelle regarded him through squinting eyes. "Then you're no better than I thought. Don't you understand, David? There's a right time and a wrong time. This is all wrong. Trina is Ivan's woman."

"Ivan's dead."

Jake pushed open the swinging door to the kitchen in time to hear David's words. A cold smile touched the corners of his lips as he offered his good-mornings.

"How's the weather?" David asked, turning his attention from Maybelle.

"The snow's stopped. At first light, they'll be able to start clearing the roads. If the police are anxious to get here, we'll see choppers by noon."

"Thank heavens!" Maybelle said. "And what about those sunrise photographs you and Bradley were going to take?"

"Too overcast," Jake said.

But no more chance of snow, Trina thought. The blizzard that had kept them safe from the outer world had ended. Soon, they'd hear the snowplows. Float planes would land. Helicopters would alight. And the outside world would beat down the door to Stoddard Lodge.

Unless they found reasons to the contrary, David would be arrested, taken from her. She couldn't let that happen.

Jake looked at his wristwatch. "I hope to be out of here by this afternoon."

"What's the rush?" Maybelle asked.

"Business. Darien Greenlee's office will be open today, and I've got a lot to do."

"You can handle a lot from here," she said. "Ivan did."

"But Ivan's office is trashed. The computer and fax are disabled. So, as soon as the road is cleared, I'll be taking the Jeep. Is that all right, Maybelle? I'll leave it in Haines."

"I suppose so," the housekeeper said. "But you be sure to make arrangements to have the car driven back here."

"Of course."

Contrary to every other time she'd seen him, Trina noticed that, today, Jake was clad entirely in black. He looked menacing, she thought. Like the hunter he was.

Maybelle clucked her tongue against her teeth. "I don't know if the sheriff is going to let you go, Jake. He's got a lot to cover. And there's all that taking of statements and witnessing and investigating and—"

"I've said all that I have to say." Jake went to the urn and refilled his coffee cup. "As David here so succinctly phrased it, Ivan is dead. There's nothing we can do for him. And the rest of life goes on.''

"I suppose you're right," Maybelle said. "Which reminds me. I'd better get ready. We're going to have a mob of guests. All those cops Reuben has been talking to. Coroners. State officials. Reporters." Maybelle was galvanized into action. She flipped open a cabinet and took out a twenty-four-muffin baking tin. "I'd better be prepared to feed everybody."

"I'll be in the barn," David said. "Trina, come with me."

Trina took a last gulp of fresh coffee that scalded her tongue, then followed David into the mudroom to begin dressing for the cold again. Peering through the windows, she saw the blank, flat, predawn sky. Though it was nearly eight, the sun had not peeked over the horizon. If Trina could have made one wish, it would be for the sun to never rise, to be sequestered here forever with David.

But that probably wouldn't happen. "We have to talk to Victor now," she said. "I don't care if he's awake or not."

David zipped up his parka. "You know, Trina, it's possible that Victor is the murderer. He wanted to inherit, and he couldn't do that until Ivan was dead."

"Why would Victor wait until now? He's had years and years to kill his uncle."

"But now, Victor wouldn't be the only living relative. He'd have to battle you for the estate. And, if the fates had been willing, you could have gotten pregnant. Then Victor would have to contend with a son or daughter."

"I couldn't have gotten pregnant."

"Because you didn't care for Ivan?"

"After I met him, that was true. But I didn't know that when I arrived here." She pulled on her hat. "I'm taking birth control pills."

"You are?" David was astonished. In her letters, she'd expressed a strong desire to have children. That was one of the reasons Ivan had thought she'd make a good bride.

"I'm not a complete idiot," she said. "I wasn't going to make the mistake of becoming a mother too soon. You can divorce a spouse, but a child is yours forever."

"True." Unbidden memories flashed across the surface of David's mind. Though he hadn't seen his children in six months, he had a drawer full of photographs from their early days, pictures they'd drawn in school, a few letters. David wrote every week and telephoned every Sunday morning, but it was no substitute for watching them grow. They were so far away. To say that he missed them didn't begin to express the depth of his feelings. They were his, forever. And they were gone. He repeated, "Forever."

"Right. And I've waited this long. I didn't want to make a mistake." She cocked her head and studied him curiously. "Are you all right?"

"I'm fine."

She remembered. "You have kids."

"A son and a daughter. They live in California with their mother."

"And you miss them. I'm so sorry, David."

"So am I."

After his divorce, he hadn't ever thought he'd want children again. The pain of missing them was too great. He didn't think he could go through that hell again. But with Trina... "I want kids," he said, half in wonderment.

"So do I. My biological clock has been ticking for ten years." Her hand dropped to her belly and she smoothed her parka. "But I want my babies to have a father who cares for them, who loves them and wants them as much as I do."

His voice lowered. The bond he felt with her tightened. "I could be that kind of father."

"Yes." Her blue eyes sparkled with unreserved anticipation, then she blinked and looked away. "If you're not in jail...."

"Right." He dragged himself back to their present dilemma. First, before anything, they had to clear his name. He flung open the door. "Let's go find out what Victor knows."

In the heavy gray of predawn, they trudged along the path to the lodge. The white aftermath of the blizzard was piled high around them. Fresh snow crunched beneath their feet, and the plowed accumulation rose four feet on either side of them.

They entered the lodge through the back door, stamping away the snow and cold, not bothering to discard their parkas, hats and gloves. In the front room, a fire glowed invitingly on the hearth. David glanced at it. "Apparently, Jake has been awake long enough that he started a fire."

"Probably got up early," she muttered, "in case there were any wide-eyed, adorable woodland creatures begging to be gunned down in cold blood."

"You really have the wrong idea about hunting."

"But the right idea about Jake. When he was describing stalking that bear..."

"Bear?"

"You know, the one that's now a rug? All I could think was, here's a guy who loves to move in for the kill."

"He's competitive," David said. "Aggressive."

"I'd say he's more than aggressive. He makes the great white shark look as docile as a guppy."

They tiptoed quietly through the rooms. Jake wasn't here. Nor was Bradley. From the Winkles' room, they heard the gentle, pleasant sounds of a Windom Hill tape. Phyllis was singing along.

Quickly, Trina and David peeked into the other two rooms on the first floor and found them cold and empty.

Upstairs, David went to the door of the room nearest the bathroom and knocked. Though there was no sound from within, he turned the knob and shoved it open.

They'd found Victor Stoddard.

The bedsheets and comforters were tangled. His limbs sprawled. The blood from a wound on his forehead splashed against the carved oak headboard. His eyes were wide, staring sightlessly.

David turned to shield Trina from the sight, but he was too late. Trina stood in the doorway, frozen.

When he went to her, she held him at arm's length. "Is there a pulse? Shouldn't we check? Oh, David, is there something we can do for him?"

Place pennies on his eyes and wish him a good journey into a better world, David thought. "He's dead."

A shudder of horror trembled through her, and she wrapped her arms tightly around herself, as if she were suddenly chilled. "We mustn't touch anything," she said.

He pointed to a small object that lay at the foot of the bed. "The gun. Smith & Wesson automatic. It's .22 caliber."

There was one item they wouldn't need to search for. David's gaze flicked around the room, avoiding the dead man on the bed. What else was here? What had the murderer wanted to hide? "Trina, go downstairs and telephone the house. Tell Maybelle what happened and tell her to send Reuben over here. Now."

She pivoted, turning her back on the sight of death. "What are you going to do?"

"Stay here and search for—"

"No, David." Her voice quavered. "Please don't mess with anything. The forensic people are going to be here soon. Don't leave your fingerprints here."

"I won't." He felt in the pocket of his parka for his gloves. On the dresser in the small bedroom, he saw an open briefcase. "I won't leave fingerprints."

Resolutely, she turned around. "I'm not going anywhere unless you come with me. Don't you see, David? You're clear of this murder. You were with me all night."

"Are you sure?"

"Yes."

"Can you say, with absolute certainty, that I didn't sneak out of the bed in the night?"

"Yes."

"No, you can't, Trina. You sleep far too soundly. I could have been tap dancing on the ceiling last night, and you wouldn't have awakened."

He went to the dresser and studied the open briefcase without touching it. Surely, there was nothing incriminating in here. The murderer wouldn't have left behind obvious evidence.

"Nice briefcase," David said. "Leather. The initials printed by the handle are DG."

"Darien Greenlee."

Inside, displayed prominently among other documents, was the last will and testament of Ivan Stoddard. David leaned down and read without touching, then he flipped to the second page and the third. The contents of these flimsy scraps of paper marked his future. For better or for worse.

In the hallway, he heard the sound of someone else arriving and he whipped around. Trina had been quicker. She blocked the doorway. He heard her say, "You can't go in there."

"What are you doing here?" David recognized the whine of Phyllis Winkle's voice. "I thought I heard somebody walking around up here. What's going on?"

David stepped up behind Trina and looked over her shoulder at Phyllis who had, apparently, decided to sleep in. She was still wearing a red negligee that hugged her skinny body and hung low in front to reveal cleavage. Her face, however, was plain and tired, a little puffy around the eyes. Had she experienced trouble sleeping? Had she crept up here during the night and fired a .22 caliber bullet through Victor's forehead?

David edged Trina out into the hall and closed the door behind them. "Let's go. We're all going downstairs to use the telephone."

"Not until you tell me what happened," Phyllis said.

David took a deep breath, not anxious to face Phyllis Winkle's reaction. When Ivan died, she had sobbed hysterically. When they learned of Darien Greenlee's death, Phyllis had fainted. How would she deal with this?

"Well?" she demanded.

David looked her straight in the eye. "Victor Stoddard is dead."

"Oh, my God! How?"

"Looks to me like he was shot in the head with a .22 caliber handgun."

The response from Phyllis was totally unexpected. She gasped, then spoke angrily. "That's impossible! It can't be! You said there weren't any .22 pistols in the house."

"Obviously, there was one," David said. "Ivan was also killed with a .22."

"I know about Ivan, but you're mistaken about Victor." Her hand reached toward the doorknob. "I'm going to take a look."

"No!" Trina blocked her way. "We're not going to touch any of this evidence. For once, we'll handle this properly. We're all going downstairs to call Reuben."

In tense, suspicious silence, they moved down the stairs in a clump. While David placed the call to the house, Trina sat beside Phyllis and asked, "Why are you so sure the gun can't be a .22 caliber?"

"I'm just going by what I've heard. I really don't know anything about guns at all. A .22 or a .45 or a .77. They're all the same to me."

Her hands twisted into a nervous knot in her lap. Her legs were crossed. Though she should have been cold in the flimsy nightgown, her cheeks were flushed almost as red as the delicate silk that flowed from her shoulders.

"What do you know about this?" Trina asked.

"Nothing," Phyllis replied quickly. "I didn't even know that Victor spent the night over here."

"Then you didn't hear anything," Trina said.

Phyllis shook her head. "Not a thing."

"Not a gunshot?"

"No."

Trina thought that the report of a pistol would be obvious in the night. Even one shot. "If you didn't hear the gun, where were you?"

"Bradley was up early, taking a shower and getting dressed. He and Jake were planning to go out and shoot some photos. You know, sunlight on the snow. I showerered, but went back to bed. Just the usual."

"The usual?" Trina questioned.

"We made love," she said. "We are newlyweds, after all."

But could they have missed hearing the shot of a pistol? Trina wondered. Of course, Victor's room was at the opposite end of the lodge, and this was a solidly constructed building. If they'd been making love, playing music... "So, you didn't hear the gun?"

"No."

When Reuben lumbered through the door, he looked as if he'd just rolled out of his unmade bed and still hadn't had time to pull himself together. Though he managed a smile for Trina, his expression was grave, close to exhaustion. "Another one?" he asked.

"Victor," said David.

Rubbing his eyebrows and twitching his mustache, the sheriff sank down on the sofa nearest the fireplace. "Victor Stoddard. I don't imagine there will be too much mourning over his passing."

The same fact had been slowly dawning on Trina. No one much cared about Victor. He'd been unpleasant, a bully and coward at the same time. He would not be missed. Still, he deserved a moment of grief, a whisper of sorrow to commemorate his death.

"About the gun," David said. "Phyllis doesn't believe it was a .22 caliber."

"Why not?" Rueben turned toward her.

She shrugged ingenuously. "I'm just going by what other people said. Everybody said there weren't any guns that small on the premises."

"I guess I should take a look," Reuben said. "You people wait here. I'll be back."

As he tromped heavily up the stairs, Phyllis grew physically more agitated. Just as she bounced to her feet and announced that she was going to her room to dress, Bradley and Jake sauntered through the door. Phyllis flew at her husband, burying her face against his chest. "Darling, it's so terrible. Victor's dead."

While David gave the limited details to the two men, Phyllis continued to cling to her husband. Her grip on his arm was clawlike.

"Reuben's upstairs," David finished. "He'll probably bring the gun down."

Phyllis looked fearful, almost panicky. She gnawed at her lower lip. "Is he going to make me look at the gun? I don't know anything about firearms, except that they smell awful and they're heavier than they look."

"So, you've handled guns?" Trina said.

"Not really."

"But you know they're heavier than they look." Trina glanced at Bradley. The more Phyllis trembled, the more stolid he became. "What about you, Bradley. I know you can aim and shoot a camera. But what about a gun?"

"I haven't always been involved with environmentalist groups," he said. "For years, I worked with the homeless in inner cities. I couldn't help but know about guns."

"Did you ever own one?"

Before Bradley could respond, Reuben came down the stairs. He had the gun inside a sealed plastic bag. When he held it out for examination, Phyllis shook her head from side to side in violent denial.

"It can't be," she said.

"But it is," Bradley said. "A .22 caliber Smith & Wesson automatic. And it belongs to me."

Chapter Thirteen

"I haven't seen the gun since before Ivan's murder," Bradley said. "I brought it with me up here because... I don't know, really...I guess I was expecting some kind of trouble."

"You got it," Reuben said. "All the trouble any man could want."

Finally, the sun had begun to rise, Trina noted. A somber light crossed the windowsills and spread across the floor. It was a morning that Victor Stoddard would never experience. Nor would Ivan. Nor his attorney, Darien Greenlee.

"At least we'll be able to get out of here today," Bradley finally said.

"Not today," the sheriff said.

"What do you mean?" Bradley asked. "We were planning to leave tomorrow, anyway. We need to get back to Boulder."

"Sorry. I'll have to ask you to stay until we've completed the ballistics tests. If we learn that this weapon killed both Ivan and Victor Stoddard, we'll need you for further questioning."

"That's not fair!" Phyllis thrust herself forward. The red silk of her gown swirled dramatically. Furious, she said, "That might look like Bradley's gun, but it can't be his. It just can't."

"Mind telling me why not?" Reuben drawled.

"I threw away Bradley's gun!"

Trina gasped. This story was becoming more and more entangled. The web of interconnections and lies had twined into an unfathomable Gordian knot.

"You know, Phyllis—" Reuben looked like he couldn't take many more surprises "—I think it would be best if you got dressed. Then you'll come with me and we can have a quiet little conversation."

"I want them all to hear," she said. "They all think they're so smart. As if they never made a mistake."

"I never did," Jake said. He went to the fireplace and rested his elbow on the mantel.

"Really?" Phyllis snapped. "I suppose you're perfect."

"Nobody's perfect," he returned. "But I don't make mistakes. A hunter can't afford to misjudge his prey."

When Trina glanced at him, he returned her gaze with a fierce intensity. His eyes riveted on her face, she felt as if he were trying to see inside her head, to read her thoughts. For an instant, she felt like prey, like a helpless creature that Jake had trapped.

"All right, I'm sorry." Phyllis spread her hands wide. "I made a mistake. Does it matter?"

"Normally," Reuben said, "I'm a forgiving sort of man. But there have been three murders. Now, if you'll come with me, we can talk about this mistake of yours."

"Come on, Phyllis." Bradley touched her arm. "Calm down, honey. You haven't done anything wrong."

She shrugged off his grasp. "When I went to the tub house to meet with Ivan, I expected trouble. So I took

Bradley's gun with me. When Ivan made a pass at me, I pulled out the gun."

Trina nodded. This explanation made far more sense than the story Phyllis told them about her prowess in self-defense. "You held him at gunpoint," Trina said. "That's how you convinced him to give you his clothes."

"Correct. You should have seen his face." Phyllis laughed nervously. "The great Ivan Stoddard, hunter. I didn't want to hurt him, only to humiliate him."

"And then?" Trina encouraged.

"I locked the door, and I stuck that little branch through the latch on the outside so he couldn't get out without help."

"Dangerous joke," Reuben commented.

"The tub house was heated, and the water in the tub was already starting to steam," Phyllis said defensively. "I didn't think he'd be cold. I figured he'd stay inside, stewing."

"Then you took Ivan's clothes to the barn and hid them in the upper loft," David said. "Why?"

Miserably, she said, "I didn't want Bradley to know what I'd done. I knew Ivan wouldn't talk. And if I said nothing, he wouldn't have to know I'd been in the tub house with Ivan." When she gazed at her husband, Trina thought she saw real emotion in Phyllis's usually vapid expression. She really cared about Bradley.

"And the gun?" Reuben said. "What did you do with the gun?"

Phyllis looked into her husband's eyes. Was the woman searching for an answer or for forgiveness? Trina wondered.

"Oh, Bradley," Phyllis said. "I didn't want to return your gun. You're so jealous. I was afraid of what might happen if you heard about Ivan...."

Though Jake gave a disbelieving snort, Trina fully accepted Phyllis's sincerity. She'd been concerned about her husband, worried that meeting with her ex-lover and hearing about yet another man who was after his bride would be too much.

And, Trina thought, Phyllis might have been right. Trina had seen Bradley when he'd nearly lost his mellowness. There was tension in him that he covered so well.

Reuben repeated, "What did you do with the gun?"

"I was in the barn," Phyllis said. "It had just started to snow. I mounted and rode to Hunter's Creek, out to the field. That's where I dropped the gun."

"Into the creek?" Reuben asked.

"No, I didn't want to pollute the water. I dropped it near that hemlock tree that stands alone. There's nothing else around, but I figured the snow would cover it over, and it would be gone."

Silence fell in the room. Had Phyllis really been protecting Bradley from his own jealousy? Trina wondered. Would Trina have done the same for David?

"What else are you leaving out?" Reuben asked.

"Nothing. That's the whole story." Phyllis paused. "Oh, except that I got the robe and slippers from the barn that night and burned them in David's fireplace. But I've already explained that part to you, Sheriff."

"Tell me again."

"I thought that if I got rid of the clothes, that part of the murder would be forgotten or overlooked. Since I hadn't killed Ivan, I had hoped that I could erase my actions, to somehow remove myself. I didn't want to have to tell this story."

She sank down in a rocking chair, and her scarlet silk fluttered around her like a slowly deflating balloon. Her energy and vivacity had faded. And, in the dawn light, Trina almost felt sorry for her. Phyllis had wanted to embarrass Ivan, but her machinations ended up causing her to look like a fool.

"When you heard that Ivan was shot with a .22 caliber bullet," Reuben said, "why didn't you mention the gun?"

"I didn't know," she said. "I really and truly don't know a thing about guns. And I threw Bradley's gun away, so I didn't think that could possibly be the murder weapon. Really, Sheriff, I wasn't trying to withhold evidence. I just didn't know."

"And you—" the sheriff turned to Bradley "—why the hell didn't you tell me you owned a gun?"

"I didn't see any point. I knew that I hadn't used it and I thought..."

Trina knew exactly what he had thought. He'd assumed that his wife had used the gun to kill Ivan Stoddard. It was a pretty fair assumption. Phyllis had gone to the tub house armed. And dangerous?

Reuben stood, solid as a spruce tree. "I should lock you all up and throw away the key. I want you all to get over to the house, but I'm not questioning anybody again. I'll leave that to the other people who ought to be arriving soon."

"How soon?" Trina asked.

"Helicopters can get through now. Very soon. I'll be in David's office."

"Reuben," Jake said, "how soon will we be done? As soon as the road is clear, I want to head out."

"Nobody's going anywhere," he said. "Not until the forensic people go over these murder sites, and not until I hear back from Darien Greenlee's secretary."

"Why?" Jake demanded. "There's no reason for me to stay."

"We'll see."

When Reuben lumbered out of the lodge, Trina glanced around the room. There were only five of them left. Four suspects. And a murderer.

TRINA TRAILED DAVID to the barn and watched while he hurried through his morning chores, checking the heat, feeding the livestock and mucking out the stalls. His ease and efficient motions impressed her. Every bucket was within easy reach. Not a single motion was wasted.

"So," she said while he worked, "according to Phyllis, here's what happened. She met Ivan, they argued and she pulled a gun. She swiped his clothes, then she hid them in the barn, saddled up, rode to the creek and dumped the weapon." Trina frowned. "How long would all that take?"

"I don't know about the argument," he said, "but hiding the clothes and riding to the creek wouldn't have taken more than ten minutes. Phyllis is an expert horsewoman. She wouldn't bother with full riding gear, just enough to get her to the creek and back."

"Then what?" Trina said. "Somebody followed her to the creek, got the gun, returned to the tub house and shot Ivan?"

"That's it." He returned a heavy grain sack to its place. "All totaled, the time from when she left Ivan to the time when he was shot would have been only about twenty minutes."

Trina frowned. "And Ivan just sat there in the tub house? For nearly half an hour? While his guests were arriving?"

"He was naked, Trina. If he yelled for help, he was going to look like a jerk. Keep in mind that he was locked in. With the shutters closed and the door barred, there's no way he could get out without breaking a window. Even if he did manage to get free, he would have had to sneak back to the house, totally nude, and hope nobody saw him." David dusted off his gloved hands. "All done in here."

"David, do you think Phyllis was telling the truth?"

"Do you?"

"I believe she was trying to protect her husband."

"Well, it could have happened the other way," he said. "Maybe Phyllis wasn't clever enough to take a gun with her. Maybe she went to the tub house and Bradley followed with his gun."

"You mean Bradley killed Ivan?"

"It's possible," David said. "If he caught the old boy in the act of seducing his wife."

"Or maybe Phyllis did it. Maybe Ivan kept coming on to her and she shot him."

David thought for a minute, then shook his head. "I don't think so. If the shots had been at such close range, the hair on Ivan's chest would have been singed. No, I'm pretty sure that somebody broke in that window and fired." He aimed his forefinger like a gun, cocked his thumb and pulled the imaginary trigger. "My guess is Bradley killed him. If you were my bride and I caught some guy trying to seduce you, that's what I'd do."

"No, you wouldn't."

"You're right. I would have told him to break it up and put on his clothes." David grinned. "Then I would have beat the stuffing out of him."

"Would you?" She rose to her feet and went toward him. "Would you do that to protect my honor?"

"Yeah." He pulled her into his embrace. "I'm a decent fighter, good with my hands."

"Yes." She sighed and leaned against his chest. "I know you're good with your hands. Very skillful."

Their bodies molded together, fitting neatly, and Trina felt a warm contentment. "The best thing about Phyllis's story is that it takes you off the hook."

"Not entirely."

"No, but you're not the main suspect any more."

"I think the title goes to the Winkles, since they own what's probably the murder weapon," he said. But David was far from relieved. There were too many loose ends, too many complications. The outside investigators might well still see David as a suspect. "There's always Ivan's will."

"That's what you were reading in Victor's room."

"It was propped up so nice and accessible in Darien Greenlee's briefcase. Wasn't signed, though. I think maybe it was just a proposed will that Darien was bringing here for Ivan to look over and study."

"Why do you think that?"

"A couple of pieces didn't fit. In this will, a ton of money was left to Victor. Most of the land and all of the existing structures—house, barn and lodge—went to Ivan's new wife. That would be you."

"I don't want it."

"Whether you want it or not, that's how he left it. Most of the land. But a large chunk, eight hundred acres, came to me. I don't know why. That was double the amount he took from my father."

"Maybe Ivan wanted to make amends."

"I couldn't say. We never talked about it." He gave her a little squeeze. "But I like the idea. I'd take it."

Ivan's generosity was too much to be believed. If David owned a portion of this land and the rest belonged to Trina, fate would have been too good. He didn't expect such good fortune. As a rule, David wasn't the kind of man who received windfalls. "But here's the kicker," he said, "the part you'd like. All this land was to be designated a game preserve. No hunting allowed."

"I'd like that," she said.

"But I don't think Ivan would. No hunting? That's way out of character. I mean, he wasn't as avid as Jake, but Ivan liked the sport. That's why I don't think he would have signed the will. I think naming this a preserve was Darien Greenlee's idea."

"Was he an environmentalist?"

"He must have had leanings in that direction. How else would he come to know a woman like Phyllis Winkle?"

"True."

He held her close, treasuring this moment of solitude before the outside investigators arrived. It wouldn't be long now. Only a couple of hours before the roads were clear. David wasn't looking forward to the intrusion. He would have preferred solitude. Days and weeks of solitude with only Trina for company in the long Alaskan nights. "Are you cold?" he asked. "Do you want to go back to the house?"

"I'd rather stay here with you."

"Good answer." He kissed the top of her head.

"One thing puzzles me about Phyllis's story. If she threw the gun away and somebody else picked it up, that would mean that they were following her. Why didn't she see them? Is the area near the hemlock tree forested?"

David visualized the location. "The hemlock tree's in the field. Nothing else around."

"If it happened the way Phyllis said, why wouldn't she have seen the person who picked up the gun?" Trina asked.

"She might have been distracted."

"Distracted?" Trina leaned away from him.

Behind her glasses, David saw the bright intelligence in her eyes.

"She'd have to be blind not to see someone coming toward her across a field of white snow," she said. "They'd stand out."

He shrugged. "Let's go take a look."

"On horseback? Isn't the snow too deep for riding?"

"There are other ways."

LUCKILY, TRINA THOUGHT, he hadn't been referring to snowshoes or skis, though either would be appropriate for a trek across the new snowfall. She'd never been on snowshoes. And her skills at cross-country skiing were minimal, at best.

The form of transporation David was talking about was kept in the garage on the far side of the lodge. He escorted her inside and pointed to a fleet of eight snowmobiles.

Trina laughed. "I've never even been on one."

"No problem. You just point the nose and drive. It's easier than driving a motorcycle or a car because you don't need to worry about traffic."

"Could I just sit on the back of yours?"

"Scared?"

"No."

"All right, then." David explained the simple driving controls and the handlebar steering. "Now, don't try to go slow or you'll sink down in the snow. You want to skim across the surface.''

''To skim?''

He turned on the ignition. The last words she heard over the roar of the motor were, ''Follow me.''

It took about three minutes for Trina to decide she loved snowmobiling. Though David was already far ahead of her, she actually did feel like she was skimming on the endless white expanse of snow. Her snowmobile dipped over the rises and bounced across moguls. The air whistled around her. Cold, but exhilarating.

They circled in the snowfield, and she noticed that no one had yet begun to clear the road leading to the house and lodge. Out here, the effect of the blizzard was more apparent. The road they'd driven only a few days ago was buried under four feet of snow.

Ahead of her, David raised his arm and waved. She banked, throwing up a splash of snow, and followed him to the single hemlock tree beside Hunter's Creek.

David climbed out of his snowmobile and sank up to his thighs in snow. He headed toward her. ''How do you like it?''

''I love this.'' An excited grin stretched her cold cheeks. ''I'm not much of a skier, but I could really get around on one of these.''

''So, here's the tree. This must be the place where Phyllis dumped the gun.''

They were still within view of the house and lodge, maybe only half a mile away. ''How long did you say it took Phyllis to get here?''

''Only a couple of minutes. She was on horseback. And there wasn't all this snow.''

"And she needed to hurry," Trina remembered. "So Bradley wouldn't have time to be suspicious of where she was."

"Right."

She stood in her snowmobile and looked around. There wasn't a sprig or tree to hide behind. "How could someone have followed her? She would have seen them."

"You're right. Against all this white, nobody could approach. Unless he was a hunter."

In her mind, she saw white. The white of snow and the blizzard-filled skies. The white of her wedding gown. Her cake, splattered against the wall in the dining room. The white of Jake's clothing. "Jake," she said. "He'd been out hunting before the party."

"In white," David said. "He wears all-white snow gear in winter. Says it gives him an extra few seconds to sneak up on the prey."

"Could he have done it?"

"He's maybe the only person who could. Especially if he followed her on skis. The guy's an Olympic champion. He could cover this distance on skis in no time. Phyllis wouldn't have heard him coming. And, blending into the snow with his white gear, she wouldn't have seen him."

"But why? What was he doing?"

"Finding himself a gun that couldn't be connected to him."

"But why would he kill Ivan?"

"I think we're about to find out." David pointed to another snowmobile, coming at them. The whine of the engine sliced the air. In seconds, Jake was beside them. His white outfit, covering him from head to toe, made him almost invisible, but Trina clearly saw the gun he held in his hand.

"I thought you might figure it out," he said.

"You followed Phyllis and got the gun."

"Correct. The situation was too perfect to pass up. When I came back from hunting, I had intended to talk with Ivan. Just talk. Though he'd been unreasonable as hell."

"About what?" Trina asked.

"The land, my dear. I expected to have it. Ivan had made me promises, and I had trusted him too much. There were even a few small loans that I collateralized with this land."

"How?" Trina asked.

"With the aid of a very helpful young lady in Darien Greenlee's office. A useful woman. But I don't know how she'll hold up when Reuben starts questioning her." He gestured impatiently with the gun. "If I could have gotten to her before this damn blizzard, I would have gotten away with everything."

"But you misjudged the weather," David said. "Thought you never made mistakes."

"I never make mistakes that can't be remedied."

Trina suppressed a shudder of fear. Why was he telling them this? Were she and David about to become a mistake that was remedied?

"This was too good to pass up," he continued. "I saw Phyllis make her dramatic exit from the tub house, carrying Ivan's clothes and a gun. I went to the tub house and told Ivan to wait there. I'd get his clothes and be back."

Which, Trina thought, explained why Ivan didn't try to escape on his own. He'd thought help was on the way. "But, if you'd been arguing, why would he believe you?"

"Because we both hated the greenie environmentalists, people like Phyllis and her wimp husband. And Darien Greenlee."

"I thought he was your attorney," David said.

"He was. And my lady friend in his offices made him extremely useful. She rewrote correspondence for me, exchanged letters and erased documents from the computer."

"Letters," Trina said. There was the COPA letter that had been removed from Ivan's files. "Did you ransack Ivan's office?"

"That's not my style. Ransacking? Lacks finesse, doesn't it? Why call attention to details?"

"It was Victor," David said.

"Of course, it was Victor." Jake sneered. "Like Phyllis, Victor had a flair for the dramatic gesture. Shooting the cake. Stabbing the dress. Oh, yes, and the initials he wrote in the tub house with his own blood. That was one step too far. I knew the forensic team would be able to pin that effort on Victor. Then they would question him. And he, being a coward, would talk."

"So you killed him," Trina said.

"His death was painless," Jake said. "He'd been loyal to me and I believe he really intended to give me this land for a fraction of the market price. I spared him the agony of a slow death. There was only one split second when he wakened and saw me standing above him. He knew he was about to die. And then it was over. It was a good death for a stupid and cowardly man."

Trina feared the death he had in mind for them. "And Ivan's murder?"

"Murder is such an ugly word," Jake said. "Ivan died less quickly. He was shot in the chest. I'm sure he knew pain before he lost consciousness. It seemed appropriate to me that he should die naked. None of his wealth or possessions could protect him."

He lowered the gun. "As for you two..."

"Wait!" David said. "What about Greenlee? How did you kill him?"

"Why do you care?"

Frankly, David said, "I'm buying time."

"Why? You know I have to kill you."

"Every minute I can be here on this land, breathing this air and seeing the sky, is precious to me."

"Noble sentiment," Jake acknowledged. "And you're a good hunter. It seems unfair to shoot you down without giving you a chance. By the way, that's what I did with Greenlee. I offered him a chance to escape before I hunted him down. He was a challenge."

"You hunted a man?" Disbelieving, Trina could only stare at this killer, this murderer. A hunter.

"I've conquered every other species," Jake said.

"Give us that chance," David demanded. "We're unarmed. Give us a one-minute head start."

Jake laughed. And yet, Trina could see that he was intrigued by the possibility. His eyes sparkled. They might have a chance.

"Ten seconds," he said. "Starting now."

Chapter Fourteen

David dove onto the back of the snowmobile behind her. "Go! Go, Trina!"

Their lives were in her hands. She fired the ignition. At the roar of the engine, she sped away. The snow churned and shifted beneath them. Their combined weight made the vehicle drag, and the engine squealed. When she swung around, aiming toward the house and lodge, the spoiler kicked up a fountainhead of white ice.

They were less than ten yards away when Jake took his first shot. She heard the crack of the gun, and her grip on the handlebars trembled. They swerved, but she managed to pull them back on track.

David yelled in her ear. "Get out of the field. Go right."

"Across the creek?"

"Yes. Toward the trees."

He was right. They were an easy target in the white field, and Jake was an Olympic-caliber marksman. They needed to find cover, to force him to pursue. He couldn't shoot while he was riding his snowmobile.

Whispering a prayer that they wouldn't get stuck, Trina plunged down the snowy embankment to the creek.

They flew across. On the other side, there was a stretch of trees.

"Up there!" David pointed past her shoulder. "Then trade places. Let me drive."

She heard another shot. Why hadn't someone come to help them? Where was the sheriff? Why hadn't the people in the house responded to the sounds of gunfire? To her ears, the snap of the gun resounded. But from the house, behind the well-insulated walls, they wouldn't hear, wouldn't know that Jake was hunting them. She and David were his prey.

A giant spruce tree shot up in front of her and Trina slowed to maneuver around it.

"Park!" David yelled.

Behind the cover of the spruce, she stopped the snowmobile. Frantically, he leapt in front and ordered, "Keep your head down."

He took off at breakneck speed. In the small riding compartment, she pressed against him, wrapping her arms around his torso. She held on for all she was worth. The route David negotiated was terrifying and reckless. He darted between trees and shrubs, whipped below branches that were only inches from the tops of their heads.

Leaning close to his ear, she asked, "What happens if we hit something?"

"Boom!" he said.

Boom? As in explosion? Trina looked over her shoulder. She could see Jake approaching. He seemed so close. Hunched over the handlebars, he looked like a white-clad demon from hell.

Aggressive, she remembered. He might already be regretting the ten seconds he'd given them. But she knew Jake would not give up. Not until they were dead.

David seemed to be working his way along a ridge, circling the house until they were behind the barn.

She glanced back again. "David! He's stopped."

"Damn."

"What does that mean?"

David slowed and stopped. The silence was deafening. "That means he's going to wait at a vantage point where he can see the whole back of the house. You didn't notice if he had his rifle, did you?"

She nodded. "He did. He had a huge pack on the back of his snowmobile, and I saw the stock of a rifle sticking up. Is that bad?"

"It's a specially adapted weapon. Really accurate. I've seen him pick fleas off a fence post with that gun."

He thought for a minute. There was enough gas in the snowmobile to cover a good distance, but not an endless supply. Jake expected them to return to the house. That was why he'd stopped. Right now, he was probably scanning these trees with his long-distance scope.

David made a split-second decision. They wouldn't go to the house. They'd go far afield before turning back. Luckily, he knew this land well. But so did Jake.

Again, they took off across the vista of snow. They dove across a narrow field, terrifying a huge, gawky moose, who galloped off toward cover.

The engine straining, the snowmobile climbed a ridge. If the machine stalled here, David knew battling Jake would be the least of their troubles. There were wolves on this land. And bear, too. Though they were hibernating, they could be wakened. David didn't want to rouse any angry grizzlies.

At the top of a snowbank outcropping, David stopped. Had they lost Jake?

The answer came in a second. The snap of gunfire. David heard the whiz of a bullet. It was so close he could feel it pass only a millimeter from his head. Jake's shot probably put a bullet hole in the brim of David's Stetson.

Again, David circled. Heading toward the house. Dodging trees. He wished for more speed, but their combined weight was already forcing the snowmobile to work extrahard.

They were within sight of the garage beside the house, heading downhill, when he misjudged and drove over a rock. The snowmobile tipped dangerously, but David managed to keep them upright. He felt the steering linkage come loose. He tried to turn, but the mechanism snapped. They were out of control.

Careening downhill with the throttle open wide, they were aimed at the side of the garage. Closer and closer they came. Their only chance to miss the edge of the building was to throw the snowmobile off course. "Lean," David yelled.

He threw his weight to the left and Trina did the same. The snowmobile veered in that direction. They might clear the garage. But there were trees beyond.

"We're going to jump, Trina."

"What?"

"When I say three."

He timed their move carefully. Jake was probably watching. He could pick them off in a second. "One. Two..."

"Three!"

He grabbed her arm and pulled at the same time as he lunged away from the snowmobile. They rolled together in the snow.

The snowmobile hit the tree. Branches splintered in the air. And then . . . boom!

The snowmobile exploded in a ball of orange flame.

David regained his footing and yanked Trina forward. He guessed Jake would shoot at them from behind. He dragged her to the edge of the garage. From there, they ran. They were only twenty yards from the house, but they wouldn't be safe from the hunter until they were inside. Even then, David didn't intend to walk in front of unshaded windows.

The explosion had roused the others. Reuben came out on the porch and Maybelle followed. Her mouth gaped wide. David and Trina raced up the stairs. "Get back inside," David yelled. "It's Jake."

Inside, with the door closed, David pulled Trina against him. "Are you all right?"

"It's a little late to be asking." She gasped. Her face was bright red from exposure and exertion. "I can't believe we're alive."

"What the hell is going on?" Reuben demanded.

Maybelle shook her head. "That's quite a blaze you started out there. Good thing the wood is too wet for the fire to spread."

"Steering was out," David said. "But I didn't want to hit the garage."

"You both sit." Maybelle herded them to the sofa. "You need tea. And muffins."

Reuben lowered himself onto a chair opposite them. "Talk," he said.

AFTER DAVID AND TRINA repeated Jake's confession, the sheriff leaned back in his chair and cogitated for a minute. Then he said, "I believe you. Every word."

David closed his eyes and savored the moment. He was no longer under suspicion. He was free. And, if the will he'd seen was accurate, he was about to inherit a sizable chunk of land.

"What do you think Jake's going to do?" Reuben asked. "You think we're in danger here?"

"I think he'll take his own advice," Trina said. "Last night, when David and I talked to him, he told David to run. He said that with the right provisions, he could last forever in the wilderness."

"He's probably right," David said. "I wouldn't want to be on the posse that was tracking him. Jake is a lethal hunter. I'm amazed that we got away from him."

Reuben rubbed his hands together and he grinned. "By golly, you two have done me a big favor."

"Swell," Trina said. "So glad to help."

"I was expecting the big city cops to come out here and have a good chuckle at how bad I'd messed this up. But, thanks to you, I might have this all solved in a tidy little package for the hotshot forensic guys. Sure would help if I could get that COPA letter from Greenlee's office."

"Did you talk with his secretary?" Trina asked.

"Sure did. She said she could fax stuff, but the fax is out. And then she suggested electronic mail, but the computer is dead."

"Not in David's office," Trina said.

"I never thought of that," Reuben said. "David, are you set up for communications?"

"No."

"But I can put it together," Trina said. "If there's a modem intact and enough of the existing software and hardware."

Within moments, she'd ransacked Ivan's office, pirating enough equipment to make David's computer operable. She sat behind his desk and settled down to work. "This isn't exactly the equipment I'm familiar with," she said. "But it's close."

"Great," Reuben said.

"We ought to warn you," she informed him, "that Jake had a girlfriend inside Greenlee's office who was purging files for him."

"Whoa, that's bad news. It wasn't his secretary, was it?"

"We don't know."

David perched on the edge of the desk, watching her. "You're good at this stuff, aren't you?"

She smiled at him. "I know computers, and this is a piece of cake. We're going to be cruising on the information highway before you know it."

Maybelle hurried into the room with a tray of muffins, which she passed around. "I can't believe Jake would do such a thing," she said. "He's an important man. A celebrity."

"Maybe that's why he wanted so much," David said. "It was a pretty clever scheme, really."

"What was?" Maybelle questioned.

"The way I figure, Jake intended to offer the land as collateral to investors, to people who trusted his reputation. Then, he would use that money to buy the lodge from Ivan."

"But Ivan never would have sold," Maybelle said.

"So Ivan had to die. Victor would have unloaded this place in a minute."

"Wait a minute," Reuben said. "You think he was planning to kill Ivan all along?"

"He didn't have much choice after he killed Green-lee," David explained. "Jake must have taken the phone call from Greenlee that said he was coming out for a week. That's why neither Maybelle nor I knew about it."

Reuben nodded. "I'm with you so far."

"Jake couldn't let Ivan and Greenlee get together and compare notes. If they did, Jake's scheme would have come to light. He had to kill both of them. And he counted on his girlfriend in Greenlee's office to strip the files for him."

"What if she already did?" Maybelle said. "Then you're out of evidence."

"There's enough," Reuben said. "I'll make this stick."

"If you ever find him." Maybelle peeled the wrapping off a muffin and bit into it. "Jake is slicker than a river otter, and he knows survival techniques. Plus, we're coming up on spring. I'm guessing that if you don't find him in the next few days, you can kiss Jake goodbye."

From outside, they heard a clattering racket, and Reuben looked up. "Chopper," he said. "How are you coming, Trina?"

"Just a few more minutes," she said.

Reuben turned to David. "Let's go out and see if we can help those hotshots from Juneau. I want you to explain Jake's scheme to them."

They all left Trina alone in the office. Within a few moments, she had contacted Greenlee's secretary by phone. While they discussed the E-mail communication, Trina asked about someone in the office who was dating Jake Poynter and learned that Jake's girlfriend had no access to the secretary's files. She was only a clerk, according to the secretary.

Trina sat back to wait for the transaction. Within seconds, the COPA letter that detailed loans against Ivan's property flashed across the screen of David's computer. Trina saved and printed the letter and some additional documents that Greenlee's secretary thought might be useful. According to all the information, Jake's scam was pretty much the way David had indicated.

Trina considered asking for a copy of Ivan's existing will, but decided against it. Let Reuben decide which papers he wanted to see and which he didn't.

Though she could have gathered her papers and joined the people in the other room, Trina wasn't anxious for this final phase of the investigation. In the first place, she would have to relive, for what seemed like the ten thousandth time, her foolishness in becoming Ivan's bride. Also, when the crimes were solved, there was no reason for her to stay in Alaska. She'd be free to go, to head back to Denver and try to pick up the pieces of her life.

And what about David? Consistently, he'd asked her to stay. But their relationship was too fast, she thought. The whirlwind of her expected love for Ivan had hardly died. She'd be crazy to jump feetfirst into another involvement.

Not wanting to face this final showdown, she flipped through the files in David's computer. Scanning. Wondering. In the word-processing section, she found a file named Trina. What was that?

She called up the file, and the screen showed a letter.

It was the first letter she'd received from Ivan. What was it doing here on David's computer? She scrolled through the file. All the correspondence was here. Every word. Every sweet, poetic phrase. David must have written all those letters, she realized. He'd signed Ivan's name.

She closed the file and allowed the screen to go blank.

Her mouth was dry. Her hands trembled. In her ears, she heard the loud hammer of her own pulse. The physical symptoms felt like shock. How could he deceive her so thoroughly?

Her foolishness was compounded a dozen times. How had she been so blind? Why hadn't she guessed? There were clues from the first time she saw David. When he spoke of the land, his words were almost lyrical. Just like in those letters. Those damned letters.

He'd known that she worked as a secretary, though she hadn't told him.

And she thought of the letter that outlined the hunting expedition with Jake. The only way David could have known what happened was if he were there. The hunters were David and Jake. Not Ivan.

"Oh, David," she whispered. Had he been secretly sneering when he seduced her? Had every word he'd spoken been a lie?

And now she'd have to face him, knowing that he had deceived her, played her for a fool. *Get it over with.*

She grabbed the information Reuben needed and stalked through the house. There were several strangers sitting with Reuben and David at the dining room table, and they all looked very important. She didn't care. She didn't want to meet them or shake hands or pretend that she wasn't dying inside.

Without looking at David, she handed the documents to Reuben and turned on her heel. "I'll be upstairs when you need me."

In her room, she grabbed her suitcase and flipped it open on the bed. Carelessly, she tossed in clothing.

Through her bedroom window, she saw the rotors of a helicopter. She would leave as soon as humanly possible. By road, by air, by sea. Any mode of transportation was fine with her as long as she could put distance between herself and Alaska. Trina had to be as far away from David St. John as one person could be from another.

He pushed open her door and entered. "What's wrong?"

"I don't recall inviting you into my room. Please leave."

"Trina, what happened?"

"I think you know." She grabbed her airline ticket and a pen. "Here, David. I have one last request. I want you to write something for me. One word. Love."

"I can explain."

"Just write."

He did as she requested.

Trina found her locket, the piece of jewelry she hadn't worn since her sham wedding to Ivan. With shaking fingers, she unfastened the catch and took out the scrap she'd carried close to her heart. *Love.* She compared the scrap with the word he'd written. The penmanship was identical. "You even signed the letters," she said. "Sincerely, Ivan. Cordially. Love."

"I'm sorry, Trina."

"Why didn't you tell me? You're as bad as he was."

"I was waiting for the right time."

"And when was that, David? After I'd married Ivan? That was the whole plan, wasn't it?"

"It just happened. Like I told you, my job was hiring and firing. I started the correspondence with you. Believe me, Trina. I never planned to deceive you."

"How could you do this?" It was inconceivable to her that he and Ivan would take her innocent trust and humiliate her so completely. "What did I ever do to you? Oh, I'll bet you and Ivan had a good chuckle about me. Have you got the letters I wrote?"

"I saved every one."

"Give them back. I don't intend to be a source of amusement for all your buddies in Osprey." She slammed her suitcase closed and locked it. "I want every page back."

"It won't do you any good, Trina. I've read them so many times that they're committed to memory."

She sank down on the bed. Nothing had ever felt so bad as this. Not the murders or the fear she'd experienced. It was nothing compared to the despair she felt. Her misery went deeper than bone marrow, her sorrow permeated her genes and nerve endings, every drop of her blood.

"I can't expect you to forgive me," he said. "I was merely interested in you. I thought you were a person I'd like to know better. Every night, I'd sit at my computer. I was alone. No one else ever saw a word of our correspondence. Not even Ivan."

She wanted to believe him, but . . .

"After the first week," he continued, "I knew something remarkable was happening. When I wrote to you, I felt like a whole man again. Not just a guy with a failed marriage, but a man with a future." He hesitated. "I never expected to fall in love again."

"You conned me. I put my heart on the line."

"And you were right," he said. "Think of it that way, Trina. You can trust the emotions that told you there was a man in Alaska who loved you. Because there was."

She'd been right? "What do you mean?"

"You never need to doubt yourself again," he said. "I love you, Trina. I love you with all my heart."

"How can I believe you now?"

He knelt before her and took her hand in his. "I want you to stay with me forever. In the cold of winter and the green of spring. I want for you to be my partner in life."

She recognized his phrase from the letters. She'd been right. She'd somehow fallen in love with the right man.

"Marry me, Trina."

"I can't." She held up her left hand where Ivan's engagement ring still sparkled. "I'm already married."

"Hell, I picked out that ring, anyway."

"You did?"

"It was Ivan's money, but I went into Juneau and found the ring."

"And the roses?" she asked.

"I sent them. I made the travel arrangements."

"Then you were the man I fell in love with." The realization dawned slowly, opening a new horizon. "David, why didn't you say anything?"

"I don't have much to offer. I'm not wealthy. Once this mess is cleared up, I probably won't even have a job."

"I don't care."

"Our life could be a financial struggle," he warned. "But I'll do everything I can. Whatever it takes, I'm—"

"Shut up, David."

"Yes, ma'am."

"Promise me that you'll never lie to me again."

He pulled her into his arms. Gently, he kissed her. Her spirits began to rise. She'd been right! Her instincts had led her to the right man. She kissed him back.

"I'll marry you, David. But it's going to be a real ceremony. In a church. With a gown and flowers and another ring."

"Whatever you want. My dearest Trina, I will always love you."

"Forever," she whispered. "And I will love you."

Epilogue

It was five months later, at the waning of summer, when David and Trina packed a picnic lunch and rode on Sol and Myrtle into the forests behind the lodge.

When all the paperwork was resolved, Ivan's property, in its entirety, belonged to his widow, Trina, and to David, whom he referred to as a friend he had unwittingly betrayed through the elder St. John's irresponsibility. Large chunks of Ivan's cash had gone to others, but there was more than enough to live on, and the lodge had become a fairly successful endeavor. Hunting was limited to residents of Alaska. Mainly the lodge was used as a retreat.

When they reached a distant glen, far away from curious people at the lodge, Trina dismounted. She spread a blanket on the moist, grassy earth and stretched out, allowing the sun to warm her face. Her hand rested on the slight swelling of her belly. Three months pregnant, she was full of life and love and sweet contentment.

She smiled at her husband. "I never turned into a rough and ready Alaskan gal, did I?"

"You're everything I want, darling."

"But I wish I was tougher."

"And that's why I brought the rifles. Today, we're going to have your first hunting lesson."

"I think I've changed my mind. Whenever I think of hunting, I think of Jake."

"He's gone, Trina. He'll never bother us again."

"Gone," she agreed. "But not erased. They never did catch him."

"How could they? He's an excellent marksman, brilliant at survival skills. He'd said that he would be able to survive in the wilderness, and he proved it."

She sighed. Nowadays, most of her thinking was occupied with what she should name the baby. "I don't want to hunt. In fact, I think we should eliminate hunting entirely from the offerings we have at the lodge, don't you?"

"I'd be lying if I said that I did."

"And you'll never lie to me again."

"Never." He kissed her forehead. "I love you."

No matter how many times she heard those words, she never tired of them. She was beloved. Her heart had been true.

During those hours, she managed to avoid the rifle lesson he wanted to give her. Trina's existence was focused on creating life, not on hunting. But when they returned to the lodge, she had second thoughts.

Reuben's pickup truck was parked in front, and he stood on the porch, waving.

"What is it?" David asked as he helped her dismount. "What's wrong?"

"They found Jake Poynter. He was way down south, near Ketchikan."

Trina felt a chill along her spine. Might be a good idea if she learned how to handle a gun. "Was he arrested?"

"He's dead. Mauled by a grizzly."

If there was such a thing as a fitting death, Trina thought Jake had achieved it. "You're sure it was him?"

"Absolutely. And he had a message for you, Trina. Before he died, he said to tell you that you were right. He missed the admiration."

"And the trophies," she said.

Jake never understood that prizes would never amount to real worth. The only true beauty was in nature, in the midnight sun and the northern lights. The only possessions worth having were feelings. Peace. Happiness. And, most especially, love.

HARLEQUIN®

⟨R⟩ I N T R I G U E ®

What if someone out there looked exactly like you...
and that someone had committed a murder?

⟨MIRROR IMAGES⟩

In July and August don't miss this special two-book subseries
by popular Intrigue author Sheryl Lynn.

Look for:

#331 DARK KNIGHT
#336 DARK STAR

MIRROR IMAGES: Only from Harlequin Intrigue!

TD-G

HARLEQUIN®

I N T R I G U E ®

Into a world where danger lurks around
every corner, and there's a fine line between trust
and betrayal, comes a tall, dark and handsome man.

Intuition draws you to him...but instinct keeps you
away. Is he really one of those...

Don't miss any of the twelve sexy but secretive men,
coming to you one per month in 1995.

In August, look for:
#333 THE EYES OF DEREK ARCHER
by Vickie York

**Take a walk on the wild side...with our
"DANGEROUS MEN"!**

DM-7

Take 4 bestselling love stories FREE

Plus get a FREE surprise gift!

Special Limited-time Offer

Mail to Harlequin Reader Service®

3010 Walden Avenue
P.O. Box 1867
Buffalo, N.Y. 14269-1867

YES! Please send me 4 free Harlequin Intrigue® novels and my free surprise gift. Then send me 4 brand-new novels every month. Bill me at the low price of $2.44 each plus 25¢ delivery and applicable sales tax, if any.* That's the complete price and a savings of over 10% off the cover prices—quite a bargain! I understand that accepting the books and gift places me under no obligation ever to buy any books. I can always return a shipment and cancel at any time. Even if I never buy another book from Harlequin, the 4 free books and the surprise gift are mine to keep forever.

181 BPA ANRK

Name	(PLEASE PRINT)	
Address	Apt. No.	
City	State	Zip

This offer is limited to one order per household and not valid to present Harlequin Intrigue® subscribers. *Terms and prices are subject to change without notice.
Sales tax applicable in N.Y.

UINT-295   ©1990 Harlequin Enterprises Limited

HARLEQUIN®

I N T R I G U E®

**KELSEY ROBERTS serves up a double
dose of danger and desire in the exciting**

THE ROSE TATTOO

In June we served up a tall, dark and delectable hero and a
sweet and sassy heroine in #326 UNSPOKEN CONFESSIONS.
Then last month, it was the hot and spicy J. D. Porter and the
sinfully rich Tory Conway sharing Southern fried secrets in
#330 UNLAWFULLY WEDDED.

On the Menu for August - #334 UNDYING LAUGHTER

Wes Porter—subtly scrumptious
Destiny Talbott—tart and tangy
Mouth-watering Mystery—deceptively delicious

Look for Harlequin Intrigue's response to your hearty appetite
for suspense: THE ROSE TATTOO, where Southern specialties
are served up with a side order of suspense!

ROSE-3

As a Privileged Woman,
you'll be entitled to all these Free Benefits.
And Free Gifts, too.

To thank you for buying our books, we've designed an exclusive FREE program called *PAGES & PRIVILEGES*™. You can enroll with just one Proof of Purchase, and get the kind of luxuries that, until now, you could only read about.

BIG HOTEL DISCOUNTS

A privileged woman stays in the finest hotels. And so can you—at up to 60% off! Imagine standing in a hotel check-in line and watching as the guest in front of you pays $150 for the same room that's only costing you $60. Your *Pages & Privileges* discounts are good at Sheraton, Marriott, Best Western, Hyatt and thousands of other fine hotels all over the U.S., Canada and Europe.

FREE DISCOUNT TRAVEL SERVICE

A privileged woman is always jetting to romantic places. When you fly, just make one phone call for the lowest published airfare at time of booking—or double the difference back! PLUS— you'll get a $25 voucher to use the first time you book a flight AND 5% cash back on every ticket you buy thereafter through the travel service!

HI-PP3A

FREE GIFTS!

A privileged woman is always getting wonderful gifts.
Luxuriate in rich fragrances that will stir your senses (and his). This gift-boxed assortment of fine perfumes includes three popular scents, each in a beautiful designer bottle. <u>Truly Lace</u>...This luxurious fragrance unveils your sensuous side. <u>L'Effleur</u>...discover the romance of the Victorian era with this soft floral. <u>Muguet des bois</u>...a single note floral of singular beauty.

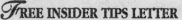

YOURS FREE!

$50 VALUE

FREE INSIDER TIPS LETTER

A privileged woman is always informed. And you'll be, too, with our free letter full of fascinating information and sneak previews of upcoming books.

MORE GREAT GIFTS & BENEFITS TO COME

A privileged woman always has a lot to look forward to. And so will you. You get all these wonderful FREE gifts and benefits now with only one purchase...and there are no additional purchases required. However, each additional retail purchase of Harlequin and Silhouette books brings you a step closer to even more great FREE benefits like half-price movie tickets... and even more FREE gifts.

L'Effleur...This basketful of romance lets you discover L'Effleur from head to toe, heart to home.

Truly Lace...
A basket spun with the sensuous luxuries of Truly Lace, including Dusting Powder in a reusable satin and lace covered box.

Complete the Enrollment Form in the front of this book and mail it with this Proof of Purchase.

PROOF OF PURCHASE

Pages & Privileges

Offer expires October 31, 1996

HI-PP3